TO HAVE
& TO HOLD

ALEATHA ROMIG

Book #5 of the Brutal Vows series

New York Times, Wall Street Journal, and USA Today
bestselling author

COPYRIGHT AND LICENSE INFORMATION

TO HAVE AND TO HOLD

Book five, Brutal Vows

Aleatha Romig's Most Recent and Upcoming Releases

Visit Aleatha's store to purchase e-books, signed books, and store exclusive items.

TO HAVE AND TO HOLD - Brutal Vows, book five - March 2025

Arranged marriage, Mafia/cartel, enemies to lovers, age-gap, he falls first, protective hero, Romeo and Juliet vibes, dangerous romance

QUEENS AND MONSTERS - Brutal Vows, book four - January 2025

Arranged marriage, Mafia/cartel, alpha hero, virgin heroine, touch her and die, family saga, he falls first, possessive hero, sheltered heroine, dangerous romance

BOUND BY A PROMISE – Brutal Vows, book three - October 2024

Arranged marriage, age-gap, forbidden, Mafia/cartel dangerous stand-alone romance

ONE STRING – July 2024

Aleatha's Lighter Ones - Second-chance, enemies-to-lovers, fake-date, little-sister's-best-friend, forbidden, stand-alone contemporary romance

TILL DEATH DO US PART- Brutal Vows, book two - June 2024

Arranged marriage, enemies to lovers, Mafia/cartel, he falls first, stand-alone, dangerous romance

NOW AND FOREVER – Brutal Vows, book one - May 2024

Arranged marriage, age-gap, Mafia/cartel stand-alone romance

LIGHT DARK – April 2024

Cult, psychological thriller, forced proximity, romantic suspense stand-alone

*Previously published through Thomas and Mercer as INTO THE LIGHT and AWAY FROM THE DARK

REMEMBERING PASSION – Sinclair Duet book one – September 2023

Scorching hot, second-chance romance filled with the suspense and intrigue

REKINDLING DESIRE – Sinclair Duet, book two – October 2023

Scorching hot, second-chance romance filled with the suspense and intrigue

Luciano Family Tree

Beginning of book one, NOW AND FOREVER

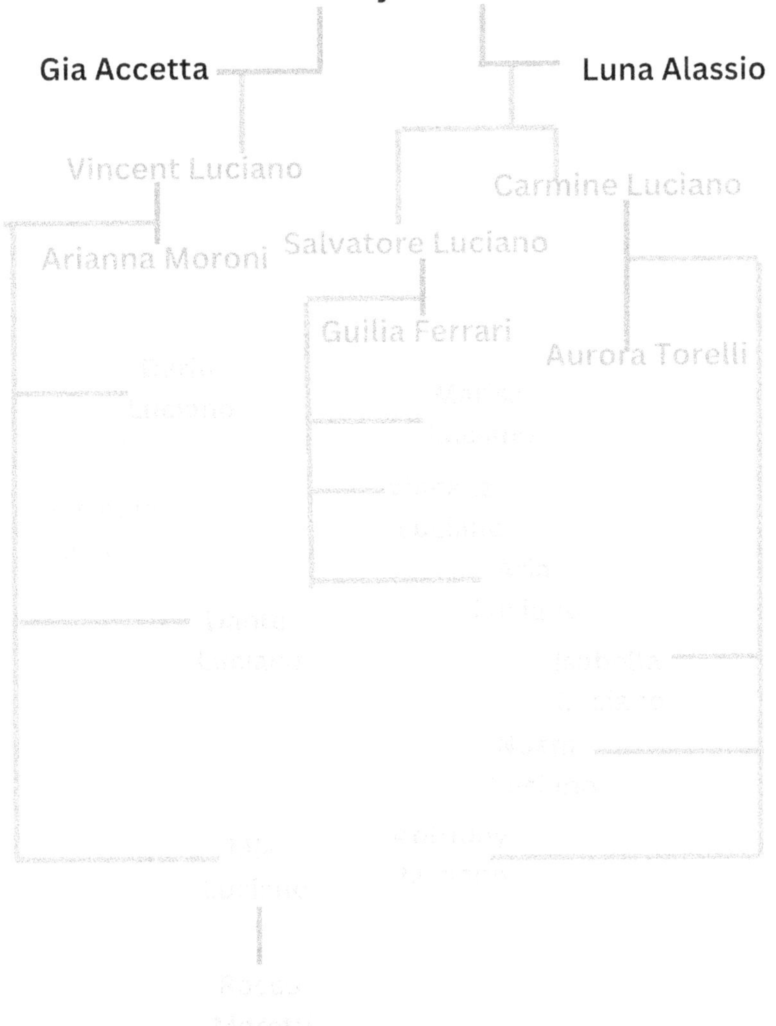

Roriguez/ Ruiz Family Tree

Beginning of book one, NOW AND FOREVER

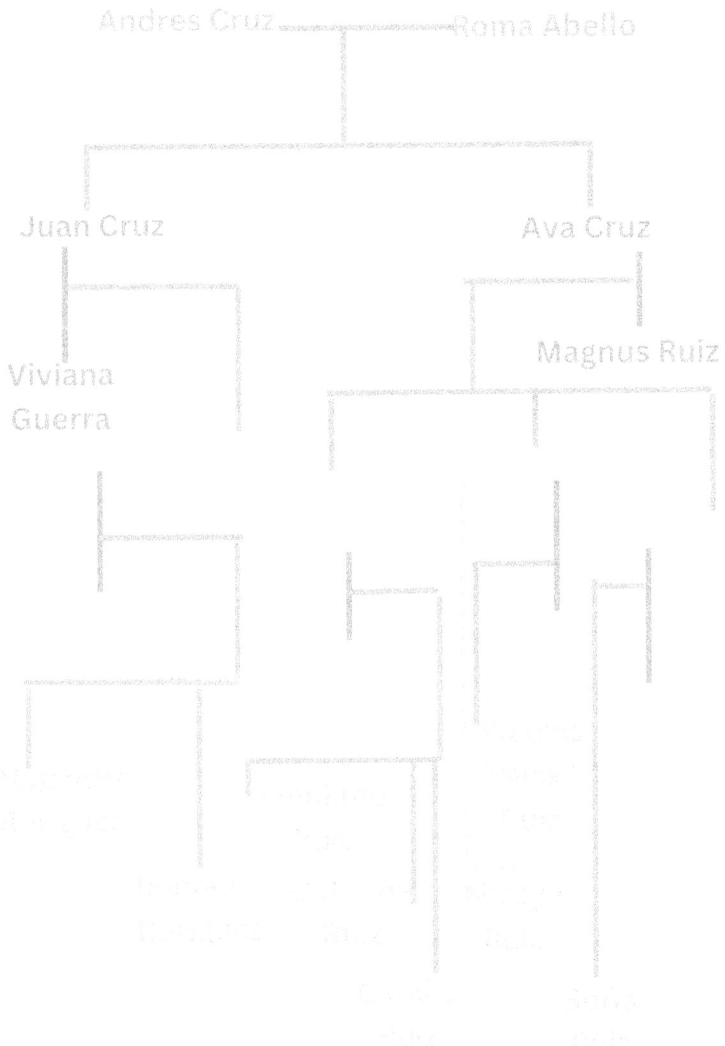

SYNOPSIS:

Arranged marriage, age-gap, forbidden love, enemies-to-lovers, forced proximity, Romeo and Juliet vibes, family saga, Mafia/cartel romance, slow burn, redemption, morally gray hero, dangerous romance

The Roríguez cartel is spinning out of control, tragedy putting the alliance and our future in question.

I'm Emiliano Ruiz and throughout the last few years, I've witnessed my sisters being doled out to members of the Luciano Mafia. The cartel has also taken famiglia women. It doesn't matter if it's the Luciano famiglia's turn to take a bride.

My mind is set—it's my turn.

I never imagined marrying a young bride until I caught sight of Isabella Luciano. She's only eighteen, and with her long yellow hair and big brown eyes, she's a vision to behold. She sees me, however, through the tinted lens of her father's hatred.

Carmine Luciano's disdain of the cartel and the

alliance isn't a secret. His opinion won't stop me. I'll prove to Isabella that even bad men can be good husbands.

No matter what her father says or what happens in our war, Isabella will be mine.

Have you been Aleatha'd?

TO HAVE AND TO HOLD is a stand-alone dangerous Mafia/cartel romance in the "Brutal Vows" series. Each arranged-marriage story is filled with the suspense, intrigue, and heat you've come to expect from New York Times bestselling author Aleatha Romig.

CHAPTER

ONE

Isabella

I stared straight ahead, seeing the reflection of my family as the elevator whisked us up to the capo dei capi's apartment in the Kansas City skyline. This was a formal event. My father and little brother were both wearing suits, and my sister, Noemi, Mom, and I were all wearing dresses. Nothing but the best for the kingpin of the Kansas City Famiglia.

Biting my lip, I felt my stomach twist with nerves. Tension rippled through the air even thicker than it had in the SUV on the way to this first-birthday celebration—a momentous milestone for the capo's daughter.

As our family drove across town, Papà reminded us of his rules—no socializing with members of the Roríguez cartel. It wasn't the first time we'd heard his lecture. If I

1

recalled correctly, the first time was before Mom, Noemi, and I flew to California for Catalina's wedding shower. Papà's bodyguards were present for our protection and to spy on our interactions.

The world of the famiglia had been turned upside down since that trip. The aftermath was easily traced to my cousin Dario marrying Catalina, the daughter of one of the Roríguez cartel's top lieutenants. Then my uncle died, making Dario the top of the Luciano famiglia, much to my father's and my uncle Salvatore's mortification. That wasn't all. Next, Dario forced his sister, Mia, to marry into the cartel. Her husband's father recently passed away, making Aléjandro the drug lord, the top of the cartel. Dario's last sibling, Dante, willingly married Catalina's younger sister, Camila, another member of the cartel.

The latest marriage came as a relief. I didn't know until later, but Dario spoke to my father about me marrying Reinaldo Roríguez, now second-in-command in the cartel. My savior was the last person I would have expected—Dario's stray, Jasmine. She was another person Father warned us about speaking to.

Sometimes I thought it might be helpful to carry a list.

Papà's deep voice cut through the waves of tension. "Remember what you were told. We will leave as soon as possible."

"Yes, Papà," my siblings and I answered in unison.

I looked down, seeing my little brother. Anthony was small for a nine-year-old. All three of us siblings shared the same coloring, blond hair and light brown eyes. I was the oldest. Noemi was next at fifteen years old. My father finally got his boy with Anthony.

At the sound of our father's reminder, my brother reached for my hand.

Smiling down at him, I gave it a squeeze. Papà wouldn't approve of Anthony needing reassurance. He was to be a man after all. If I was asked, I'd say it was our father's fault that the three of us and even Mom were battling nerves.

Trips to Dario and Catalina's home never ended well. Someone would say or do something to set Father off. Usually, it was the capo himself. We all knew that if it wasn't for our father's devotion to the famiglia, he'd turn down the invitation.

I sucked in a breath as the elevator doors opened to the large open foyer. The sounds of voices and the melody of music replaced the earlier silence.

"Mr. Luciano," one of Dario's guards said with a nod. "Mrs. Luciano," he greeted Mom, and then turned toward the room. That was the way it was when you're young in this family. You were invisible.

My father was the third son of our grandfather, Anthony Luciano. Vincent, Dario's father, was the first son. Vincent's mother had difficulty having more children. From what I've been told, after her death, Anthony remarried, wedding our grandmother Gia.

The different wives accounted for the age difference between Uncle Vincent, Uncle Salvatore, and my father, Carmine Luciano. That was also why Uncle Salvatore's and my father's children were much younger than Uncle Vincent and Aunt Arianna's. Papà was sixteen and a made man when his nephew, Dario, was born. It's understandable why he and Uncle Salvatore didn't appreciate taking orders from Dario.

Papà turned, inspecting his family. "Isabella, let go of your brother's hand," he growled in a hushed whisper. His dark eyes narrowed at Anthony. "You are a man."

"Yes, Papà," my brother said.

"We must greet the capo," Papà said, turning his attention to the living room filled with people. His neck straightened and his shoulders stiffened at the sight of members of Catalina's family and the Roríguez cartel. "Anthony, come with me to the capo's office."

"Carmine," Mom said softly, "he's only nine. Perhaps he should stay with us."

Ignoring Mom's concern, Papà laid his large hand on Anthony's back and directed him toward Dario's office doors.

Noemi hugged Mom's arm. "Tony will be fine." My sister scanned the crowd and whispered, "Where is Aunt Giulia or Aunt Arianna?"

Jasmine's flaming red hair caught my attention. I rolled my eyes. "Jasmine is back."

"You know how your father feels," Mom warned. Her eyes opened wide. "There's Arianna with Catalina. We can greet the hostess and then stay near your aunt."

Mom led us through the crowd. Ariadna Gia, the birthday girl, was sitting on Aunt Arianna's lap. "Catalina," Mom said with a feigned smile. "It was nice to be invited to the celebration." She gazed down at the one-year-old dressed in layers and layers of lace. "Goodness, time flies. Ariadna Gia is growing so fast."

Catalina stood.

Despite Papà's disapproval of anyone from the cartel, since the first time we met, I'd liked Catalina. As time passed, I admired her ability to stay strong while surrounded by so many who didn't approve of her as Dario's wife.

She reached for Mom's hand and squeezed. "Aurora, I'm happy you could make it." She turned her attention on Noemi and me. "Talk about time flying...Isabella and Noemi, you are both growing up—beautiful young ladies. I haven't seen either of you since Isabella's graduation." She looked at me. "Are you registered for classes this fall? Camila is currently enrolled at MSKC. I'm sure she'd be happy to show you around."

I'd shared with Catalina at my graduation that I wanted to study.

Before I had the chance to answer, Mom replied, "Carmine and I think it would be better for Isabella to spend this next year learning about ways to help the community. As you know, I chair multiple boards for some of Kansas City's most recognized philanthropic organizations."

Catalina glanced at me.

I made an almost imperceptible shake of my head, hoping she wouldn't share what we'd said. Her knowing would only upset my parents.

Catalina's lips pressed together before she forced a smile. "That sounds lovely. I'm sure, Aurora, you'll be able to show Isabella the ropes."

"We could use your help with the food pantry. If you could find time." Mom's voice lowered. "There's an increasing number of non-English-speaking people in need." Her eyes widened. "I'm sorry to assume. You are bilingual, aren't you."

Catalina nodded. "Yes. I speak Spanish and English."

I stifled a laugh at the order of her answer.

Mom continued, "Let me know if you could volunteer a few hours a week. I'm sure the director would be thrilled..."

Tuning out their conversation, my gaze wandered around the large room. I let out a breath of relief as I saw my cousins. I reached for Mom's arm. "Excuse me. Marisa just arrived. I'm going to go see her."

Mom nodded.

Noemi and I made our way toward the foyer and our cousins—Uncle Salvatore and Aunt Giulia's children. I imagined they'd received the same lecture on their way here. I caught up to their three daughters as Uncle Salvatore walked toward Dario's office and Aunt Giulia headed toward Mom and Catalina. Due to our similar ages, Noemi and I had always been close with these cousins. Marisa was seventeen, Aria was sixteen, and Vincenza—Cenzi—was fifteen.

Marisa's stare met mine and her smile grew.

I reached for her shoulders. "God, I'm glad you're here."

"Yeah," Noemi said, "if we had to listen to Mom ramble on about the burden of the ever-increasing number of Spanish-speaking people at the food pantry..."

"No," Marisa said. "Please tell me it wasn't in front of anyone from Catalina's family."

"To Catalina," I replied.

Marisa shook her head before looping her arm with mine. "Whose father do you think will leave first, ours or yours?"

"Who is that?" Aria asked.

We all turned to look.

I recognized him right away. "Catalina's brother, Emiliano."

Aria's eyebrows danced. "I don't remember him being so buff."

Marisa nudged me. "Have you seen your almost-husband?"

"Ugh. Don't say that. For once, I appreciate Jasmine."

"Is she here?" Aria whispered.

I nodded. "When I saw her, she was with *her* husband." I emphasized the word. "I haven't seen—"

My words stopped as the elevator doors opened, and our cousin Mia stepped out carrying her baby, Jorge, named after Mia's late father-in-law. The new *el Patrón,* Mia's husband, Aléjandro, was a step behind her.

"Does he look more intimidating than before?" Cenzi asked in a hushed tone.

"They're all scary if you ask me," Marisa replied. "But I do want to see the baby."

A crowd gathered around Mia and *el Patrón.*

Aunt Giulia joined our small circle. "I'm sure Catalina wouldn't mind if you girls wanted to get some punch from the dining room and go back to the library for a while. I'll let you know when the party begins."

That was code for *get away from the cartel until you must absolutely be present.*

Watching her mother walk away, Aria grinned. "I'd rather stay out here and drool over some of the scary men."

My gaze scanned the room. If I could look at the cartel members without the knowledge that they were all criminals, murderers, and most likely rapists, there were some who were drool-worthy. I straightened my neck. "Our parents wouldn't approve."

Marisa was the one to respond. "Izzy, you're eighteen. Uncle Carmine shouldn't be telling you who you can and can't see or speak to." She lifted her chin. "As soon as I'm eighteen, I'm leaving this city."

"And going where?" Noemi asked.

She shrugged. "Anywhere but here in this testosterone-dominated world."

"So you're leaving the planet?" I asked. "Is NASA taking candidates with a high school diploma?"

Marisa nudged my arm before we all began walking toward the dining room. On the long table was a big cake that read *Happy 1ˢᵗ birthday, Ariadna Gia.* Based on the delicious aromas coming from the kitchen, we'd have more to eat than cake.

Patiently, I waited as others filled their cups. All the time, I nibbled on my lip and watched the cartel's interaction. Despite my father's constant warnings, everyone appeared jovial, smiling, talking, and laughing.

As I walked away from the punch bowl, I paid special attention to my cup, not wanting the red punch to spill on the marble floor. Near the fireplace, I stopped suddenly, almost running into a rock-hard obstacle. Looking up, I blinked, seeing the man I knew to be Catalina's brother. "Oh, I'm sorry. Did I get any punch on you?"

Emiliano smiled and looked down at his shirt—a blue button-up with sleeves rolled up to show his muscular forearms—then his dark stare came back at me. "No harm, no foul."

The aroma of tobacco and spice filled my senses. "That's good." I took a step to the side. "If you'll excuse me."

"You're Isabella?" He tucked his chin in a charming way, grinned, and offered me his hand. "I'm Emiliano."

Staring down at his large palm and long fingers, my heart raced in my chest. In the span of seconds, I suddenly felt as if I might faint. I scanned the room from side to side. If my father so much as heard that I spoke to this man, I'd be grounded to my room or worse.

Not taking Emiliano's hand, I scooted another step back and lifted my chin. "We've met, I believe." I shrugged. "Weddings." As my circulation warmed, I searched for my sister or cousins. "I need to go."

"The party hasn't even started."

"Not leave...but my father...I..." I swallowed. "I really should find my sister."

"If she's with a group of girls, I think I saw them head down the hallway toward the theater room."

"Library."

His eyebrows arched. "You'd rather read than watch a movie?"

The answer was yes, but we weren't conversing.

I straightened my neck. "Goodbye."

Emiliano winked. "I'll save you a seat for the gift opening. I'm sure it will be enthralling."

"That won't be necessary."

The punch in my cup quivered from my trembling as I walked away and toward the library.

TWO

Isabella

Red punch dribbled down my wrist as I pushed open the library door and rushed inside. Closing the door behind me, I shut my eyes as my heart thumped against my breastbone. Upon lifting my eyelids, I saw four sets of eyes staring at me.

"Izzy, what happened?" Noemi asked as she stood from the lounge chair she was sharing with Aria.

"How could you leave me out there alone?"

"You were hardly alone. There's two worlds of people out there," Marisa said, standing from the chair she was sharing with Cenzi.

Aria chimed in. "We thought you were with us. What happened?"

Now all four of the other girls were standing and coming closer.

"Emiliano…Catalina's brother." I set the cup of punch on a nearby table and looked for something to clean my fingers and wrist.

Cenzi hurried from the room, only to return in seconds with a towel from a nearby bathroom. "Did he do something to you?" she asked as she handed me the plush white cloth.

Holding the bright white hand towel, I wasn't sure of anything. Looking up, I said, "I don't want to stain their towels."

Noemi took the towel and wiped my hand and wrist. "I'm sure the capo can afford new towels." Her chocolate brown eyes met mine. "Emiliano…what happened?"

"I was carrying my punch back to you, and I almost ran into him." I shook my head. "I don't know. I might have run into him."

Everyone's eyes were wide.

"I didn't get punch on him." Rolling my lower lip, I nibbled on it and shrugged. "He talked to me. I tried to get away, and he kept talking to me."

"Did Dad see the two of you together?" Noemi asked.

I shook my head. "I don't think so. I hope he's still in the capo's office. Mom might have seen. I was so frightened; I couldn't wait to get away from him."

Aria's smile widened. "I'd like to talk to him. Hell, I'd like to do more than that with him." Her little sister nudged her with her elbow. When no one said anything, Aria went on, "Come on. You can't deny that Catalina's brother is hot. If the cartel men were as bad as our fathers say, why does Mia look so happy? She's with the scariest one of the group."

"I got a peek at Jasmine," Marisa said. "She looks different, more confident." She shrugged. "Like she isn't a stray any longer."

"She's married to the second-in-command to the drug lord," Noemi said. She let out a long breath. "But you're right. Jasmine doesn't seem scared either."

My nose wrinkled. "But we've been told since Dario's engagement how dangerous the cartel members are and how horribly they treat women. The cartel runs a whorehouse. Dad said Catalina and Camila were fortunate to get out of that life."

Cenzi scoffed. "Uncle Carmine is upset about the alliance. Our dad is too. But it's not like Catalina and Camila were going to be put to work in prostitution."

"It isn't a whorehouse," Marisa said. "It's a club with women who...you know, have sex. Newsflash, that's what Emerald Club is."

The small hairs on the back of my neck stood to attention. "No, it isn't. Mom said Emerald Club is just a dance club."

"Well," Marisa said, "I'm not sure why she's lying to you, but it's more than a dance club. I've overheard Dad telling Mom about some of the problems brought on by the bratva and cartel."

"Whatever. You're saying the cartel is causing our famiglia problems."

Noemi took her place back on the lounge chair. "We've been to Catalina's childhood home—for Mia's wedding. It's not as if the Ruizes are living in an abandoned warehouse like they show on television. Catalina left a home on a cliff overlooking the Pacific Ocean for

Kansas City. And if Mom's lied to us about Emerald Club, maybe there's something to what Aria is saying. Maybe they're not all murderers and rapists."

"But," I continued, "the whores in *their* club have been sex trafficked. That's what they do. They get women and girls who are trying to cross the border."

Marisa shook her head. "You've been watching too many videos. Sex trafficking is a problem everywhere, even here. When I leave, I'm staying away from truck stops."

Could I be seeing things through the lens of my parents' bigotry?

I sat next to my sister. "There was something about the way Emiliano looked at me. I can't describe it. My stomach was instantly in knots, and my circulation was going so fast, I thought I might faint right in the capo's living room." I laid my head back. "Papà would have gone ballistic."

My cousins shared a grin, sat down together on the other lounge chair, and turned to me. Marisa was the one to speak. "Maybe you weren't scared." Her eyebrows danced. "Maybe you were attracted to him."

Pressing my lips together, I shook my head. "No. And Papà would never—"

"Are you forgetting that he already did?" she asked. "Uncle Carmine agreed to offer you to Reinaldo."

My heart was again beating too fast. "It's because Dario didn't feel Jasmine was enough of an offer for *el Patrón's* son. And Papà wasn't happy about it." I stared at everyone. "It was Dario's doing, not Papà's."

"You know if Dario tells Dad to jump, he'll jump,"

Noemi said. "Dad talks shit about the capo, but he won't stand up to him, not on something like this."

Aria leaned back. "Look at you. All three of you have beautiful blond hair. You stick out." She peered over at Noemi and me. "Stick out—in a good way. Men notice you. Women will notice Tony when he's older too."

Her comment reminded me that our father had taken Tony into the capo's office. I couldn't help worrying about him. Papà was harder on him than he was on Noemi and me. That wasn't to say he was easy on us. It was just different.

When my thoughts came back to our conversation, Aria was speaking. It didn't take me too long to realize she was talking about Emiliano.

"…at Dario's wedding, I wasn't sure what to think of him. I mean, he kept looking at Dario like he wanted to kill him."

Marisa scoffed. "He probably did. Catalina's his little sister."

Cenzi nodded.

Aria went on, "He's bulked up since then and doesn't seem so uptight."

"Dealing with Dario makes everyone uptight." I was thinking about what Marisa said. "I forgot that he's older than Catalina. How old do you think he is?"

"He's older," Aria said. "Maybe thirty."

Noemi responded, "That sounds old, but it really isn't. Dante's in his thirties and Camila is like twenty." Her checks pinkened. "I think I'd rather be with an older man who knows what he's doing. Some of the girls at school talk." She swallowed. "I think it sounds awkward to fumble around with a guy who knows as much about sex as I do. Which is only what I can read in a book or see in a movie. And that's not real."

"I hate that we're so sheltered," Marisa said. "Attending an all-girls Catholic school, I don't even have any guy friends my own age to compare." She sat taller. "And I've heard the stories at school, too. I think they're lying and talking for attention. I mean, there's no way that they're getting all that action and we're sitting here in an all-girls library while the living room is full of eligible men." When we didn't respond, she added, "That's why I'm taking off after I'm eighteen. I want to see the world. Learn about guys and everything the world has to offer."

The library door opened inward. Aunt Giulia peeked inside. "Contessa announced that the meal is ready. It's a buffet. You girls should get your plates and come back here to eat."

As we all stood and began to file out the doorway, my aunt reached for my arm. She lowered her voice. "I thought you should know. Mia has been talking to your mom about you helping her out in San Diego with the apartment house she's running."

My eyes narrowed. "Mia's running an apartment house?"

Aria and Cenzi were farther away, but Marisa's and Noemi's eyes opened wider.

"Go on," Aunt Giulia said to the other girls before turning back to me. "It's Mia's project. She had an old school renovated into apartments for the whores from Wanderland, the cartel's club."

Club?

"Is their club any different than Emerald Club?" I asked.

Aunt Giulia pressed her lips together and shook her head. "I don't know for sure, but the basics are the same. Your uncle claims Emerald Club is better. Anyway, now with Jorge born and Aléjandro's new position, Mia could use help. When Aurora said you were taking a year off from college to do philanthropic work, Mia latched on. I guess some young woman from Catalina's family is helping, but she can't do it alone."

"Do they keep them locked up?"

"Who?"

"The women working in the club."

My aunt tilted her head. "No...why would they?"

"What if they want to leave?"

"Then I guess they leave. Mia said that the change in housing has had a positive effect on the women."

"Women. You just said whores." I wrinkled my nose. "I don't want to go to San Diego." My eyes opened wide. "Where would I live? I couldn't live with Mia—not with *el Patrón*." Tears threatened the back of my eyes. "What did Mom say?"

"She said she'd talk to your father."

I let out a breath. "He'll never agree to it."

Aunt Giulia feigned a smile. "You're probably right. I just wanted you to know in case Mia says something to you about it."

My nose wrinkled. "Work with whores? Is that even safe?"

Aunt Giulia kissed my hair. "Don't worry about it,

Isabella. Just be prepared if the topic comes up." She tilted her head. "Now, let's eat, watch Ariadna Gia—or Catalina—open presents, and get out of here before a fight breaks out."

"Sounds good."

CHAPTER

THREE

Emiliano

Even though Isabella avoided me for the rest of the party, I did my best to keep my eyes on her. She was easy to spot with her long golden hair. Whenever our gazes would meet, she would look away. Of the throng of girls, the only one who would make eye contact with me was the middle sister from Salvatore's family. I learned from Cat that her name was Aria, and she was sixteen. Definitely off-limits. Besides, there was something about Isabella.

Yes, her hair was beautiful, but her sister had the same color hair. I didn't feel a pull toward her sister. There shouldn't be a pull toward Isabella. She was of age, but that still meant young. I'd be thirty at my next birthday.

Maybe it was watching Jano and Rei settle down that

made me want to do the same. Knowing the dislike Dario's uncles had for the alliance, I'd be better off to talk to Jano about a daughter of one of his lieutenants. Rei oversaw many soldiers in Northern California.

With my back against the wall and my arms crossed over my chest, I watched as Catalina sat on the floor with Ariadna Gia. Dario was sitting behind them on a sofa, smiling and nodding as Catalina opened presents and showed them to the baby and then to her husband.

If anyone would have asked me when our father was first discussing Cat's arranged marriage to Dario Luciano if I thought it would work, I would have said no. Seeing him interact with his wife and daughter was as if the man who sat behind the desk in the big office had two personalities.

I found Isabella seated with her sister and cousins, all crammed on another sofa. It was pretty obvious that they were only present because of their fathers heeding Dario's invitation. Dante and Camila were next to the capo. Camila was writing each gift and the giver's name on a tablet.

My mother and Mrs. Luciano were seated close on two chairs. Mrs. Luciano was holding Jorge. My dad and Uncle Nicolas were about as far away from Dario's uncles as they could be and still be in the same room. It seemed evident that while some people were trying to make the alliance work, others would be just as happy if it dissolved.

"*Ey*," Nick, my cousin, said as he settled beside me against the wall. He lowered his voice. "We have Herrera to deal with and instead, our top brass are in Kansas City at a one-year-old's birthday party. This is *mierda*."

Bullshit.

I stifled a laugh. "*Sí,* but look at Jano." We both turned to see *el Patrón* sitting with his arm around Mia's shoulders. "He needed this break. Even if it's only for one day."

Nick nodded. "He's doing well. Jorge would be proud."

"The resistance is wearing on him. The confirmation of Herrera being alive has him working 24/7."

"Have you talked much to Rei?" Nick asked. "How are things going up north?"

"You know about as much as I do. I know he and Jano talk every day."

"Em."

I turned my attention to my sister, the one on the floor.

Her smile grew as she held up a little LA Chargers cheerleader dress. "It's adorable."

"Adorable," the capo said dryly, "but she'll never wear it."

Catalina turned and smiled at her husband and turned back toward me with a wink. "She'll wear it."

"Not if they're playing the Chiefs."

Laughter rumbled through the room.

Nick whispered. "You're not making points with the capo."

When I turned to the capo, I saw the gleam in his eye. To say our relationship had improved since he married Cat would be an understatement. I whispered back, "I think I am." A quick turn of my head told me what I suspected. Salvatore and Carmine Luciano weren't sharing in the camaraderie. At least my father and Nicolas were grinning.

After the last present was opened, Catalina invited everyone into the dining room for cake. As we squeezed in, I made it a point to get closer to Isabella. I eased in behind her as Catalina put Ariadna Gia into a high chair. It was when Contessa came from the kitchen with a tiny cake with a candle that we began to sing.

As soon as "Happy Birthday" ended in English, we sang it again in Spanish.

Even Dario took part in helping the little girl blow out the candle. My mother and Mrs. Luciano fussed over the fact that Catalina left Ariadna Gia in her lacy dress as she trepidatiously pushed her hands into the frosting.

Phones came out around the room as pictures were taken.

I leaned forward and spoke near Isabella's ear. "I think I'd rather have a piece of the cake on the table."

Isabella startled and turned toward me and immediately away.

Keeping my voice low, I said, "I promise I won't bite." I was about to add *unless you like that*, but I sensed that she was truly afraid of me.

Her voice was barely audible. "Please don't talk to me."

"Making friendly conversation."

The little brunette turned to me. "Hi, I'm Aria."

"Girls," a deep voice bellowed.

I saw Carmine looking our way.

"It's time to go," he said.

"There's cake for everyone," Catalina said.

"We must be going…"

The capo stood tall. "I'm sure you can stay for one piece of cake."

The capo had spoken. No one was leaving before the cake was served.

As soon as the cake was eaten, Salvatore and Carmine excused their families and boarded the elevator in two groups. Catalina, our mom, and Mrs. Luciano tended to an icing-covered one-year-old, and Jasmine and Camila helped Contessa with carrying the dishes into the kitchen. I followed Rei and Jano toward the capo's study. To my surprise, the capo and Dante were already present.

The room was regal, with cherry wainscoting and bookcases filled with books. Large floor-to-ceiling windows allowed the early evening summer sun to illuminate the space with a warm glow.

"How are things going out on the West Coast?" Dario asked Jano.

Jano took the chair to Dario's side.

There was something about this den that was different from Dario's office. In this space, it felt as if we were on a more level playing field.

Dante tapped my shoulder and moved behind a small bar. "Drink?" He grinned. "One that's not punch."

"Tequila?"

"Of course." He pulled out a bottle of Clase Azul Reposado and poured two fingers. "Ice?"

"I'm good." I took the glass as Rei appeared at my side.

"No ice for me either."

"Where did Mia go?" I asked. "I didn't get a chance to see much of Jorge. He was the second main attraction."

Rei answered, "She and her cousin, Giorgia, took him upstairs to feed him and get him down for a nap."

His answer made me smile. "You're getting the uncle thing down."

Dante lifted his glass filled with two fingers of an amber liquid. "To uncles." He lowered his voice. "All the fun without losing sleep."

We clinked glasses and emptied our tumblers.

Dario and Jano were focused on their own conversation. Rei leaned forward. "We waited to tell anyone until after we told the capo." He paused. "Jasmine and I are adding another baby to this alliance."

Dante's grin grew from ear to ear. "Fuck, my brother's going to be a grandpa."

We all laughed.

"That title is his for the taking," Rei said. "To be honest, it would mean the world to Jasmine if he used it or anything similar—*abuelo* or even *nonno*. But we're talking about the capo, so who knows?"

"Were you nervous about telling him?" I asked.

Rei stood tall, pressed his lips together, and shook his head. "Me? No. You know me, Em. I'm never nervous."

"You were armed, admit it," Dante said as he refilled our glasses.

"I still am."

We all were.

I turned to Dante. "Do you think Carmine would have allowed Rei to marry Isabella?"

Rei lifted his hands. "Wasn't interested. Not interested now."

"I know, but...?" I looked again at Dante.

His eyes narrowed. "Is there a particular reason you're asking?"

"Maybe. I should talk to the capo."

Rei shook his head. "No, *hombre*. If you want to pursue Isabella or anyone, you go through Jano."

"Fuck. *Sí*. I wasn't thinking. You're right."

"Wasn't thinking about what?" Dario asked, he and Jano coming toward the bar.

"Pour me one of those," Jano said to Dante.

FOUR

Isabella
A month later

Outside the windows, the Kansas City summer sun baked the ground, turning the green grass to brown. If I wasn't planning a trip, I'd be outside in our pool or lying in a chair on the pool's deck. Instead, here I was in my bedroom. "I can't believe they're making me do this," I moaned as I filled my suitcase with whatever I thought I might need for a month's stay in San Diego.

Noemi sat cross-legged on my bed beside the suitcase. "It could be worse. You're not getting married, just going to help Mia."

I sank to the floor, wrapped my arms around my legs, and tucked my knees beneath my chin, fighting the chill of the air conditioning on my bare legs. "I've tried everything to get Mom and Papà to change their minds." I shook my head. "I can't even look at Papà. He's being completely unreasonable." I lifted my chin, staring up at my sister. "Did I tell you what he said when I told him I didn't want to stay with Mia and *el Patrón*?"

Noemi shook her head.

"He said maybe I could live in the apartment building."

My sister's mouth opened but no words came out.

"Yeah. With the whores." My nostrils flared as I exhaled. "I called and spoke to Mia. She sounds excited to have me there. She said where I live is my choice. Another option is to share an apartment with Liliana, the Ruiz who is also helping with the apartments." I shrugged. "She's not a lot older than us."

"An apartment in California. Is that safe?"

I shrugged. "I think the cartel has her guarded. I assume."

"If she's that young, why is she living away from her family?"

"It sounds like she got some freedom with Mia's help. When I first heard about Liliana, I thought that she was Catalina's cousin, but Mia explained that she was actually married to Catalina's uncle. Liliana is like twenty years old, Catalina's step-aunt, and a widow."

Noemi shook her head. "Damn, sounds like she's been through a lot." Wrinkling her nose, she added, "I'm so scared for you. I can't imagine going out to California all alone."

"Rafaele is going to travel with me. I don't even get to use a famiglia plane."

"It's only for a month. You'll be back."

"I should have pushed for attending college." It was too late for that. Fall semesters were ready to start all over the country. Noemi was about to begin her sophomore year in high school. People were moving on with their lives—people who had choices.

Sighing, I stood and walked toward the closet. "What will I even wear?" I ran my fingers over my clothes—dresses, slacks, blouses, and skirts. A glance down at my shorts and I knew they wouldn't meet my mother's approval for traveling clothes.

The click of my bedroom door opening summoned me out of the closet. Tony barreled toward me. His collision nearly tackling me as he wrapped his arms around my hips and buried his face in my breasts. "Izzy."

I lifted his chin, bringing his reddened soft brown eyes to mine. "What happened? Are you okay?"

"Mom just told me you're leaving."

My chest ached as I lowered myself to my knees and took his hands. "I don't have a choice."

"She'll be back in a month," Noemi added.

"You should." His cheeks were damp with tears. "You should have a choice." His little face contorted with anger. "I hate Dario."

My gaze scanned from Tony to Noemi and back to my brother. "It's not Dario's fault. Mia asked for me to help her."

His head shook from side to side. "No, the day of Ariadna Gia's party, I went with Papà to Dario's office. I heard them talking."

"About what?"

"About you. Dario said it was time for Papà to make a sacrifice for the famiglia."

Noemi joined the two of us on the floor. "He said *sacrifice*?"

Tony nodded.

My voice trembled. "How am I a sacrifice?"

"I don't know. They all were talking fast. I was trying to act brave. I forgot about it until Mom said you're going away to California."

I swallowed. "Dario made Papà say yes." I stood and after making a complete circle scanning the room that had always been my bedroom, I sat on the edge of my bed. "No wonder he won't budge on the subject."

"Because he won't stand up to the capo," my sister said.

Inhaling, I watched as Noemi sat at my side. "I'm looking at this all wrong."

"What's the right way to look at it?"

I thought of my cousin Marisa. "If I stay here, Mom will have me attending all her club meetings, social engagements, and pet projects, pushing me into her society circle. I don't want to be there. I want to get out of this bubble too. If I do what Mom has planned, I'll be stuck." My own words were bringing a seed of hope to life within me. "Instead of dreading California, maybe I should appreciate the opportunity. It's an escape from here." My gaze met Noemi's. "You know, like Marisa was talking about?"

"But...the cartel." She reached for my hand. "I'm scared for you."

Tony was now standing at my side. I wrapped one

arm around him and squeezed my sister's hand. "I'll make you a promise, both of you." I inhaled. "I'm going to look at this month as an experience helping me to grow up and break free. Remember at Ariadna Gia's party?" I asked Noemi. "We were talking about being sheltered. We have been. This trip is my chance to see at least a little more of the world."

"Whores?" my sister asked with her nose wrinkled. "*El Patrón*?"

"Papà and Mom have painted us their version of the cartel's reality. Mia and Jasmine are happy. Mia even said I didn't have to live with them. I could live with Liliana in an apartment. Papà would never permit that back here in Kansas City. Heck, he'd never let Mom make that decision. Maybe *el Patrón* is different?" I feigned strength for my siblings. "Who knows, I may want to stay more than a month."

"Don't say that," my brother said. "I'm going to miss you."

"I'm going to miss both of you. You still have each other. Noemi is here for you, just like I would be."

My sister nodded.

"When are you leaving?" Tony asked.

"Tomorrow morning. Rafaele is flying with me and delivering me to Mia. Papà said that Mia would arrange a bodyguard for while I'm out there."

"After you finish packing," Tony said, "could the three of us watch a movie in your room and eat popcorn?"

"You want to get popcorn crumbs in my bed?" I asked jokingly.

Tony nodded quickly. "Please."

"I think it sounds like a great plan."

Three hours later, after a tense dinner, Noemi, Tony, and I all lay on my bed watching *Toy Story* for what could very well be the hundredth time, when a knock came from my bedroom door. After climbing off the large bed, I opened the door and found Franco standing in the hallway.

"Miss Isabella, your father wants to see you in his office."

A sense of dread rippled through me. I'd just shared a meal with my father, and he'd hardly said two words to me. My flight was set for ten the next morning. I tuned back to my siblings. "Don't wait for me. I know what happens next."

Wearing the comfy clothes I'd changed into after dinner—leggings, an oversized long-sleeved shirt, and footie socks—I followed Franco down the hallway and down the front stairs to Papà's office. The door was slightly ajar and golden light spilled through the passage. Beyond the windows in the foyer, the summer sky was beginning to darken with impending nightfall.

"Mr. Luciano," Franco announced my arrival.

His office smelled of tobacco and books. Papà looked up from his desk. His suit coat and tie he'd had on earlier during dinner were absent, and the sleeves of his shirt were rolled up to his elbows. There was a tiredness to his presence.

"You wanted to see me?" I asked, standing before him.

Papà's dark eyes scanned me from my loose hair to

my socks. His nostrils flared as he leaned back against his large leather chair. "I think it's best for us to discuss the next month."

"Since I'm leaving the house by seven thirty tomorrow morning, I guess it's now or never."

His jaw clenched. "Isabella, sit down and show some respect to your father."

I sat on the edge of one of the two chairs facing his desk.

When I didn't speak, he did. "You know your mother's and my feelings regarding the Roríguez cartel."

I nodded.

Crimson seeped from Papà's collar. "I expect verbal answers, young lady." His voice grew louder. "You will be representing the Luciano famiglia. That is a very important—"

"Sacrifice?" I volunteered.

He stared at my interruption. "Responsibility was the word I was about to use."

"I know your feelings," I said, leaning forward. "I don't understand why—if you feel they're all so dangerous—you are sending me there." I hesitated, not wanting to get Tony in trouble. "Is it because of the capo? Is he making you do this?"

Papà sat forward. "Mia is the one who brought your travel up to your mother. Aurora believes strongly in charity. After giving the proposal consideration, we decided this would be an eye-opening experience for you. One you can bring back to Kansas City and see our world in a new light."

"Dario had nothing to do with this?"

Papà slammed his palm on his desk. "Damn it, we are part of the famiglia. Of course, the capo was involved." He exhaled and leaned back. "I won't tolerate receiving any reports of promiscuous activities. You are there to aid your cousin with her project. Remember that unlike the stray, you are a Luciano. You have worth that will not be squandered on the likes of the cartel." He inhaled. "I decided to inform you before you left…I've spoken to the capo about Aldo Ricci, the son of the consigliere in St. Louis."

"Spoke to him about what?"

"Marriage, Isabella. With the dangers we're facing, uniting outfits, especially with the close proximity of St. Louis, is beneficial. You're beautiful, and you could be the way to bridge the gap we've had with the St. Louis famiglia in the past."

"Is it set? My wedding?" I asked.

"No, that's Dario's job. I am not privy to his timing. I'm certain it won't be set until after you return from San Diego. I wanted you to know that you are spoken for. Therefore, your interaction with the cartel will be by necessity only. Stay close to Mia and do as she asks. I don't want you living with *el Patrón*, but under the circumstances, I feel it will be the safest place. Mia will look after you." He brought his hands to the arms of his chair. "Mia mentioned living with a widow. I don't approve. Rafaele will accompany you to Mia's home. I want your word that you will reside there."

My mouth felt suddenly dry. "I'd like to meet Liliana."

"You will be working with her. I'm sure you'll meet.

Remember, you're going out there to represent the Luciano famiglia in a unique way." He repeated, "You are a Luciano. Mia is too, but she has a different last name. The stray...well, she never has been famiglia. While you don't yet have a ring from Aldo Ricci, you are not available."

"You don't want to marry me to the cartel?" I lifted my eyebrows. "Then why did you tell Dario I could marry Reinaldo?"

"You dodged that bullet, Isabella. Praise the Father and thank the saints daily for your fortune. Stay as far away from the cartel men as possible. If I learn that any one of them so much as touches you, there will be a war on our hands that even the capo won't be able to stop."

Emiliano

S ilas opened the door to *el Patrón's* home, allowing me entry. *"Buenos días,"* I greeted. Silas was the final guard at the last point of entry. Since Aléjandro ascended to the top position in the cartel, his home was even more guarded than before.

"Señor Ruiz, el jefe esta en su oficina."

With a nod, I headed toward Aléjandro's office. As I approached, I heard voices. It didn't take me long to realize Mia, Aléjandro's wife, was also present.

"Em," she said, turning to me as I entered. "Maybe you could add your two cents to our discussion."

Aléjandro Roríguez was seated behind his desk. If one were to enter this home, they'd surely mistake Silas for *el Patrón*, the man in charge of Aléjandro and his family's safety. He was always dressed in a suit, often a three-piece suit. On the other hand, the true leader was behind his desk with a five-o'clock shadow, despite it being morning, and wearing a white t-shirt, blue jeans, and by the one foot on his desk, black boots.

Mia was also dressed for comfort in her sundress and flat sandals. Her long hair was tied back in a low ponytail. At this rare moment, she wasn't holding her son.

I bowed at the waist. "Always happy to be of service, *señora*."

"My cousin Isabella is arriving this afternoon. Jano thinks Silas should watch over her while she's here because he's older, not intimidating to her, but I disagree. Silas has sworn his oath of service to not only Jano, but to Jorge and me. I think sending him away could create a void around here." She sighed. "I know that I'm still hormonal. Nevertheless, after what happened to..." She paused. "Jano's father, I don't want to risk Jorge's safety."

She said quite a bit, but honestly, my brain latched on to her first sentence. "Isabella Luciano is coming here. To San Diego?"

Mia turned to Jano. "How doesn't Em know that?"

"Shit, Mia," he said, lowering his foot to the floor. "We're on a twenty-four-hour search for news about Herrera and Volkov." He stood. Placing his hand over his heart he stalked toward his wife. "*Pido disculpas.*" He turned to me. "Isabella Luciano is arriving later today. She will be here for a month—initially. Mia needs help at the apartment building and not surprisingly, Liliana isn't getting it done."

Mia reached out to her husband's arm. "I know this

isn't as big of a priority for you as it is for me. She's coming out here because I pressured Dario. Once he approved my request, I assured my uncle that Isabella would be safe. I also don't want to compromise our safety in that process."

"Your safety is my priority."

"What will she be doing in your stead?" I asked Mia.

Mia sighed. "Being me until I can figure out how to get back there. I've developed a system to keep track of each woman, ensure we have their up-to-date information, everything. It's also supposed to monitor their work hours as well as when they're at the apartments, away to work, or out. It's not that complicated, but every time I check online, the information is outdated. Somehow, Liliana is consistently a day or two behind. Something could happen to one of the women and we wouldn't know for forty-eight hours. That's not acceptable. The women are trusting us with their information and safety." She took a seat across from Jano's desk. "I don't want to fire Liliana, but she needs help. According to Catalina, Isabella is a fast learner. She graduated high school with honors and wanted to attend university." She pressed her lips together. "Of course, Uncle Carmine doesn't see the need."

I tried to get a feel for what would be required of Isabella's bodyguard. "I assume she's staying here with you?"

Jano rolled his eyes.

Mia replied, "Her father wants her here. I get the feeling that she's intimidated. Uncle Carmine and Aunt Aurora don't have high opinions of the cartel. I told her she could stay with Liliana if she preferred. She has an apartment at Estate 3301."

My eyebrows rose. "High-end real estate."

"She's been through a lot. It's a three bedroom. José and Renata Pérez are her bodyguard and her live-in help. That leaves one free bedroom if Isabella would be more comfortable there."

"I know José. I didn't realize he was married," I said.

Jano answered, "They had previously been with Gerardo and felt protective of Liliana. They're a married couple in their forties. From what I hear, Renata is almost as good of a cook as Viviana." That would be Silas's wife.

Mia stood and lifted her eyebrows. "I thought you were going to say almost as good as me," she said with a smirk.

Jano wrapped his arm around Mia and tugged her toward him. Whatever he whispered caused her cheeks to flush with crimson before she kissed his cheek.

I cleared my throat. "I volunteer."

Jano turned to me. "No." He released his wife and moved back around the desk. Strewn over the surface were paper maps, ones I knew he'd studied backward and forward. "I need you. I need you on the streets and at Wanderland. Shit went down last night. You have connections through *tu padre,* and you're one of the best hackers I know next to Rei. It would be too much of a loss to have you babysit Isabella."

"But it's not a loss if Silas does?" Mia pleaded.

"This house is safer than Fort Knox," Jano said. "Silas

can be gone during the day and once Isabella is done at the apartments, he will be back with us."

"What if she lives with Liliana?" she asked.

"He can still return. José is capable of keeping two girls safe in a luxury apartment."

Mia wrapped her arms around herself. "Do you know the last time I heard that saying—safer than Fort Knox?"

Jano let out a breath. "Bella."

She nodded with tears in her eyes. "Bella."

Jano came around the desk, leaned against the surface, and pulled his wife between his long legs and into his embrace. "What happened out there will not happen here."

"If we hadn't taken so many of the guards…Jorge was left shorthanded." She palmed Jano's cheeks. "*Por favor, estoy asustada*."

El Patrón's Adam's apple bobbed as he turned to me. "Find a soldier we can trust with Isabella."

"You can trust me."

"Em, find me a soldier and have him here by noon. Isabella arrives after two. He can accompany Silas to the airport."

I wanted to argue my case. I could also see the turmoil Mia was still experiencing from what happened to Jorge Roríguez I. Mostly, I understood that I'd just received a direct order from *el Patrón* himself. As a soldier myself, I wasn't in a position to argue.

My thoughts filled with capable soldiers. We had them—men who would lay down their lives for Jano, Rei, and the cartel. This wouldn't be that simple of a request.

Cue the other important person running through my

mind—Isabella Luciano. She was famiglia. Whomever I chose would have to swear to protect her as if she were cartel. One day, she would be.

After all, Isabella was coming to me. I'd concede that I wasn't the exact reason she was coming to California. Nevertheless, I had one month to show her that I wasn't the monster she'd been led to believe. I'd show her that in essence the cartel and Mafia famiglia were more similar than she realized. We had different products and similar products. We both worked in an underground world that everyday people chose to ignore.

The Mafias of the past were renowned, filled with the lore of honor and duty. The likes of Al Capone, Carlo Gambino, and Frank Costello romanticized the realities of their livelihoods. Movies such as *The Godfather* and *The Untouchables* made mere men into legends.

The cartel needed to up its public relations. As we witnessed with the news and social media coverage of the death of Jorge Roríguez I, cartels were viewed with less allure. *Scarface* and *Savages* portray us as cruel, greedy, and bloodthirsty.

The reality was that the Mafia and cartel were different sides of the same coin. No one could claim that either organization was filled with boy scouts. We both dealt within the illegal world of drugs, prostitution, and extortion. *El patrón* was especially bloodthirsty to avenge his father. Yet the man the world never saw was the one who moments ago made his wife blush, showed her compassion, and listened to her concerns. Perhaps the world would never see that side of the Roríguez cartel.

As I drove away from Jano's home, I wasn't concerned about the world. I was thinking about one particular woman—a young woman but a woman all the same. I would spend what time I could over the next month showing Isabella Luciano that cartel members were also men of honor and duty.

My first order of business was to find a soldier who would protect Isabella with his life while at the same time understanding that if he crossed a line with her, his life would be over.

SIX

Isabella

Rafaele and I deboarded the airplane at our final destination. Exiting first class, we were some of the first passengers to make our way up the long jet bridge. With each step, I tried to remind myself of the promise I'd made to my siblings, the promise to use this experience to learn, to explore, and to see more of the world. As we stepped into the San Diego airport, I glanced out the large windows, seeing rows of commercial airplanes parked at gate after gate. This wasn't exactly seeing more of the world, but it was a start.

"Miss Isabella," Rafaele said as we stepped away from the parade of people. "Wait with me as I call Mr. Ramírez and let him know we've arrived." When I didn't respond, he added, "Silas Ramírez is the head of *el Patrón's* security."

I nodded my response.

These were names I'd need to learn. I nibbled on my lower lip as Rafaele spoke discreetly into his phone. There were so many uncertainties running laps through my thoughts. Taking a deep breath, I straightened my shoulders. There were things I couldn't or wouldn't allow myself to concentrate on. For one, eighteen years old was hardly old. I couldn't drink alcohol, and I'd never learned how to drive. Nevertheless, I was officially an adult. Even if my father and the capo didn't agree, I could legally make my own decisions. My thoughts went to Aldo Ricci. Marrying him wouldn't be my decision.

As I waited by Rafaele's side, I had the epiphany that I'd always had a bodyguard, one of my father's men, at my side. It wasn't as if I gave any thought about trusting them. I simply did.

What would happen when it was no longer a famiglia guard?

The questions came faster than the answers. Despite the mayhem multiplying in my mind and wreaking havoc on my emotions, I stood tall, refusing to display my insecurities. I may never know why the capo demanded this of me, but I wouldn't let it bring me down. I'd show Mia and the others that I was ready to attack the world head-on.

After his call ended, Rafaele sent a text message and placed his phone in the inside breast pocket of his suit coat. "Mr. Ramírez is waiting in the car. Mr. Horace Torres will join us in luggage return."

"Torres?" I asked. "Who is he?"

Rafaele inhaled as he led me through the long hallways and connecting walkways. "He has been assigned to you."

"My new bodyguard." I verbalized my recent thought. "How do I know if I can trust him?"

"I've sent a text message to Mr. Luciano. Dante will send a report quickly, and we'll know all we can about him."

I let out a breath. "Do you always do that...background checks?"

Rafaele nodded. "No one gets near the famiglia who hasn't been vetted."

That made me think. "But all the cartel that show up at the capo's home. Surely, they haven't all been vetted."

His jaw clenched. "Every one of them."

"So, they're not murderers and rapists?"

"A spotless crime report isn't required. Understanding and trust is."

We walked through the crowd in silence, following the signs. As we neared the terminal with the luggage return, I asked, "What about Papà, Uncle Salvatore, or even Dante? If a crime report was to be run on them, would it be clean?"

Rafaele shook his head. "There's much the police don't know."

Before I could give this train of thought more of my attention, a man wearing a dark suit not too different from Rafaele's, holding a tablet that read *Miss Luciano*, caught my attention. My heartbeat accelerated as I scanned the man up and down. It was difficult to judge, but I'd guess that he was older than Rafaele and younger than my father. Physically, he appeared to meet the unwritten bodyguard code—tall, fit, and buff. The gold band on his left hand let me know that he was also married.

"Miss Luciano," he said with a bow of his head.

I wasn't sure why I expected him to have an accent. He didn't.

"Yes," I replied. "And you are Mr. Torres?"

"I am Horace Torres. You may address me as Horace. I'll be at your service throughout your stay." He turned to Rafaele. "You will join Miss Luciano until we reach Señora Roríguez's home."

Even though it wasn't a question, Rafaele answered in the affirmative. As Rafaele gathered my checked bags, Horace kept a watchful eye on the crowd. Once my bags were accounted for, Horace led us out to the street. I was immediately hit with the contrast to Kansas City—the presence of palm trees and the lack of humidity. While the air was warm, it wasn't the oppressiveness I was used to during a Missouri summer. We came to a waiting black SUV, and Horace opened the rear door for me.

"Welcome," an older man, also wearing a suit, said from the driver's seat. Unlike Horace, his accent was noticeable.

"Thank you. Are you Mr. Ramírez?"

"*Sí*. Please call me Silas."

It appeared we would all be on a first-name basis.

Rafaele took the seat to my side as Silas pulled the SUV away from the curb and began to drive. I'd never been to Mia's home. I'd only been to Catalina and Camila's parents' home for Mia's wedding.

Some questions came to mind. Not wanting to be

overheard, I took my phone from my purse and sent text messages to Rafaele.

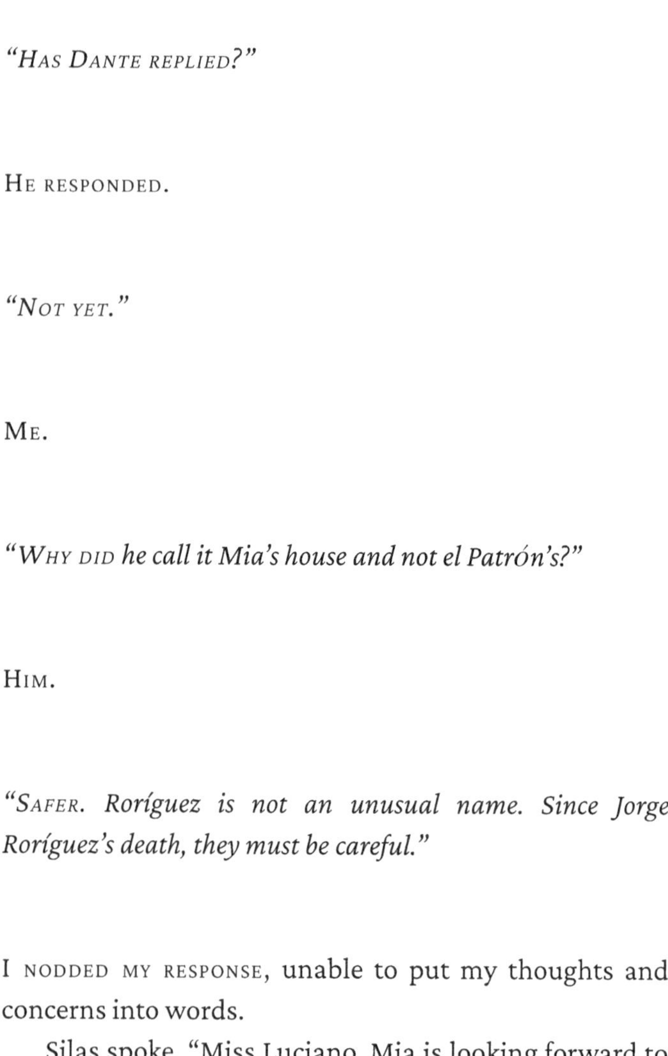

"Has Dante replied?"

He responded.

"Not yet."

Me.

"Why did he call it Mia's house and not el Patrón's?"

Him.

"Safer. Roríguez is not an unusual name. Since Jorge Roríguez's death, they must be careful."

I nodded my response, unable to put my thoughts and concerns into words.

Silas spoke, "Miss Luciano, Mia is looking forward to your arrival. You will spend today and tonight at her home, and tomorrow, Horace will take you to Mia's office at the apartment building."

"Please, call me Isabella."

Silas nodded.

We were on a highway only for a short time. Once off, the streets wound around with no true grid pattern. The passing scenes beyond the windows were nothing like I was used to. Tall palm trees lined the streets, bushes sported large vibrant flowers of all colors, and the sky was cobalt blue. Beautiful homes with varying architecture could be seen on both sides of the street until they couldn't. The homes were replaced with elaborate gates and shrubbery.

My phone vibrated in my grip. I looked down and read Rafaele's text message:

Dante's report came back. *Horace passed.*

I turned to him and nodded.

Thank you, Dante.

Silas drove up to a solid gate painted white with gold filigree. He passed a badge beneath a scanner and the gate moved slowly to the side. A wide driveway made of bricks led to an ultra-modern home. My attention went to the pair of armed cartel guards, one on either side of the inside gate. They weren't making any attempt to conceal the long guns they had strapped over their shoulders. If my mother or Noemi were present, I'd reach for one of their hands. Instead, I clutched my purse tighter.

Silas stopped the SUV on the bricks and Horace hurried from the front seat to open Rafaele's door. As Rafaele stepped out, the two guards began to approach. Silas, now also out of the SUV, said something to them in Spanish, and they both retook their original spots. It was Horace who offered me his hand as I exited the SUV.

The only words I recognized as Horace addressed the guards was my name. They merely nodded. My attention went to the surroundings as I passed through the gate. Large pavers and rocks covered the ground between the gate and house. Smaller sandstone rocks decorated the exterior of the lower level. There was also a trellis covered in vines that sheltered what appeared to be a small patio. Before I could take more in, the door opened, and my cousin appeared.

"Isabella," Mia said. "I'm happy you're here." She came forward and wrapped me in a hug. With her arm around my shoulders, she led me into her home. "I wasn't sure we could convince your mother to let you come out west. I'm glad we did."

We.

Did she think I was for this trip in any way?

Along a hallway, we passed by a closed door. The sound of male voices speaking in a language I didn't understand gave me a cold chill.

"That's Jano's office. Just ignore it."

Before I could reply, I saw the front—or would it be the back—of their home. Large glass doors were open to a stunning patio and pool. It was what was beyond that caught my attention. The Pacific Ocean. "Oh, Mia. This is amazing." I took a step toward the doors, feeling the summer breeze and smelling the salty aroma of the ocean. "Your home. I had no idea it was…" I turned to her. "I remember your townhouse in Kansas City."

Mia pressed her lips together and nodded.

"This is…it's so much nicer."

"Everything here is nicer than Kansas City. Don't tell my brother I said that, but it's the truth."

As if chatting with the capo was ever on my agenda.

Rafaele, Silas, and Horace appeared behind me with my suitcases.

"Did you leave any clothes at home?" Mia asked as she scanned the three large suitcases and a smaller carry-on.

"I had no idea what to pack. What I will wear when I'm working. If I'll need anything nicer…"

She laughed. "I guess you just packed it all." She turned to Silas. "Please take her things up to the spare bedroom we discussed." She turned back to me. "After you meet Liliana tonight—she's coming over for dinner so we can talk shop—if you want to live with her instead of here, that's still your choice."

"Papà said—"

Mia shook her head. "I promised Uncle Carmine you would be safe. You will be protected in either place. Consider this month a taste of what it's like to make your own decisions. I sure as hell wish someone would have shown me that when I was your age. It would have saved a lot of pain."

Mia's the wife of *el Patrón*. She couldn't possibly make her own decisions.

Could she?

She turned to Rafaele and extended her hand. "It's nice to see you again."

"Mrs. Mor—" He stopped. "Mrs. Roríguez."

"That's right. And if you report anything that I just said to Carmine or Dario, you will live to regret it."

Rafaele's eyes opened wide, and he grinned. "My job was to transport Miss Isabella safely to you."

"And you've done a fabulous job. Would you like a drink or something to eat before you leave?"

"No, ma'am." He turned to me. "Miss Isabella, are you satisfied if I leave for Kansas City now?"

Satisfied.

Holy shit.

I wasn't sure who this new Mia was, but I was excited to find out. "Thank you, Rafaele. As Mia said, you did a fabulous job." I took a step closer to Mia. "I'll be fine."

CHAPTER
SEVEN

Emiliano

Jano sat at his desk swearing in two languages, his stare transfixed on the video on his screen. Much was grainy and pixelated. From reports from soldiers on the street, a gun fight broke out at Pacific Beach last night. Two people were killed and three wounded. None of them cartel or bratva soldiers. It was the innocent who paid the highest price.

The press blamed the entire incident on the cartel despite the street camera footage showing that our soldiers were fired upon first. My cousin, Nick, also a soldier growing in stature among the Roríguez cartel, stood behind Jano, pointing out specifics. I sat across the office at my laptop. With access to the cartel's larger computer network, I had access to other cameras, from those of residents' doorbells to commercial-grade security systems.

This was the hacking *el Patrón* wanted me to do. My job wasn't to find evidence to change the mind of the police. They'd never be convinced that we didn't start it. This diligent search had another purpose: to provide Jano with the proof of who needed to pay.

"It's Kozlov's men," Nick said.

"You don't think it's Volkov? We know Volkov is communicating with Herrera."

Nick shook his head and squinted toward the screen. "Stop the video there." He had my attention. "Go back. Stop."

I stood and walked around the desk to see what they were seeing.

Nick pointed at the screen. "Can you zoom in on that man, the one who just fired his gun?"

Jano pulled the picture to increase the zoom while at the same time decreasing the clarity. "Fuck."

Fuck was right.

Nick pointed. "Look at that tattoo. That's definitely Kozlov's mark."

Jano sat back against his chair and raked his fingers through his hair. His dark eyes smoldered black and his nostrils flared. "Fucker is upping the attacks. Herrera is funding him. I feel it. I know it."

"We should up the number of guards at Wanderland and the apartment building," I said, thinking of the woman arriving today. "With both the Herrera cartel and the bratva watching us and willing to take out bystanders to make their point, we must protect what is ours."

Jano roared as he stood, slapping his palms on the maps littering his desk. "How did they know we had a crew at Pacific Beach? We've changed our pickup schedule, and they still fucking knew."

"They could have gotten lucky," Nick said. "Casing places in case we show up."

"That takes a lot of men," I said.

Jano clenched his jaw. "Or someone told them we changed collection day."

"No one would do that," I replied. "Jano, the dealers know not to double-cross you."

He paced to the wall and back. "I need more men."

"Bring some down from the north," Nick suggested.

"No. We're vulnerable there too."

"Mexico?" I suggested.

"No. Except for a few, our men in Mexico are compromised." Jano stopped walking and turned to us. "It's time to call in a debt."

"Which debt?" I asked.

"Rei and I went to Kansas City and took out Myshkin. Now, we need the famiglia to back us up out here in our territory. Fucking alliance works both directions." He rubbed his fingertips over his beard growth. "Herrera isn't risking his own men to bring us down. Somehow, he's convinced Kozlov to do the dirty work. We need reinforcements to get Kozlov out of the way so we can get to Herrera."

There was no arguing with Aléjandro. Ever since the

execution of his father, he had been hell-bent on Herrera's destruction.

El Patrón stood tall, looking more like the boss than he did a few months ago. With the stress of his new position, he'd lost weight but not muscle. His cheekbones were more defined and a vein in his forehead bulged with each word. "Tonight, I want all the lieutenants and available soldiers at the warehouse. Leave a skeleton crew of soldiers on the streets." He turned to me. "And keep Wanderland and the apartments well-guarded. Everyone else is to be there, including both of you. Ten o'clock. Be my eyes and ears when I can't be. I need to see their faces, to watch their eyes. If there's a *traidor* among us, I'll fucking gut him in front of an audience."

"Do you want me to keep looking for more evidence?" I asked.

Jano went back to his tall chair behind his desk and shook his head. "Both of you, go. Tell your fathers what's happening. Have them deal with Wanderland. Em, secure the apartments and Nick, get word out about tonight's meeting. If any soldier isn't where you tell them to be, there will be consequences."

"*Sí, jefe,*" we said in unison.

Aléjandro picked up his phone. "I'm calling the capo."

As we were walking out, Jano called to me. "Em, so I can tell Dario, who did you find to babysit the princess?"

The princess.

"Horace Torres. He works with the whores at Wanderland. That familiarity will help Isabella." Plus, he was married to the same woman for over fifteen years.

He'd kept his hands clean of abuse with the women at the club. I believed I could trust him with Isabella. I may also have threatened him.

Jano nodded. "He should stay here tonight during the meeting. I'll take Silas with me. The outside guards stay here too. No one is using our meeting as a time to get to my wife and son."

He forgot Isabella, but I wouldn't.

"I'll tell him when he gets here."

"He's here. I received the message a half hour or more ago."

My eyebrows rose. "They're here...Isabella is here?"

"*Sí*," he said dismissively. "*Vete*."

Stepping into the hallway, I closed the office door behind me. Despite the hell that was happening on our streets, a strange twinge of excitement sped through my circulation at the knowledge that Isabella was in this house.

I contemplated going out the front door, but that would be disobeying an order. Jano told me to talk to Horace. That would be my first stop. If I happened upon Isabella in the process, all the better.

Walking toward the living room, I scanned beyond the open doors to the pool and the glistening ocean beyond. Nothing was as beautiful as the sight of Isabella seated under an umbrella at a table with Mia. The two of them had glasses and plates before them and were looking at the screen of a laptop.

As I passed through the living room and by the kitchen, I saw Silas's wife, who was *el Patrón's* cook and housekeeper. "Viviana," I greeted.

Her smile grew. "Emiliano, *quieres almorzar?*"

"No, gracias." I could ask Viviana if she knew where Horace was, but that wouldn't get me out on the pool deck.

I squinted against the sun as I stepped out onto the travertine pavers. "*Buenas tardes.*"

Mia and Isabella looked up. While Mia smiled, Isabella turned her attention back to her lunch. Determined, I walked closer.

Mia stood and reached for my arm. "Thank you for your help. Horace is the perfect choice for Isabella. I don't know why I didn't think of him. And he'll be able to help her with the names of the club workers." She waved her hand. "Honestly, pregnancy brain doesn't go away when you give birth." She turned to Isabella and back. "Em, you know my cousin, don't you?"

Isabella's stunning chocolate orbs were once again looking my direction, and her slender shoulders were back, making her pert breasts push toward the material of her sundress.

I bowed at the waist and stood tall. "Isabella, it's nice to see you again."

"Hi."

"Oh," Mia said, "of course, you've been together as recent as Ariadna Gia's birthday. I just figured with Uncle Carmine's overprotectiveness, you hadn't been properly introduced."

"We spoke," Isabella said with more confidence than she showed in Kansas City.

"Yes," I replied. "And not to worry. The punch came out of my shirt."

Isabella's eyes opened wide. "No, there wasn't a stain. Was there?"

I felt my cheeks rise. "No. I am just teasing you." I spoke to Mia. "I need to discuss something with Horace. Do you know where he is?"

"Yes, he's out in Silas's security building. Felipe took Rafaele back to the airport so Silas could show Horace the equipment he's installed to make this house as safe as possible."

"Thank you. I'll go out there." I tipped my chin. "It's nice to have you here. I'm certain Liliana will appreciate your help."

"I'm trying to get Isabella accustomed to my program." Mia looked at me. "Em, you and Nick helped me design this. Could Isabella call you if she needs help?" She rolled her eyes. "I'm mostly on house arrest. My husband is a little stressed."

"In his defense, he has good reason." I grinned. "Of course, Isabella. Mia will give you my number. Call or text anytime."

"Perfect," Mia said.

Isabella's only response was a pink glow to her cheeks.

"I'll go find Horace," I said as I turned and entered the house.

"Emiliano," Viviana called. "I made one too many beef sandwiches." She smiled. "Could you be so kind as to take one off my hands?"

Shaking my head, I walked to the long kitchen island. "If you make it to-go. *El Patrón* has my afternoon scheduled."

She handed me a small paper bag and a bottle of water. "You men must eat to stay strong. It is easier to attract the *damas bonitas*."

Pretty ladies.

My Adam's apple bobbed as I smiled. "*Me mataría si mirara a Mia.*"

"*Sí*, he would. I don't think that's who you were looking at."

I lifted my finger to my lips. "Can you keep a secret, Viviana?"

"How do you think I've worked for the Roríguezes for so long?"

"*Gracias.*"

Taking my homemade lunch—a hell of a lot better than what I usually picked up from a food truck—I went in search of Horace.

EIGHT

Isabella

"I promise I'm fine," I said to my sister. Holding the phone tightly to my ear, I walked around the bedroom Mia assigned me. "This house is unbelievable. I'm currently standing at the bedroom window and looking out at the Pacific Ocean."

"Aren't you scared?"

I inhaled. "I'm nervous."

"What about *el Patrón*?"

"I haven't seen him. He's been in his office all day. Mia told me to ignore it or him." I scoffed. "She seems different than she was back in Kansas City."

"Different how?"

"You know how we said Jasmine seemed different, like she was no longer a stray?"

"Mia's never been a stray," Noemi said. "She was the daughter of the capo...before Dario."

"I don't know how to explain it. And she showed me the program she wants me to work with at the apartments. As she was explaining it, she would go off on stories about the different women."

"The whores?"

I pressed my lips together. "Mia sounds like she knows them and even respects them. I think I could have been wrong—no, I'm sure I was wrong that the women were trafficked. According to Mia, besides their job—"

"Having sex," Noemi interjected.

"It's their choice of profession. No one is making them work there. And now they have other options. Mia started an incentive for education. She said nearly ten of the women have completed their GED, and two are enrolled at an online community college."

"Izzy," Noemi said in a hushed tone. "You almost sound like you will like working with them."

"Maybe I will. On the airplane, I was trying to figure out why the capo thought it was a good idea to send me out here. Forgive me for not having a high opinion of him, but if he sent me out here to fail, I want to prove him wrong."

"Have you met that other girl yet, the one who married Catalina's uncle?"

"Liliana. Not yet. She's coming over tonight for dinner so I can meet her before work tomorrow morning."

"What about Jorge?"

"What about him?" I repeated. "He's not quite six

months old, cute, little, and doesn't do much. Viviana, Mia's housekeeper, and Mia seem to have a schedule worked out. I think Mia wants to get back to the apartments, but *el Patrón* won't allow her, not with Jorge still so young."

"It gives me chills. How terrifying it must be to be married to a drug lord."

It sounded terrifying.

"Maybe." Standing at the window, I stared out at the ocean glistening with millions of diamonds and peered down to the pool. "Tell Mom that I'm good. There are a few hours before Liliana gets here. I think I'm going to lie by the pool." A smile curled my lips. "I'm glad I brought a bathing suit. I'll talk to you in a few days."

"Call me tomorrow after you go to the whores. I'm worried about you."

"How about we call it the apartments?"

"Fine."

"Okay. Give Tony a hug for me." I disconnected the call.

As I changed clothes, I wondered if I was wrong to not want to live in Mia's home. The guards with the guns were scary but also reassuring. And for the first time I could remember, I enjoyed being around Mia.

With a book, sunglasses, and towel in tow, I slipped from my bedroom. Almost to the landing on the stairs, I heard heavy footsteps coming my direction. Pressing myself against the wall, I watched as *el Patrón* stalked up the staircase. Wearing a white t-shirt, blue jeans, and a scowl, his boots echoed on each step. It wasn't until he reached the landing that he realized I was there.

He stopped, his dark orbs scanning from my hair to my toes. The sharp edge of his jaw clenched, and his nostrils flared. He was much taller than I realized, and big. His wide chest was only inches away from me. In a word, he was terrifying.

"*Ni una palabra.*"

"I-I'm sorry."

He lifted his chin and waved his hand up and down. "This is…" He inhaled. "I conduct business here." His accent was like Silas's—more obvious. "Cover yourself before you go to the pool."

I nodded quickly as panic rang in my ears. "I didn't think."

"Start thinking. Cartel soldiers come and go from here. Mia wants you to be safe." He did another scan over my skimpy bathing suit. "I don't want them to get the wrong idea." With that, he continued upward.

Once he reached the top and turned the opposite direction from my bedroom, I let out the breath I was holding. With my heart racing, I followed him up to the second floor. Once I was in the bedroom again, I closed the door and shut my eyes. As I held onto my own hand, I realized they were trembling and a tear streamed down my face. My stomach was suddenly in knots.

The pool could wait.

I considered calling Noemi back to tell her what happened.

Would that be admitting defeat?

After taking off my swimsuit and putting my sundress back on, I quietly opened the bedroom door, listening carefully for the sound of heavy footsteps.

Slowly, I made my way back to the staircase. The sound of childish music came into range. When my feet hit the first floor, I saw Jorge in a round contraption in the middle of the living room, bouncing up and down. Mia was by him on the couch.

She looked up from her book and turned toward me as I came closer. "Did you decide against getting some sun? The pool is refreshing especially after traveling."

Shrugging, I sat on a chair in the same grouping. "*El Patrón* works from home?"

Mia closed her book on her lap. "Mostly. He goes out too."

"Do a lot of his soldiers come and go from here?"

"Lieutenants mostly, like Em and Nick, who were here earlier. I guess technically they're soldiers, but Jano trusts them, more so than some of the others." Her eyes opened wide. "You're safe here, Isabella. I'm sure you saw the guards when you came in. Silas has everything under twenty-four-hour surveillance and more soldiers stationed around the property, including on the ocean side."

"I packed a swimsuit, but I didn't think about a cover-up. Do you have one I could borrow?"

Mia's smile grew. "Of course. I'll bring it to your room if you want to change now."

I tapped the book I'd brought downstairs with me. "Today, I'm okay just sitting outside. Is there more you want to tell me about what my day will be like tomorrow?"

The music in Jorge's jumper was still playing, but the bouncing had stopped, and his little head lopped backward before it fell forward on the padded seat. Mia smiled. "Enjoy some sun. I need to put him down for his afternoon nap, and then we can talk."

The baby barely stirred as she picked him up and laid him on her shoulder.

I was about to go out to the pool when *el Patrón* came down the stairs. I watched in stunned silence as the scary persona I'd encountered on the steps disappeared. His cheeks rose and his lips curled as he cradled Jorge's head. Running his palm over the soft hair, he whispered something I couldn't hear, and then kissed Jorge's head and Mia's lips.

He didn't turn my way or acknowledge my presence. I sat speechless as his boots echoed on the tile, his long legs leading him toward his office.

How could that be the same man as the one who frightened me?

Isabella

It wasn't until I was out on the patio in the sunshine that the time difference between San Diego and Kansas City hit me. I'd left early this morning from Missouri, and while it was now late afternoon here, if I was to make it past dinner without falling asleep, I decided I needed rest.

I met Mia at the top of the staircase. "Did you want to discuss more about the apartments?"

"It can wait for Liliana. I wanted to be sure you understood the rules around here."

I rolled my eyes. "I've lived my entire life with rules."

"These aren't so strict. If you want to leave the house for things other than work—well for work too—it's not a problem. You just need to tell Horace, and he can drive you. Do you have his phone number?"

"Yes, we exchanged numbers. Right now, I think I want to lie down. Being out in the sun made me tired."

Mia smiled and tilted her head. "Isabella, I want you to know how much I appreciate you coming out here to help. I think when you meet Liliana, you'll understand why she's having difficulty. Unfortunately, she has gone through a lot for someone so young."

"She's a widow."

Mia nodded. "Sadly, that's not the worst of it. I want her to be happy and find purpose. If working at the apartments isn't what she wants to do, that's okay too. I've been trying to boost her self-esteem." She tilted her head. "While I'm asking you to take the lead and help her, to her, I'll ask the same. Please don't take offense. If I'd known Uncle Carmine would let you come out here, I would have had you out here a lot sooner."

"No offense will be taken. I'll do my best to not overstep."

"Oh, there's no overstepping. All you can do will be appreciated. Don't hold back. But if in the process, you can make her feel more confident, it would be nice."

"I'll do my best."

"Go ahead and rest. Liliana will be here about six and dinner will be at seven."

I nodded.

As I started to walk away, Mia turned back my direction. "I left a cover-up for you on your bed."

"Thank you."

The long white lacy cover-up would reach all the way to the floor and had flowing sleeves to shield me from the sun if I wanted. It was perfect. At the same time, looking at it reminded me of my encounter with *el Patrón*, sending shivers and goose bumps over my skin.

For some reason my thoughts went from *el Patrón* to the guards I'd recently met, Silas and Horace, to Silas's wife, Viviana. With the exception of Mia's husband, all the cartel members were surprisingly pleasant. My lips curled as I recalled Em coming out on the sun deck and teasing me about the punch. If I were to have the same thoughts about members of the *famiglia*, I could pinpoint those who are friendly and helpful and others that could be considered scary.

Before resting, I chose to take a shower and wash away the travel and sunscreen.

What was it like for Mia to marry into the cartel?

As I added conditioner to my hair, I thought about Jasmine.

How could they stand the dangerous life and dangerous men?

I mean, now that I was out here, I was curious about the dangerous men...in a way that caused my nipples to bead.

"Stop that," I said aloud, referring to my treacherous body. "You're not out here to further cement the alliance. These men may seem nice but remember how *el Patrón* made you feel."

Wearing panties and a loose t-shirt, I closed the blinds to the beautiful ocean and climbed between the cool sheets. Despite my concerns about sleeping with the cartel around, I drifted off without any effort and woke to the sound of the alarm I set.

It was five-thirty.

I twisted my unruly hair into a messy bun, applied some mascara and lip color. Next, I donned another sundress. This one was golden and went all the way to the floor. At the last minute, I grabbed a half cardigan to cover my arms. I wasn't looking for another lecture about being covered up.

The delicious aroma of whatever Viviana was cooking met me before I reached the landing. As I stepped onto the first floor, I saw Mia and a young girl out by the pool. The too-thin dark-haired girl was holding Jorge and bouncing him on her hip. My first thought was that this girl couldn't be Liliana. She looked younger than Noemi.

Maybe she was the daughter of someone Mia knew.

"*Señorita* Isabella," Viviana said as I passed the kitchen area.

"Viviana, whatever you're cooking smells delicious."

"*Gracias*." She lifted her chin. "Mia and Liliana are outside. Mia wants to eat out there. It's a beautiful evening."

Okay then. This waif of a girl *is* Liliana.

I thought about Viviana's greeting. Papà would be furious that she spoke even a little Spanish. Instead of feeling the same way, I grinned at the little knowledge I had of the language. While it wasn't extensive. I could say please, thank you, and yes.

"Isabella," Mia said.

Liliana turned, her large brown eyes meeting mine. My first thought was of a Margaret Keane painting, ones where the eyes were giant, often of children and women.

"Hi, Liliana," I said. "Nice to meet you."

She let out a sigh. "You are young." The tips of her lips moved upward. "I know they sent for you because I'm not very good at the job."

"No," Mia and I said in unison.

I walked closer and ran my hand over Jorge's soft hair. "Honestly, Liliana, I'm here because Mia knows what it's like to be out of high school and in the Luciano family." I pressed my lips together and looked at my cousin. "The men in our family can be overbearing."

"*Sí*," Liliana said. "I know that feeling."

"Mia's giving me a chance to spread my wings, and I'm grateful." My speech wasn't prepared and while I thought I was bending reality to make Liliana feel better, maybe there was more truth in my statement than I realized.

She sat on a chair near the pool and adjusted Jorge, so he was sitting up on her lap as he held tight to one of her thumbs. "I still need help."

"Good," I replied. "That will give me something to do."

Mia reached for Jorge. "Let me get him changed for dinner." His shirt was wet from drool. "You two can get to know one another."

I sat on a chair near her. "Can I ask you something?"

Liliana nodded. "Were you scared to work with…" I didn't say whores. "…the women from the club?"

"*Sí*, at first." Her cheeks rose as her smile grew. "But once I met them, I wasn't afraid. Some were so nervous themselves. They're apprehensive around new people.

Some have confided in me that they fear being judged. I understand that."

"Then why do what they do?"

"First, they aren't all sex workers. Some are only dancers. We had a bartender, but she didn't get along with the other women well, and truly, she makes more money than they do. But even the sex workers have their reasons for their profession. For most, they have long-term goals."

I let out a sigh. "I didn't know that there were women at the apartments who didn't have sex. Will I know who does what?"

Liliana laughed. "Not by looking at them. In their apartments, everyone is the same. No makeup or costumes. No false eyelashes. Just women and girls. Like you and me."

"What about communicable diseases?"

"The apartments have a clinic, open daily until five. They have required testing as well as healthcare available when requested." She leaned back, allowing her long brown hair to fall over her shoulders and down her back.

I was struck by how pretty Liliana was as she closed her eyes and looked up toward the sky. I hadn't noticed her delicate features or long eyelashes until now. "How old are you?"

"Nineteen. Almost twenty."

"Sorry," I said, "if I'm being nosy, but how can you relate to the way the women in the apartments feel?"

"Because I've been judged." She shrugged. "Wrongly

or rightly. It doesn't matter if the judgment is founded, it can still hurt."

I sat back and turned my attention to the setting sun over the water as Liliana's words took root in the depth of my soul. When I turned back, my eyes were moist, probably from the bright sunshine. I wiped a tear from my cheek. "I should have brought out my sunglasses."

She nodded.

"I'm guilty," I confessed. "Ever since Mia asked my mother about me coming out here, I've been judging the women." I forced a smile. "Thank you for helping me see that was wrong."

"I hope that helps you when you're there. They need to trust us for Mia's plans to work."

My gaze went through the open glass doors into the house. "Do you like Mia?"

Liliana's large eyes grew even bigger. "Mia is fantastic. She's done so much for the women and for me. I have an apartment. If *el Patrón*—not Aléjandro but his father —had his way, I would have been sent back to live with my parents."

"Mia challenged Aléjandro's father?"

"I don't know if she challenged him. All I know is I have a life now."

"Would moving back with your parents have been a bad thing? I mean, you're only nineteen."

She sat still for a moment and exhaled. "It would not have been a good thing." She turned toward the house. "I'm going to see if Mia or Viviana needs help."

"I'll go with you."

There was more to Liliana's story. I could feel it. I found myself wondering if eventually she'd share. And then I was surprised I wanted to get close enough to this cartel girl I barely knew.

Liliana and I set the outside table with utensils, napkins, glasses filled with ice water, and plates. Silas carried Jorge's highchair out next to the table. All the while everyone was talking and relaxed as if we weren't in a drug lord's home.

When we sat down and Viviana carried the tortilla casserole out to the table, I expected *el Patrón* to appear, a dark cloud over our friendly conversation. He didn't.

"Isn't your husband home?" I asked Mia.

"He is. Viviana took his dinner to his office." She shrugged. "He works hard. Too hard. I don't know the details, but something happened last night and something else happened today. Whatever they are, they have him extremely agitated."

"He's not usually agitated?" I asked.

Mia's smile returned. "No, he's a good husband and father. Remembering my father running the famiglia, I know that sometimes, it's better to let him be. He'll come to me when he's ready."

To my surprise, Viviana and Silas joined us. We were almost done eating when Silas received word of a car arriving to the front gate. He turned to Mia. "Rei and Jasmine are here."

My eyes opened wide.

"Good," Mia said. "I feel better if they're here."

I lowered my voice. "You want *Jasmine* at your house?"

She nodded. "I made a lot of mistakes in the past. Instead of dwelling on them, I chose to move forward. After all, she's now my sister-in-law." She grinned. "We have the same last name."

Roríguez.

I had never thought of that.

CHAPTER

TEN

Emiliano

T he headlights of my Mercedes-Benz AMG GT 63 illuminated *el Patrón's* gate as I flashed my badge beneath the sensor. The gate moved slowly to the side. A new set of guards stood at either side of the interior gate as I parked amongst many other vehicles.

"Busy place," Nick said as he unfastened his seat belt.

My skin prickled as I scanned the different cars, noticing my father's. This was more visitors than would usually be at Jano's house after nine on a weeknight, filling the confined space. Nick and I had gotten word out about tonight's meeting, and this gathering crowd was no doubt here for the same reason.

The guards nodded as Nick and I opened the inner gate. The usually quiet courtyard contained more than a handful of cartel guards, soldiers, and lieutenants. Nick walked toward his father, my Uncle Nicolas, while I made my way to Horace Torres who was talking to José Pérez, Liliana's bodyguard.

"*Hola*," I said. "How has your first day with Isabella been?"

"Quiet. She's been content inside. *Mañana*, we go to the apartments."

Yeah, I wondered how that would go. Currently, there were too many other things at play for me to give Isabella too much thought. I turned and nodded toward the house. "Jano in there?"

"*Sí*. Rei too. *El Patrón* wants everyone to stay outside." Horace looked at the growing crowd. "I don't blame him. He said he'd talk to those of us gathered before we head over to the warehouse."

José lowered his voice. "The rumors aren't true, *o sí*?"

Rumors?

What I knew: Kozlov's men attacked our soldiers, or we could have a traitor among us.

I flashed a grin. "I guess you'd need to be more specific. What rumors have you heard?"

"Kozlov is gone. Volkov's men gunned him down."

The fuck?

My expression stayed stoic, despite my shock. This wasn't a rumor I'd heard. "When and where did you hear this?"

"Happened last night," Horace said. "Stories started circulating on the streets this afternoon."

"Took him out at his home," José said, "Up in Hidden

Hills. That's why Rei is down here. It could be a fucking game changer."

"Well, fuck, that's news to me." I searched for Nick in the growing crowd. He was still with his father and mine. I joined them and kept my volume below the growing din. "Is the news about Ivan Kozlov real?"

"I hope not," my papá replied. "If Kozlov is gone, Volkov is even more powerful. Add Herrera to that equation and shit's going to get real."

As if shit wasn't already real.

Everyone turned as Silas came out of the house. He scanned the men, his gaze landing on us. "Emiliano and Andrés, come with me."

I immediately stepped forward. It wasn't lost on me that my papá hesitated. Taking orders from Jano and Rei was upsetting but taking orders from Jano's guard... Papá made up the difference and got to Silas at the same time as I did.

"What do you need?" I asked.

"The first wave of reinforcements from the famiglia will arrive soon—ten men. Dante Luciano is with them." Silas scanned the cartel men. "Jano wants a friendly welcoming committee." He lowered his voice. "We don't need anyone with a stick up their ass about the alliance causing problems."

Papá and I were friendly. Dante was married to my sister, Papá's daughter. And my other sister, his other daughter, was married to the capo dei capi himself.

I nodded. "Silas, is the rumor true about Ivan Kozlov?"

He pressed his lips together in a straight line and

nodded. "Found the same way Jorge was found. We didn't get the official news until after you spoke to Horace. They took out his wife, two children, staff, and guards. I heard his fucking dog was shot." Silas shook his head. "An akita. I only hope it took a bite out of the motherfucker's leg who slaughtered them."

"Why would Volkov do that?" Inhaling, I closed my eyes and exhaled. "Kozlov's men attacked our soldiers last night. Why kill him?"

"The aftermath is eerily similar to Bella."

My mind was swirling with a tornado of thoughts. "Are you suggesting that it was Volkov's men who attacked the Bella instead of Kozlov?"

Silas shook his head and shrugged. "We don't know. As for Kozlov's soldiers, either they're now with Volkov or they're dead." He gripped my arm and tugged me a few feet away. "With Myshkin gone in Kansas City, the bratva world is fighting for supremacy."

"Is there any proof that Herrera's in on this?"

"Dante wants to talk to Jano in person before the meeting. I need you and your father to meet Dante at the airport. Keep word of their arrival under wraps. We're keeping our trusted close. Nicolas, Nick, Felipe, and Diego need to lead these men" —he gestured with his chin— "to the warehouse. Tell them to keep the crowd there until Jano, Rei, and Dante arrive. Tell Nick not to mention anything about the famiglia coming until they're all in the warehouse."

"Will do." I gritted my teeth. "These men are expecting to hear from Jano."

"They will—at the warehouse. This crowd is getting

too loud. They need to go. We don't need any uniforms showing up." He started to head toward the door and turned back. "Oh, and if you see José Peréz, tell him Liliana will spend tonight here. There's no use spreading people out."

I nodded as I pushed my way through the growing crowd. Once I'd passed on Silas's message to José, I found Nick. "Silas said for you, Felipe, and Diego to take the lieutenants and soldiers to the warehouse."

Nick narrowed his gaze. "They expect to hear from Jano."

"I know. Silas said they will at the warehouse."

"Where are you going?"

"Taking my father" —I looked around— "with Horace and José" —I need to tell them— "to meet Dante Luciano's plane. He's bringing ten men with him. I'll need a few drivers."

Nick's jaw clenched. "What the fuck about Volkov and Kozlov?"

"Seems to be true. It's fucked."

My cousin nodded. "I'll round up everyone and head south toward the warehouse."

"I need to get Papá, José, and Horace. We'll meet you as soon as we can with the reinforcements. Don't mention the famiglia until you're all contained."

There was a rumble of discontent that *el Patrón* hadn't addressed them.

"He will at the warehouse," Nick reassured.

After gathering my papá, José, and Horace, I took one last look at Jano's house. The noise level had lessened as more and more soldiers made their way out of the inside gate. I turned to Horace. "Should you make one last check on Isabella?"

"Everyone within those walls is safe. It's those who are outside those walls that concern me."

With each of us driving our own vehicle, we set off for the private airport while the others made their way to the warehouse. Our caravan arrived at the exclusive small airport minutes before their plane was scheduled to land. This was the airport the Lucianos frequented when they came out west. Getting out of my car, I leaned against the hood and surveyed the land.

By the look of the chain-link fences and pole-barn-style structure housing offices, it wasn't exclusive in a luxury sense of the word. Not as frequented would be a better definition. Narrowing my eyes, I scanned beyond the fences. There were plenty of open fields. A sharp-shooter could possibly hit a target.

My father stepped from his SUV driven by Carlos, his trusted bodyguard for most of my life. "Silas spoke privately to you, not to me."

"What are you talking about?"

"Jano is pushing us older lieutenants out."

I shook my head. "That's not true."

He leaned against my car and faced the runway. "You know what they're saying?"

"Who?"

"Our men." Papá shook his head. "Some are blaming the famiglia for our war. Before Dario and Catalina married, we were friendly with Herrera."

"You agreed to have Cat marry. Do you think that was now a mistake?"

"Fuck," he growled. "*El Patrón* didn't leave me a choice in the matter. And now Camila…"

I repeated my question. "Do you think it was a mistake, either on your or Jorge's part?"

He pulled a pack of cigarettes from his inside suit coat pocket and offered me one. I shook my head. It wasn't that I never smoked, only that when I did it meant I was stressed. I refused to admit to that state of mind at the moment.

Dad removed a lighter from his slacks pocket, lit the cigarette, and took a long drag. The thing was that my stress smoking came from an example in my life.

"You're stressed about this?" I asked.

He blew a cloud of smoke into the breeze. "It wasn't a mistake on either of our parts." He tipped his face up toward the sky. "Dante is my son-in-law as well as Dario. I trust them, more than I did their father. Jorge made an alliance with the Kansas City Mafia. Herrera made an alliance with the Volkov and Kozlov bratvas. I'm concerned we chose the wrong ally."

"Herrera and Volkov have fucked Kozlov. That doesn't sound like an ally."

"Jano doesn't have what it takes to be *jefe*. He's too young. This new turn of events is making our ranks concerned. Do you know what frightened soldiers do?"

"They fight."

"They run," he said. "And they'll run to Herrera."

I shook my head. "I refuse to believe that."

"Youth has a way of blinding people, always seeing possibilities when experience would tell you that the fucking house is on fire. I can smell the smoke. Either we get out or go down in flames."

I turned to face my father. At over a quarter century my senior, he was the man I always looked up to and admired. Maybe it was youth. Maybe it was that Nick and I were closer to Jano and Rei than our fathers were. Whatever the reason, this moment felt earthshaking in a way I wasn't ready to internalize. "If you're not for the Roríguez cartel, Papá, then you're against it. I never imagined you would be a traitor."

Shaking his head, he released another cloud of smoke. "A traitor is by definition a person who commits treason. I haven't betrayed anyone or any organization. I swore an oath to Jorge and to Señor Cruz before him." His dark stare met mine. "You're a man now, Em. Start thinking like one. Two of my daughters are married to Luciano men, two very powerful men. I will never turn to Elizondro Herrera, but I'm not above asking my sons-in-law for clemency. This ship feels as if it will go the way of Bella."

"My oath was to Jorge and since to Jano. As long as my sisters are under the protection of the famiglia and the alliance is intact, I will support both sides. The only clemency I may ask for will be for Mama if she finds herself a widow."

The bright lights of a Cessna preceded the rumbling sound of engines as the plane carrying Dante and his soldiers touched down on the runway.

Papá tossed the remains of the cigarette to the ground and stubbed it out on the tarmac. "Be careful, Em."

"Jano sent us here because of our connection to the Lucianos—a friendly welcoming crew, remember?"

ELEVEN

Emiliano

Dante Luciano, the consigliere of Kansas City, was the first to step from the cabin of the private aircraft. Ducking his head at the opening, he then stood erect at the top of the platform and scanned the illuminated tarmac. His dark stare settled on Papá and me. A single nod was our greeting as he climbed down the stairs. There was no doubt that his sports coat concealed at least one holster with a gun. I'd say two if I was a betting man. There were most likely a few knives beneath his blue jeans. A parade of men dressed in black and carrying duffel bags followed in his wake.

The convenient thing about private air travel was the ability to carry weapons of all sizes across state lines. Judging from the bags over the men's shoulders, they were in possession of multiple weapons, including long guns.

Dante extended his hand first to Papá, his father-in-law. "Camila and Catalina are safe."

Papá shook his hand and nodded. "That's reassuring to hear."

"Thank you for heeding Jano's call," I said, also shaking his hand.

"*Ju familia es nuestra familia*," he said with a grin. "Camila has been trying to teach me. I'm trying but not the fastest of learners."

"You'll ride with me," Papá said. "We have four vehicles to drive all of you to Jano's home. I believe Silas has arranged vehicles for you to drive."

Dante nodded.

The entire drive back to *el Patrón's* home, my mind was filled with questions about my own father—questions I never imagined entertaining. When he told Dante to ride with him, I almost intervened. Then I recalled what he said about Silas speaking to me privately. I was certain that if I insisted on driving Dante, I'd upset my papá. Instead, I was transporting Piero, a guard I knew. He was Jasmine's bodyguard before she married Rei. In the back seat were Lorenzo and Adrian. If I'd met the last two before, they hadn't left a lasting impression. There was, however, an incident with Piero having to do with Jasmine and me in the capo's theater room that I hoped wouldn't be spoken of during this trip.

I spoke to Piero, "Silas, Jano's head of security, texted me. He has beds for the ten of you in the back of Wanderland."

"Strip club?"

"Private club. Dante explained that you'll sleep in shifts. The room was renovated when Jano moved the women out of the club to the apartments." I shrugged. "It's more of a barracks or dorm when it's needed."

"Not used by customers?"

I chuckled. "No. Backup space. You never know when you'll have to put up soldiers or even women new to the club. Currently, it's empty. The space has a couple of bathrooms and a kitchen area. I wouldn't call it the Ritz, but you'll be comfortable."

Piero nodded as he watched the passing scenes through the windshield. The closer we came to the ocean, the darker the sky grew, going from a navy blue to a velvet black. Streetlights created circles of illumination, and palm trees swayed in the breeze. The tension built as Piero asked about what went down with Kozlov.

"Why did Volkov take him out?" I asked rhetorically. "We don't have an answer. Only, we're damn sure Volkov's men aren't getting close to the Roríguez cartel."

"How do you plan to accomplish that? Someone's men got to the last *el Patrón*."

The muscles in my jaw pulled taut. "Mistakes were made. Jorge was left with a skeleton crew of guards."

He lowered his voice. "I find it difficult to believe that he didn't have an escape plan."

"He did. He wasn't notified in time."

"Was his body identified?"

With each of his questions, my grip of the steering wheel tightened. "I suggest that neither *el Patrón* nor Rei hear you ask about their father's execution. It's something they both live with every minute of every day."

Piero lifted his palm. "No offense intended. I heard a rumor that Jorge was only identified by partial dental records. His face was gone."

I'd seen the pictures that Jano only allowed a few people to see. The scene on the Bella was gruesome. The occupants present on the superyacht were made to kneel on the helipad with their hands bound. One by one they were shot in the back of their heads. Jorge's gold watch was still on his wrist, and his recognizable body with his customary linen shirt and pants was crumpled forward.

We don't believe the terrorists were there to steal or plunder. Their one mission was assassinating members of the Roríguez cartel. However, that was our theory. To date, neither Jano nor Rei had received any pertinent information regarding what remained on Bella. The government seized it all, from Josefina's jewelry to the furniture and kitchenware. The number of dinghies remaining was still a mystery. If anyone had made it off the yacht on one of the small dinghies, they hadn't contacted Jano or Rei.

"Jano and Rei identified their father from the photographs. To think otherwise after six months would be ludicrous."

Thankfully, Piero dropped the subject as we approached Jano's home. We were following behind Papá's car as Silas manually allowed the gate to remain open to allow all four vehicles to enter. As we got out of our cars, Jano and Rei appeared from the front door.

"Thank you, my brother," Jano said, shaking Dante's

hand. He turned to everyone who had recently arrived. "*Es hora de que nos vayamos*. Dante will ride with me and Rei to the warehouse. I'll speak to everyone at once. That way there will be no miscommunication."

"Gentlemen," Silas said. "Your vehicles are at the warehouse. *Vamos*."

"Who's protecting *el Patrón's* home with most of his men at the warehouse?" Piero asked.

We watched as Horace, Jose, and Felipe exited vehicles, to be replaced by other soldiers. "Those men are the inside guards. Silas has this property protected layer after layer."

Piero nodded.

Once through the gate, I headed south, varying my route to avoid appearing like a parade to announce our intent. The closer I came to the warehouse, the more the scenes beyond our windows transformed from palm trees, flowering bushes, and gated homes to cracked streets, concrete walls, and graffiti. The streetlights that worked illuminated sidewalks littered with trash and weeds the size of bushes pushing through the cracks.

The other occupants of my vehicle remained silent as I pulled up to an inconspicuous gate. After entering a code, the gate moved, and I drove us onto the cartel's grounds. Dust stirred up from the gravel road surrounded the car in a cloud. Finally, I reached the warehouse that seconded as a safe house. The large garage door was open, and the area filled with more cars than had been at Jano's earlier in the evening. I pulled in, parking beside my papá's SUV.

The building reverberated with the sound of

formidable men climbing the metal steps. Jano, Rei, Dante, and Silas were nearly to the top, followed by other soldiers on their way to the safe house stories above. The door above was guarded but would quickly open for *el Patrón*.

By the time my occupants and I made it to the stairs, *jefe* was inside. More of the famiglia soldiers followed. Once the last man entered the large room at the top, the guard closed the door, proceeded by the clicks as a series of locks engaged. The room was filled with picnic tables. There was enough space for over a hundred men. While not all the seats were filled, when I added the dozens of soldiers standing around the perimeter of the room, the count was close to one hundred, if not over.

The soldiers' expressions were unreadable as Jano stood to speak. The prelude of his speech was in Spanish, a reassuring gesture to the cartel members that he was responsible for each man here as well as families they have at home. He expounded upon his praises for the Roríguez cartel, our accomplishments, our alliance with the famiglia, and our future. As if a switch was turned, his volume rose, his expression darkened, and his words came faster.

"What happened between the bratvas, what Volkov did to Kozlov and his family," Jano emphasized, "is nothing short of terrorism. Terrorism funded by Herrera." His tenor hardened. "We now have reason to believe Volkov was responsible for carrying out Herrera's extermination of *mí padre*."

The room filled with mumbling.

Jano lifted his hand. "The attack on Kozlov was too similar to what happened on Bella for it not to have been carried out by the same soldiers, or soldiers with the same training. It's clear Volkov is working for Herrera. We're leveling the playing field." He changed to English. "Dante Luciano brought me evidence of a large deposit of money into Volkov's offshore account." He patted Dante on the shoulder. "Our alliance with the Luciano family is and will remain strong. Dante has brought ten famiglia soldiers and promised more." He looked at Dante.

Dante nodded.

Jano continued, "I will let Mr. Luciano tell you what else the famiglia has arranged. As the consigliere and my wife's brother, listen to him."

Nick nudged me with his elbow. "What the fuck?"

I shrugged, completely unsure what Dante would say.

Dante stepped forward. "The success of the Roríguez cartel is the success of the Luciano famiglia. In the last six months, the Myshkin bratva and now the Kozlov bratva were brought down by the assassination of their leaders. Elizondro Herrera is using the unrest in the bratvas to his benefit." Dante spoke louder. "When the Roríguez cartel was hit with tragedy, you did not crumble."

All the eyes in the room were on Dante.

"You didn't fall. You didn't split or rush to Herrera. That is what he wanted. That was what he expected. Your strength is in your solidarity, and in the famiglia's solidarity with you."

Shoulders straightened and chests inflated around the room.

"Our capo dei capi, my brother, has been cultivating a relationship with Andros Ivanov, the pakhan of the bratva in Detroit."

Murmurs filled the air as Nick and I exchanged glances.

Dante shook his head. "Our country—no, the world—is watching. Ivanov sees the possibility of increasing his reach, his kingdom, so to speak."

I turned to Nick. "Is he saying Ivanov will help us?"

Dante's voice filled the air. "When we work together to take out Volkov and Herrera, the Roríguez cartel, the Luciano famiglia, and the Ivanov bratva will all be the richer and stronger."

Dante looked my direction. No, he wasn't looking at me, but at Adrian, one of the soldiers I'd driven from the plane.

Adrian stepped forward. "I am Adrian."

Hearing his Eastern European accent, I realized I'd never before heard him speak.

"Sovietnik of the Ivanov bratva. Andros Ivanov sent me here with the famiglia to demonstrate our willingness to aid in this war. We have two planes on their way with more guns and ammunition. This war will end and when it does, as Luciano said, we will all be victorious."

Jano stepped forward. "Who in this room is willing to die for the Roríguez cartel? *Levantese.*"

Throughout the room, soldiers stood, pledging their allegiance.

My gaze went to my father.

Would he refuse?

Relief washed through me as he too stood.

"Tonight," Jano said, "resume your regular duties and patrols. Tomorrow, each captain will meet with our lieutenants. Tonight, we have Nicolas, Andres, Em, and Nick in attendance. You will meet with them wherever they tell you to be. Security is essential." Jano laid his fist on his chest. "You have my word. If you fuck with Roríguez, I will watch you die."

"Did we just get promoted?" Nick whispered.

"Fuck, I think we did."

TWELVE

Isabella

I tried to keep calm as Horace and José drove Liliana and me to the apartments. No matter how much Mia told me about my new job, the reality was terrifying. A sheltered life doesn't prepare someone to work with whores. Smoothing my slacks, I rubbed away the moisture from my palms.

As we drove, the scenery around us changed. There was no longer the opulence of Mia's neighborhood and no more gated homes. Houses became smaller and manicured lawns were replaced with stones, weeds poking through the white gravel. My heart beat against my breastbone as yards filled with broken-down cars. I even saw a washing machine. Looking over at Liliana, I spoke low. "Are you ever scared at the apartments?"

She looked up from her phone. "Scared? No."

"Probably because you're used to the cartel. You know who you can trust and who you can't."

Her lips curled slightly on the ends. "I trust Mia. She's done everything possible to give the residents a safe haven, and that includes us." She tilted her head toward the front seat. "José is always there. Horace will be too. And the building is heavily guarded."

I gave that some thought. "Okay, no one is getting in to harm us. That still leaves the...tenants."

"It's really rather simple. Be nice to them, and they'll be nice to you."

It was my turn to smile. "I think I'm guilty of over-thinking and overanalyzing this. Did you do that when you started?"

She shook her head. "Mia asked me to help when the project was still in the planning stage. My husband had recently died, and Sofia and I moved into Valentina's home."

I nibbled my lip. "I'm sorry. You just said a lot of names that sound familiar....?"

"I was married off to Gerardo Ruiz, the brother of Andrés—Catalina and Camila's father," she added.

Multitudes of questions came to mind. I recalled something. "Oh, and Valentina is their mother."

"Em's too."

My cheeks unexpectedly rose at the mention of his name. "You lived there, with all of them?"

"Catalina was gone, but the rest, yes, for a while."

I wanted to push for a more personal opinion of Emiliano. Instead, I asked, "Who is Sofia?"

"Sofia is my husband's daughter." Liliana shrugged.

"She's my age. We were best friends until…" Her smile dimmed. "Anyway, after Gerardo's death, *el Patrón* wanted us to live with people he could trust."

"Where is Sofia now?"

"She moved back to Sacramento. She's working on her degree."

"College, really?"

Liliana nodded. "I'm not suited for that." Her big brown eyes opened wider. "Are you going to go to college?"

My attention went to my hands on my lap. "My parents don't see it as a priority."

"Catalina went," she said. "Camila is in college."

"My mama says it's a waste of money. Look at Catalina. She has her degree and spends her time shopping, popping out babies, and catering to Dario's needs." I looked her direction. "You don't need a degree for that."

"Catalina majored in art. I can't remember the whole name, but Valentina told me that she's on the board at some art museum in Kansas City. She has done some good things through there. Including scholarships."

I inhaled. "Shit. I didn't know any of that."

"But you live near her, don't you?"

"Yes, but my dad doesn't have a positive opinion of…" I hesitated, wondering if the men in the front seat were listening.

"The cartel," Liliana offered.

"Yes." I lowered my voice. "And honestly, of the capo."

Liliana's eyes opened wide. "He's the capo," she said,

aghast. "Your opinion isn't a choice. Just like an opinion of *el Patrón*."

Technically. My father saw it differently. Instead of pursuing that conversation, I decided to change the subject. "Did you hear all those men outside last night?"

Liliana nodded. "Something big was happening. That's why Mr. Luciano was there last night."

"What? Which Mr. Luciano?"

"Dante." Her cheeks pinkened. "Camila got lucky with that one."

I scoffed. "He's my cousin, but I guess you're right." I sat taller. "How didn't I know he was there?"

"You'd already gone to bed. I'd assume he was out of the house before us this morning. I only saw him last night. Really only for a second or two. He and *el Patrón* were busy in the office."

I looked around at the neighborhood. The houses were small but well kept.

"Oh, that went faster than usual." She smiled. "Probably because I had you to talk with." She turned toward the window. "We're almost there."

A large limestone building came into view. The outside was pristine with landscaping of rocks and succulents. We approached an enclosed parking lot with a guarded gate. As José pulled the car into the parking lot, I saw that the area wasn't all parking spaces. There was a grassy part with picnic tables and a fountain surrounded by flowers.

Liliana must have known where I was looking. "Mia recently had the area added. It used to be a playground with broken-down playground stuff. This is better for the residents. Isn't it nice?"

"It is," I answered, pleasantly surprised.

The breeze blew my hair around my face as I stepped from the car. With Horace at my side, we made our way toward the front doors. The entrance reminded me that the building was originally a school. The first set of doors opened to a foyer. Through a window at the side was a guard. Like the ones outside Mia's home, the man was armed with an array of weapons, including a long gun.

Horace spoke to him. The only part I recognized was my name. A buzzer sounded, and the next set of doors opened. To my surprise there was a second guard by a metal detector. Horace motioned for me to walk through.

I did.

No alarms beeped.

Turning back, I watched as Liliana walked through, but both of our bodyguards walked around.

"You get a free pass?" I asked Horace with a grin.

"*Sí.* My job is to protect you. Being armed is part of that assignment."

If I'd lived a normal life, I would probably have an issue with the tiers of security. My childhood in the Mafia was far from normal. Having an armed bodyguard was part of life. Even though I didn't know Horace well, his presence was reassuring.

The lingering scents of new construction filled my senses. Our shoes tapped on the vinyl plank flooring. Liliana led me into the front offices. I imagined that back in the day, this would be where the secretaries and principals had offices. She opened a door to a large private office. "This is Mia's office," Liliana said. "She said you could use it since she's still at home."

I turned a complete circle, taking in my surroundings. On one side, a large window faced the street with a small white table and four gray swivel chairs. A large white-lacquer-finished desk with a sleek white leather chair was centered near the back wall. The monitors were attached to a pole mount. Matching white bookcases and cupboards ran along the other side wall near a door. "What's in there?"

"Oh, Mia has her own bathroom."

Shaking my head, I met Liliana's gaze. "This is very nice." I walked behind the desk. "Why are the monitors on this arm?"

She came forward and pressed a button on the corner of the desktop. The middle section rose, lifting the keyboard with it. The arm extended, lifting the monitors. "This adjusts so she could stand and work. Mia says it's unhealthy to sit behind a desk all day."

My eyes widened. "I've never seen anything like that before."

"We all have them."

I looked around. "Is it always this quiet around here?"

A large clock near the window told me it was nearly ten in the morning.

"Let me show you around. Many of the women are still asleep. The club doesn't close until three a.m."

The club. Where these women get paid to have sex.

I continually told myself to not show my parents' prejudices. It wasn't easy to ignore the views and biases of the people who raised me. Then again, if this time in San Diego was going to broaden my world, maybe it needed to start with reexamining those beliefs.

That didn't mean I wouldn't freak out when I came upon a woman with too much makeup, teased hair, wearing a silk robe over X-rated lingerie and high heels, and smoking a cigarette. My imagination had been running wild ever since Papà told me I was going to San Diego.

Keep it together, Izzy.

Liliana showed me where to leave my purse and started my tour.

THIRTEEN

Isabella

I took three deep breaths in Mia's office before venturing out into the unknown. The first hall we went down led to double doors that opened to a library filled with books. There was an English and a Spanish section. Both contained everything from how-to books to fantasy and romance. Besides the shelves and books, the furnishings included multiple tall tables with chairs as well as couches and comfy chairs. As we stepped out to leave, a woman nearly ran into us.

She was pretty in a nondescript way. Wearing blue jeans and a white tank top, she was easily ten years my senior, which didn't make her old.

"Liliana," she said, surprised.

"Isla," Liliana replied. "Are you working in here today?"

"*Sí*. I'm a little late. Tell Mia I'm sorry. After what happened at the club, it was hard to fall asleep."

Club.

Is she one of the whores?

No. She looks too normal.

Liliana smiled. "I don't know what happened, but you're fine. I think other than us, you're the first to arrive." She turned to me. "This is Isabella Luciano. She's going to help around here while Mia's out."

"*Hola, Señorita* Luciano." Her eyes opened wide. "Luciano. You're related to Mia. That was her name."

"I am." I extended my hand. "Nice to meet you, Isla. Please call me Isabella or Izzy."

"Izzy." Her cheeks rose. "Thank you for helping Mia. We miss her."

"I'm glad to be here." I looked around. "I think I'll get lost."

"Ask any one of us. We're here to help."

Liliana's advice came back to me. 'It's simple. Be nice to them, and they'll be nice to you.'

"Thank you," I said.

After she walked away, I lowered my voice to a whisper. "She isn't one of the club's whores, is she?"

"We told you last night that they are simply women who choose their employment." I let that sink in as we again passed the front offices. Horace and José could be seen in the front office working on their tablets.

"Why aren't they following us?" I asked.

"Men aren't allowed beyond the front office unless they're guarding the back doors, but they're covered by surveillance." She shrugged. "It makes the residents more comfortable. Of course, if there was to be an emergency" —she pointed at a red button on the wall— "these will sound an alarm, and they'll come."

"I saw one of those in the library."

"Yeah. They're all around even in the residents' apartments."

This was a lot to take in. As Liliana led me down another hallway, I asked, "What do you think happened at the club last night?"

She shrugged. "I don't ask questions. I would suspect it is connected to the men at the house, Dante arriving, and Mia wanting me to stay with her."

Despite all the security, a cold chill ran through me. I rubbed my palms over my arms. "Are we safe?"

She simply smiled and led me into the dining room. Each location was spotless and perfectly suited. This room had a high ceiling with modern light pendants hanging on long poles. The sunshine coming through the skylights made the glass bulbs glisten. The aroma of breakfast foods met us as we entered. There were only a few residents sitting at two of the available tables. I counted twelve round tables, each seating six chairs. The ladies present were deep in conversation that I mostly couldn't understand. They didn't seem to notice us or care as we walked through the large room.

"Mia took a poll," Liliana said. "The original tenants chose a dining hall over having the ability to cook in their rooms. That said, almost every cooking or baking class that's offered is filled up within hours. Earlier this week they had the chance to bake flan."

"What is flan?"

"Oh my gosh. It's delicious." She pursed her lips. "It's like what you might call baked custard covered in caramel. You must try it."

I nodded.

Through a swinging door, she took me into the industrial-sized kitchen. Three women in white uniforms appeared to be cleaning after breakfast and getting ready to prepare lunch.

"*Hola*," the women greeted.

After Liliana introduced me—I didn't know how she could remember all the names—she went on with her tour. "They also vote on dinner entrees. Breakfast and lunch are more generic, the regular choices."

"Who pays for all of this, the cartel?" I asked as we walked back to a hallway.

"Mostly, but from the onset, Mia applied for grants and has received a few." Liliana smiled. "All she needs to do is smile at *el Patrón* and she gets what she wants."

I recalled our brief encounter. "He doesn't seem that easy to please."

"Mia knows the secrets."

"Are all cartel men as eager to please their wives?"

A shadow passed over Liliana's expression. "Not all. Let me show you the classrooms. Today is Thursday. There will be two different classes in session." We walked down a second hallway. "Thursday mornings, we have English as a second language. While all the women speak some English, many voiced a desire to be better at reading and writing it."

Through the window in the door, I saw a woman standing, and her lips were moving. While I couldn't hear what she was saying, the ladies in the front row were listening and taking notes.

Liliana pointed to the other side of the hall. There was another closed door with a window. "This is GED prep. It's more facilitated learning than traditional instruction."

"I should know what that means."

She paused. "Self-led. Each woman is at a different place and takes a different speed in her own education journey. A facilitator guides the students to help each person find their answers. Research shows that facilitated learning is better retained." When I didn't respond, she asked, "How does a child learn that a stove is hot?"

"Either they touch it, or they are told." A smile curled my lips. "Touching it—learning it for themselves—will be remembered."

"Exactly."

"Have you thought of becoming a teacher?"

She shook her head as pink filled her cheeks. "I'm not smart enough for that."

"Are you kidding? You're blowing me away right now."

The quiet, introverted Liliana I met last night was gone. In her place was a more confident woman. I wondered if needing to step up since Mia gave birth had transformed Liliana more than Mia realized.

"Is participation in education mandatory?" I asked.

"No. All voluntary." Liliana went to the next room with the same windowed door. "This room is the computer center. Everyone has access to the internet."

"Kind of normal."

She shook her head. "Not for some of these women. This one feature has been life-changing."

Life-changing?

"Computers?"

"The ability to research," Liliana said, "have online accounts, monitor their bank information. When we first opened, not one woman had a bank account. Even if they're in the computer center scrolling on social media, that's research beyond their small slice of life. The availability of this technology has broadened their world."

"Wow. I never thought of it like that. Don't they have phones?"

"They do. This center is protected against malware and has better security than their phones."

Her answer short-circuited my mind. I never questioned the security of my phone or other technologies.

The door opened and a woman stopped when she saw us, and her eyes grew wide. She started speaking quickly in Spanish to Liliana. As she spoke, I scanned her from head to toe. Her dark hair was tied back in a ponytail, and her face was clean of makeup. She was wearing a San Diego Padres t-shirt, shorts, and canvas loafers. If I passed her on the street, I would have no idea of her profession.

With each word, the woman's excitement bubbled out.

Liliana replied before turning to me. "This is Julia. Julia, this is Isabella Luciano. She's helping here while Mia is out."

"*Hola.*"

"Hi, please call me Izzy. It's nice to meet you, Julia. What's all the excitement?"

"I was telling Liliana. This morning, I received the email. I was accepted to community college. Online." Her entire body vibrated with energy. "I want to be a nurse."

"You will be," Liliana said.

"I didn't know you could be a nurse with online classes."

She nodded. "After I pass the classes, I will need to work in a hospital for the clinical."

"That's fantastic."

She bounced up and down. "I need to tell Angel, my roommate. She'll be happy like me." Julia hurried down the hall the direction we'd come.

"They have roommates?"

Liliana nodded. "When they were housed at Wanderland, they lived in a dorm-style room. Here, each classroom has been renovated into three small bedrooms, a common area, and a full bathroom. This gives them privacy while also providing the camaraderie of one another." We started walking in Julia's wake. "It's good that they voted on communal eating. In the blueprints when kitchens were included in each classroom, the number of bedrooms was only two. Originally, there were seventeen classrooms, five bathrooms, and a gymnasium. Part of the gym was converted to the cafeteria, and the communal bathrooms were removed. The other half of the gym became housing units. Overall, there are now twenty units, each capable of housing three women."

"Wow! Does the club employ that many wh—women?"

"If you include all staff, yes and more. But after a few early rough patches, Mia decided to keep these apartments for the entertainers. They were the ones who were housed in the back of the club. The bartenders, managers, cooks, cleaning crew, and other females were living on their own. They make more money."

"Oh, Mia did say something about that."

By the time we returned to the offices, I was introduced to two more women who worked as secretaries for Mia and Liliana. Their names were Reina and Celeste. I also learned that the various jobs such as secretary, librarian, cook, or custodian were paid positions the women could do on the side to earn more money. They paid well above California's minimum wage. Liliana said the goal was to provide a pathway to move beyond the women's current status, if they wanted to. If not, this was a safe, clean place for them to live.

"Do you want to eat lunch here or go to a restaurant. There's a cute café not far away," Liliana asked.

I was having difficulty wrapping my mind around all I'd seen and heard. Getting away for a while might help. "A café sounds nice. Will Horace and José accompany us?"

Liliana rolled her eyes. "Always."

As I gathered my purse, the noise level in the front office rose.

Peering around the corner, I saw what or more accurately who was the cause.

FOURTEEN

Isabella

Emiliano Ruiz.

Ever since I'd felt his stare on me at Ariadna Gia's birthday party, I'd had a hard time forgetting him. However, other than our brief talk about punch, I was too nervous to look directly at him. Yesterday, at Mia's I had a chance. To say I was affected in some way by this man was an understatement. I'd thought about him as I readied for bed last night. I also realized that him being older than Catalina, there was zero chance he would be interested in me. That didn't mean I couldn't stare.

From the safety of my new office doorway, I could appreciate what a handsome man Emiliano was. I'd never had this unabashed opportunity before. He was obviously distracted by Reina and Celeste turning up the charm.

I nibbled my thumbnail.

Starting at the top of his head, I noticed his dark hair was longer on top than on the sides. A trimmed layer of facial hair covered the edge of his chiseled chin. His brown—almost-black—eyes glistened beneath a prominent brow. My insides twisted as my scan went lower still, to his wide shoulders that tapered into toned abs. A tattoo of a snake's tail wound around his muscular right arm, disappearing beneath the sleeve of his black t-shirt. His long legs were clad in low-riding blue jeans, and on his feet, he wore black boots.

"The woman I'm looking for."

The sound of his deep voice pulled me with a jolt from my trance. I quickly brought my gaze up to his. "You're looking for me?"

"I am." Celeste and Reina dejectedly turned back to their desks as he came my way.

I sucked in a breath as he came to a stop about a foot away. A fresh, clean scent filled my senses. "Why?"

"Mia asked me to help you with the program she set up. I thought we could look at it together."

"Liliana and I were about to go out to lunch."

Em shook his head and turned toward our bodyguards. "Didn't you receive word. There's no extracurricular movement for the next few days?"

"*Sí*, we did."

I pressed my lips together. "Well, we didn't ask." Irritation was audible in my tone. "Honestly, I didn't realize we needed to."

Em's lips quirked in a lopsided grin. "Fear not. You won't starve. The cafeteria has a taco bar on Tuesdays and Thursdays."

"Eat here?"

"Or if you prefer, I will be happy to go get something and bring it back."

"But I can't leave." It wasn't a question.

"You can. You can go back to *el Patrón's*. What you may not do is walk around San Diego with only Horace."

"Mia said..." Something in Em's expression darkened, causing my words to fade away.

"Things have changed since yesterday."

That reminded me of what Isla said. "Something happened at Wanderland?"

"It's not your concern."

My fist went to my hip and my volume rose. "If whatever happened is suddenly restricting my freedom to walk the streets of San Diego, then it's my concern."

His smile broadened. "What happened to the scared little girl at the capo's home?"

"I wasn't scared. And I'm not a little girl."

"I believe one out of the two." His smile was back. "As a rule of thumb, I prefer not to be lied to."

Swallowing, I straightened my shoulders. "I'm not lying. I believe Dario sent me out here expecting me to fail. I've decided that isn't going to happen. And for it not to happen, I need to push my own boundaries. Mia stands up for herself. She's different." I shook my head. "Honestly, none of this is any of your business."

"Why would you think that Dario would send you out here to fail?"

I exhaled. "If you want to help me with the program, fine. Personal information is on a need-to-know basis." I lifted my eyebrow. "You, Emiliano, don't need to know."

"Need—no. Want—yes."

"I'll eat tacos."

He pressed his lips together and tilted his face. "Here's the thing. Unless there is an emergency, men aren't allowed any farther into the apartments than the front office or guard stations." He flashed a predatory smile. "These women deal with men enough. Mia wanted a safe male-free zone." His eyes twinkled. "It's not as if anyone would be afraid of me."

Fear. I was scared at the capo's house. Maybe it was fear of my father's reaction, not so much Emiliano himself. Nevertheless, even now, I had the common symptoms of fright: racing pulse, shortness of breath, and fluttering in my stomach.

"Liliana told me that." I tilted my head. "If you can't go back there, how do you know about the menu?"

"I usually ask whoever's working the front desk to get me an order." He paused. "I could ask you."

I crossed my arms over my breasts. "Ask Celeste or Reina. They seemed pretty smitten with your attention."

"You're not?"

I shook my head. "Nope." I lied again.

"You won't get me some tacos so that I can help you get started on the program?"

My arms fell to my sides as I peered around his solid body and met Liliana's gaze. "What do you think? Since we're apparently forbidden to walk outside, should we get Emiliano lunch from the cafeteria?"

Liliana smiled. "Em, yes." She turned to José. "You, no."

To my astonishment, José smiled. "You know how I like my tacos."

"Oh, does this mean I'm also getting Horace's?"

He nodded. "*Gracias.*"

Fifteen minutes later, Liliana and I were back in the front office with food for everyone, including Reina and Celeste. Instead of taking ours to our offices, Liliana, Reina, Celeste, and I went into a conference room I hadn't noticed before.

As we sat with our to-go containers and bottles of water, I remembered my question to Em. If he wouldn't tell me what had changed, I could find out another way.

After taking a bite of the delicious food, I hummed.

"They're good, no?" Celeste asked.

"Oh my gosh. This is the best taco I've ever had."

Liliana smiled. "Luz makes the tostadas herself. None of that store-bought crap."

"She could open a restaurant."

"We all tell her that," Reina said.

I cleared my throat. "If it's none of my business…" I had everyone's attention. "Did you two work at the club last night?"

They both sat straighter. Celeste was the one to answer. "We did."

I lowered my voice so the men wouldn't hear. "What happened? Isla said something about after what happened at the club last night, she had trouble falling asleep."

They both seemed to relax. Reina looked out the door

toward the men and leaned forward. She spoke quietly. "Two of Kozlov's men made it past security. It all started around two this morning."

Liliana gasped.

"Who is Kozlov?" I asked.

Celeste rolled her eyes. "You have some catching up to do if you're going to work with us."

"Great. Catch me up."

Celeste went on to tell me about the bratvas in California. Apparently up until recently, there were two. Ivan Kozlov was the head of one. He was assassinated Tuesday night. The Russians at the club were there to ask *el Patrón* for clemency. He wasn't at the club, but his brother, Reinaldo, was in town for a big meeting. The men were taken downstairs. Rei showed up to question them.

"Nobody trusts them," Reina said. Her smile broadened. "I'm sure Rei got the truth out of them."

Celeste giggled.

"What do you mean?"

Liliana answered, "Rei Roríguez is well known for his success at interrogation."

"What does he do?"

The other three looked at one another and shook their heads.

"How am I supposed to be caught up if you don't tell me?"

Reina asked, "You're a Luciano, right?"

I straightened my shoulders. "Yes. I don't know what that has to do—"

Liliana laid her slender hand on the table. "Rumor is that Dante has a similar reputation."

"Dante oversees Emerald Club."

"Seriously," Celeste said. "Izzy, it's time for you to wake up. Rei tortures answers out of people. The only thing different in his interrogations and your uncle's is the language they speak as they cut off body parts."

My stomach twisted. "Dante is my cousin. And I can't..."

"You could ask Julia," Liliana said. "Nicolas sent her into the private bathroom to *thank* Rei for his help after one of his questioning sessions. She said the water was red from all the blood."

I pushed my container of remaining food away. I remembered Julia. She was the one who was accepted to school and wanted to be a nurse. "Did she?"

"Did she what?" Celeste asked.

"Thank him?"

Reina pressed her lips together. "No one refuses Nicolas Ruiz. He knows how to make life unbearable."

"But Rei is married." I pushed my chair back. "Jasmine married a killer."

"I don't think they were married at that time," Liliana said. "As for marrying a killer, I did. So did Camila and Cat. We don't judge."

"Did..." I could hardly formulate a question. "Did you see the two Russians after they went downstairs?"

"No, Nick cut off entry. They closed down everything except VIP. At three we were all escorted back here. There was a rumor that *el Patrón* was brought in through a back door." Reina shrugged. "The fact they made it in at all had us all pretty wound up."

"The Russians didn't make it to the back rooms, did they?"

Celeste and Reina shook their heads.

"There was an incident a few years back," Liliana said. "Russians killed two women in the back. Shot them up with a lethal dose of heroin." She turned to Celeste and Reina. "If Nicolas or anyone else at the club does anything to make life unbearable, come to me. I'll talk to Mia. You know we're here for you."

They both nodded.

I stood and reached for my water bottle. "I think I've had enough catching up for one day." I gestured toward the food container. "If anyone wants that, I've lost my appetite."

FIFTEEN

Emiliano

Two of the residents came up to the front office after all the women went into the conference room with their lunches. Both residents had appointments out of the building that they'd scheduled. A look at Mia's program confirmed the appointments were scheduled, but they would have to be missed. Other than here or the club, anyone connected with the Roríguez cartel was on lockdown. The news didn't go over well. Nevertheless, they're still safe within these walls.

When we were alone again, José asked, "What's the word on Kozlov's men?"

"They're alive," I replied. "For now."

Horace took a bite of his lunch. When his gaze met

mine, he lowered his volume. "Fucking shame they weren't telling the truth. *El Patrón* could use them to get to Volkov."

That was the plan. It was better not to have that plan widely known. At this point, *el Patrón*, Rei, Nick, Dante, Adrian, and I were the only people who would know that the two men ultimately survived Rei's interrogation. The capo's connection with the Ivanov bratva paid off with translation.

Tonight, after dark, the men would be moved to a safe house with their wives. They gave up valuable information about the Kozlov bratva. As long as it could be confirmed, the Roríguez cartel would protect them.

Soon, the official word would be that Kozlov's men died. Rei was in the process of finding two bodies to pass off as the Russians after an intense car fire. With the unrest between the bratvas, even the cops wouldn't question the authenticity of the murders. It would be obvious that Volkov was cleaning house.

I looked up as Isabella stepped from the conference room. She stopped outside the doorway with her hand over her stomach and her face down. When she looked up, her complexion was pale, and her breathing rapid, as if she'd run a race.

"What the fuck?"

She turned my way. "I'm not feeling well." She turned and hurried toward Mia's office.

Horace began to stand.

"No," I said. "I'll check on her."

"She's my detail."

Standing, I changed my tone. "I said that I'll check on her."

He lifted his hand. "Go ahead. Emotional little girls aren't my thing."

"She's an adult." That was the last thing I said as I headed down the hall toward Mia's office, my proclamation running on repeat.

Adult.

Adult.

A spunky, beautiful, determined adult.

The office door was shut. For a moment, I debated barging in. As a newly appointed lieutenant, I could justify the action. Then again, Isabella was frightened of me in Kansas City; there was no need to give her a reason to fear me. Taking a breath, I knocked on the door.

"Horace?"

Turning the knob, I pushed the door inward. Isabella was a vision, standing facing the window with her long golden hair cascading down her back, falling in waves to just above her slim waist and her round ass.

She stifled a cry and took a ragged breath. "I'm ready to go back to Mia's..." Her voice faded away as she turned to face me. Her cheeks had more color, but her makeup gave away the fact she'd been crying Her irises appeared almost black. "Em."

I closed the door behind me and took a step toward her. "You want to leave already." I crossed my arms. "I guess Dario was right."

It took a second before recognition of my statement showed on her beautiful face. The earlier sadness morphed before my eyes into something akin to fear and then to anger as the muscles in her temples pulsated. "Dario, my father, Dante, all of them..." Her volume rose. "They sent me here with no knowledge." She gasped for breath and slapped her hands on each side of her hips. "They sent me to the middle of a war with no weapons or realization that there was a war."

"The famiglia and cartel have been together in this war since the alliance formed. How did you not know?"

Panting, she shook her head.

Lowering my arms, my lips curled. "A weapon. You want a weapon? I'll give you a weapon." I lifted the hem of my t-shirt revealing a Beretta 22 Bobcat in my holster tucked into my jeans. "Do you want it?"

Her eyes opened wide. "No." She sniffed and wiped the tears from her face. Even with the dark smudge under her eyes, she was stunning. "What happened at the club last night?"

I took another step toward her.

"Stop," she demanded. "Answer my question."

"Two Russians from the Kozlov bratva made it past our security. It could have been a deadly mistake."

"Are they dead?" Her voice quivered. "Did Reinaldo kill them?"

Fuck, someone had told her.

The damn whores in that conference room.

I worked to keep my voice calm. "Isabella, I don't know what you heard."

She wrapped her arms around her midsection. "Do you kill people?"

"I have."

A tear slid down her cheek. "And *el Patrón*, Reinaldo…?"

"We live in a dangerous world. Often, it's kill or be killed. It's not like we go out each day and say to ourselves, I wonder how many people I can kill today."

She scrunched her nose and lips as if she'd swallowed something sour. "And my family? Dante?"

I nodded. "The Mafia and cartel's businesses aren't that dissimilar. We each have our specialties."

Letting out a breath, she dropped her arms to her side. "My father owns part of Emerald Club. He oversees the restaurants."

I shook my head. "Your father is a dangerous man. He wouldn't have lasted as long as he has if he wasn't."

"I knew he was a made man by the time Dario was born. I thought that was in the past."

Again, I shook my head.

"Emerald Club has whores."

"If that was a question, the answer is yes."

Isabella spun toward the window again. "Isn't it dangerous to have a window to the street?"

Her thoughts were obviously scattered.

"It's reflective and bulletproof glass. You can see out, but no one can see in. If *el Patrón* could, he'd have Mia in a bulletproof bubble 24/7."

I took two steps toward her. She didn't move. From a distance, I watched her shoulders tremble.

"Isabella, how can I help?"

She tipped her face forward. "You can't. No one can."

"You're shaking."

Gently, I reached forward lightly, gripping her shoulders. She stiffened under my touch. Slowly, I ran my hands up and down over the soft sleeves of her blouse. Over time, her muscles relaxed. "I think you're on the verge of shock."

She shivered. "I-I'm cold."

"Turn around."

When she did, she tilted her chin up, meeting my gaze. Her pupils were solid black. "Give me your hands."

"My hands?"

I reached for them. It was as if her circulation had ceased.

"Let's get you to the chair before you pass out."

Instead of arguing, Isabella nodded and walked to the desk chair. I spun it to the side and crouched near her knees. "Look at me." She did. "Your pupils are dilated. Your hands are like ice." I held on to them again, my finger landing on her wrist. "And your pulse is rapid."

"I don't know... what's happening."

There was a water bottle on her desk. Reaching for it, I unscrewed the cap. "Drink some water."

She took the bottle and drank before setting it back on the desk.

I continued to run my thumb back and forth over her fingers. "If I'm ever fortunate enough to have children, I wouldn't want them to bear the burdens of the true workings of our business."

"I'm not a child."

"No, Isabella, you're not. You're a fucking gorgeous woman who just had her entire understanding of her life blown to smithereens." I lifted my hand and caressed her cheek. "You have a pure heart, and your family didn't want to darken it."

"They sent me out here."

"You said you wanted to go back to Mia's."

She nodded.

"Do you want to go back to Kansas City?"

Isabella swallowed. "If I go back, Dario will have been right."

"Fuck Dario. What do you want?"

Her eyes closed and her nostrils flared. When she opened them, a halo of the softest brown eyes I'd ever seen surrounded her shrinking pupils.

"Your pupils are better. I can see the light golden brown of your beautiful eyes."

Her lips curled and her cheeks rose. "I'm hardly beautiful. I'm a basket case."

"Breathe, beautiful."

She took a ragged breath.

"Whatever you want to know, ask. I'll never lie to you."

"Did Reinaldo kill those men?"

"No."

Isabella let out a long sigh. "What's going—"

I laid my finger over her lips. "I won't lie to you, Isabella. But there are some things I can't elaborate on. I believe your next question was one of those things. Do you understand?" I moved my finger away.

"Yes." She nodded. "Are the Russians the reason we couldn't go out for lunch?"

"Yes. Volkov is looking for Kozlov's men. If he

suspects we have them, he'll do anything to get them back."

"Why does Volkov want them?"

"He knows they have information. He'd kill them before letting them talk."

Isabella inhaled. "What is *anything*?"

"Imagine if he could get you, Liliana, Mia, or Jasmine...imagine the power over *el Patrón* he'd have."

"I get it. What about the women here?"

"Not the same, but they're valuable to the cartel. We've sworn to protect them." I stood and stretched my legs. "If you want to go back to Mia's, I'll take you."

"I lied to you earlier."

I lifted my eyebrows. "You did?"

"If you won't lie to me, I shouldn't lie to you."

"What was your lie?"

"At the capo's apartment during the birthday party, I was frightened of you."

My lips curled. "I knew that."

"My father has strict rules about interacting with Catalina's family or members of the cartel."

"Are you breaking his rules right now?"

Isabella smiled. "I am. He sent me to war. I need to identify my allies."

"You found one in me. Liliana too." I turned toward the door and back. "Do you want to call it a day?"

"Nope." Isabella spun her chair toward the desk, rubbed her temples, and exhaled. "Let's look at this program." She forced a smile. "I don't want you wasting your afternoon. I'm sure you have bad guys to kill."

Damn, she was impressive.

"I'm the bad guy."

"I'm beginning to doubt that."

I reached for the doorknob. "I'm going to tell Liliana to get word out that we're on lockdown, and then I'll be back."

"Thank you."

"For?" I asked.

"Being honest with me."

"Always."

CHAPTER

SIXTEEN

Isabella

As soon as Emiliano shut the door, I hurried to the attached bathroom and turned on the light. I wasn't certain what had happened. Was it shock? It might have been brought on by the sight of Em's six-pack abs or were they eight? When he lifted his shirt, I barely noticed the gun.

With my hands on the top of the vanity, I stared into the mirror. My reflection was far from beautiful. If someone asked, I'd say I looked ghostly. My insides buzzed in an unfamiliar way. I touched my forehead. My skin felt clammy as if I'd run a fever, but that was impossible. I was too cold for that.

Reaching for the faucet, I ran the water until it warmed. My fingers ached as the water turned my skin pink. I splashed more water on my face, rubbing away the mascara that had smeared. As my body began to warm, I felt the rise in temperature on the back of my neck. A quick search of Mia's drawers in the vanity and I found a hair tie. As I was securing my hair in a ponytail, I heard a knock.

"Come in," I called as I peeked out into the office, expecting Em's return.

"Izzy?"

"Liliana. I was expecting Em."

"He said he'll be back here soon. I wanted to check on you. I came earlier, but he was in here with you."

I nodded. "He talked me off a ledge, so to speak."

Liliana peered toward the window. "Yeah, that window doesn't open and if it did, there would be about a foot to the ground. Not much of a ledge." She sat in one of the chairs at the small table. "I'm sorry about the lunch conversation. I didn't expect it to get so graphic."

I took the chair opposite her. "Don't be sorry. I need to know what is happening if I want to help the...residents." I feigned a smile. "I've lived eighteen years of my life in a gilded cage, not even fully realizing what was happening around me."

She nodded. "I get it."

"Did you always understand the cartel?"

Liliana shook her head. "I had a crash course when I married Gerardo."

"Em said something that made me think."

"What did he say?"

"My mind is a bit jumbled, but it was about protecting children from the burdens of the family businesses. I don't know if I hate my parents for doing that or love them for the same reason. I mean" —I gestured around— "this is a lot to comprehend. Could they have eased me into it, or was it better to have eighteen years of ignorant bliss?"

She grinned. "You're very philosophical."

I scoffed. "Not normally. It must be a side effect of the shock."

"Well, Em gave Celeste and Reina an earful."

"No." I stood. "He shouldn't have done that. I'm here to help them. I can't do that if they're afraid to tell me things."

"Maybe you should clear the air."

Nodding, I went to the door. As I opened it, Em was standing there with his fist ready to knock, his bicep bulging as if the matter of a closed door could never stop his entrance. Gathering my courage, I asked, "What did you say to Celeste and Reina?"

His dark gaze went to Liliana and back to me.

"We don't lie to one another, remember," I said.

"Thanks, Liliana."

She was now standing. "I think that's my cue to leave."

"Don't blame her. What did you say?"

"Most people would be appreciative of a lieutenant stepping in."

"What did you say to them?" I repeated.

"I told them not to overwhelm you. That you're having a lot of realities thrown at you all at once and to go easy."

My fist went to my hip. "Thank you, but I don't need a lieutenant or a knight in shining armor." I kept my stare locked with his, unwilling to let myself think about the toned abs beneath his shirt as he blocked the doorway. "If you'll excuse me, I need to talk to them before I get my lesson on the computer program."

Em took a step back, his nostrils flaring and his lips pressed together.

Back in the front office, I went to the tall desk. "Ladies." Reina and Celeste turned my way.

"We're sorry if we scared you," Celeste offered.

I shook my head. "You did, but don't be sorry. I'm here because Mia can't be. I can't help her if everyone here is afraid of scaring me. Forget what Emiliano said. My door is always open, and I want to do everything in my power to be here for you and all the residents."

They both nodded.

"I'm going to go back to the office, and Em's going to help me with Mia's program. But that doesn't mean I'm unavailable."

Reina grinned. "Got it, *jefe*."

"Yeah, I need to work on my Spanish as well."

"Boss," Celeste translated.

"Nope," I corrected "A better term would be coworker."

When I returned to my temporary office, I stopped in the doorway. Em was sitting behind the desk in the white chair, his attention on the large screens. I stared at his profile, the sharp cut of his jawline, his prominent cheekbones, and his plump full lips pressed together. Being in his presence had become reassuring and at the same time frightening.

Maybe my father was right that the cartel was filled

with murderers. What he'd failed to mention was that so was the Mafia.

Em turned to the sound of my footsteps on the vinyl flooring. His lips curled. "Are you ready for your first lesson?"

"Not my first. Mia worked with me yesterday."

"Then your second." He stood and took a seat in another chair he'd moved around to behind the desk. "I have no doubt you'll have this up-to-date in a week or less."

I sat in the leather chair. "Okay, *jefe*, tell me what to do."

Em stilled at my side.

I turned toward him, seeing his darkening stare and the pulsating of a vein in his forehead. "Did I say something wrong? They told me that means boss."

The tendons pulled taut in his neck as he moistened his lips. "It does."

"Then why are you looking at me funny?"

"Is this one of those moments I'm not supposed to lie?"

"Of course," I said, leaning back against the chair.

"If I tell you, you'll go back to being scared of me."

"I doubt that."

"Having you call me boss and asking to be told what to do took my thoughts to an inappropriate place."

My mouth felt suddenly dry and my core unexpectedly clenched. "I'm afraid you'll have to be more specific. I'm as uneducated on inappropriate places as I am on cartel and Mafia specifics."

"Truth, not elaboration."

As he began to give an overview of the program, my mind went to places I'd only thought about with movies and books. His large hand gripping the mouse made me wonder what it would be like to have it touching me. And then I remembered he had touched me, my arms, and held my hands. I couldn't recall all that happened, but his touch had been comforting.

"Do you have any questions?" he asked.

Taking a deep breath, I struggled with telling him I hadn't heard a word he said. I reached for the mouse. "Let me try."

It was about three o'clock when Em received a phone call. He took it out into the hall. When he returned, his smile was present, but his eyes weren't glistening.

"Is everything all right?"

"I have to go." He jutted his chin toward the computer screens. "Are you good? You can do this. You have been doing it by yourself for the last hour."

"Honestly, I'm nervous." I scoffed. "I have been all day, so what's new?"

"If you want me to take you back to *el Patrón's*, I can now. Otherwise, Horace will need to do it."

Em would take me. Why? Yet the thought of being alone with him in a car made my body react. I shifted my shoulders. "No. I'll stay here until at least five."

"Okay. You have my number if you have a question."

"I hardly think that if you're in a life-and-death battle, you want me to call about a spreadsheet."

"If I don't answer, I'll call back."

"Good, don't get hurt out there."

"Would you really care if I did?"

His question caught me off guard. "A few months ago, probably not." I lifted my cheeks in a smile. "Now I care."

He nodded and walked away.

Letting out a breath, I leaned against the chair, wondering how I could have been so wrong about not only him but so many things. In Mia's program, she has information on each tenant. When I saw names I recognized, I pictured the woman's face.

Julia, the one who was excited about being accepted to community college passed her GED less than two months ago. Luz, the one who cooked the delicious tostadas, told Mia she wanted to be a chef. The two ladies in the front office were younger than I realized. Reina was twenty-three and Celeste was nineteen. The list went on and on.

A world of misconceptions.

As the clock neared five, Horace came back, knocking on the doorframe. "*Señorita* Luciano."

"Izzy."

"Miss Izzy, are you ready to go home?"

I assessed the work I'd accomplished. If tomorrow went as well as this afternoon, I'd have Mia's program up-to-date by the end of the day. "Yes." I pushed the chair back.

"Have you decided where you want to stay, *el Patrón's* or *Señorit*a Liliana's?"

I'd forgotten I had a choice.

"I'd like to talk to Mia about it. So, I'll stay there tonight if she won't mind me being there."

Liliana appeared beside Horace. "You're tired of me already?"

"No." I stood and turned to Horace. "I'll be ready in a few minutes."

As he walked back toward the front of the offices, Liliana leaned against the doorframe. "I'm tired too. I'll get my purse."

When we were in the car with José and Horace, I asked Liliana, "Tell me what your day usually consists of when you're not giving tours or inputting information."

"Since Mia's been gone, I've been busier with the residents. This afternoon I spent nearly an hour in one of the apartments trying to deescalate a misunderstanding between roommates."

"Did you do it?"

She nodded. "I think it is resolved."

"They really trust you."

"I feel like I'm helping even if it is just letting each side voice their viewpoint."

SEVENTEEN

Isabella

J osé dropped Horace and me off at Mia's. As soon as Viviana answered the door, Mia was there with Jorge in her arms.

"You never called. How did your day go?"

"Other than a minor issue of going into shock, it improved." I grinned. "I should have your program up-to-date by the end of the day tomorrow."

"Tomorrow? Wow, you're fantastic."

We walked together past *el Patrón's* closed office door, past the kitchen where Viviana was creating magical aromas, and finally out onto the pool deck. Mia placed Jorge in a colorful small fenced-in area with soft rubber flooring and enough toys for a toy store. Once he was content, she stood straight. "I'm worried about Liliana. What did you think?"

"I think she's amazing," I answered honestly.

Mia's eyes opened wide. "Tell me more."

"She knows every woman's name. They talk to her, confide in her, and go to her for help. And when she's there, she's a different person. She knows so much." I lay back against the lounge chair, stretching out my legs, and stared up at the bright blue sky. "Something did bother me."

"What?"

"At one point today, Liliana was explaining the classes you offer." I turned to my cousin. "She was incredibly knowledgeable. I asked if she'd ever considered becoming a teacher. Her response was that she wasn't smart enough for something like that." My volume rose. "She is."

Mia nodded. "Without going into what is Liliana's to share, her self-confidence has taken a hit. I'm thrilled to hear your assessment of her at the apartments. It sounds like she's doing better than I realized."

"I think the only reason the program is behind on her input is because she's not sitting in her office, or standing," I added with a grin. "She's physically out among the women. My guess is she's doing what you were."

"Now, tell me about the minor case of shock."

I shook my head. "I'd rather not talk about it."

"Okay. Just know if you want to talk about it, I'm here."

Placing my feet back on the travertine pavers, I stared at Mia as tears burned the back of my eyes. "Did you always know what your father did, what your brothers do?"

Mia's eyes opened wide, and she licked her lips. "I'm sure I didn't know at some point. Once you learn, it's impossible to forget."

"Celeste who works in the front office is only a year older than me."

Mia nodded.

"I want to call Noemi and talk to her, but I feel like I can't."

"She's your sister. I'm sure she'd like to talk to you."

With my elbows on my knees, I supported my head. "I don't want to be the one who bursts her bubble."

Mia reached out and placed her hand on my knee. "I'm sorry. If I'd have known your lack of understanding, I would have prepared you better. May I ask how you learned...what you learned?"

Inhaling, I sat straighter. "Liliana and I wanted to go to a café for lunch. Em arrived at that same time and told us that we were on lockdown. Isla had mentioned earlier in the day that she had trouble getting to sleep after what happened at the club last night." Suddenly, it occurred to me that Mia may not know. If *el Patrón* didn't want her to know, I didn't want to be the one to tell her.

My forehead furrowed. "I-I um...do you know?"

She nodded. "Jano had to leave late at night. He told me what happened."

Closing my eyes, I shook my head. "I didn't know about any of it. I've heard the word war from my father, but I didn't realize..." I stood and paced near the crystal-blue pool.

The sunlight danced on the Pacific Ocean like millions of shimmering diamonds.

When I turned back, Mia was waiting patiently. "I didn't know there was a literal war. People are dying. People are being tortured." I took a deep breath. "Dante..."

"Reinaldo and Jano," Mia added. "Dario, Uncle Salvatore, and Uncle Carmine."

"My dad."

She pressed her lips together and nodded. "It's a lot to take in." She forced a smile. "I bet Uncle Carmine didn't send you out here to lose your innocence."

Dropping my hands to my sides, I stood taller. "Dario did. He thought I'd break."

Mia's eyebrows bunched as she stood. "No, he sent you out here because of me." She came closer. "I'm not one to stick up for my brother, but he didn't send you out here to fail. He sent you out here because I need help, and we both believed you would succeed."

A lump formed in my throat.

"Thank you. I didn't know that." I looked back at the pool. "What time is dinner? Do I have time to swim a few laps?"

"I'll talk to Viviana, but I'm sure we have time. Does this mean you're going to stay here?"

I nodded. "I like Liliana, but one thing my father made me promise was that I would stay with you. Seeing as I'm breaking a million of his rules, I can at least follow that one."

Mia wrapped her arms around my shoulders. "I'm glad." She took a step back. "I miss the apartments and especially the tenants. It can get lonely here, even with

Viviana and Silas. Jano is so busy…" She smiled. "I'm very glad you're here, Izzy."

I lowered my volume. "Your husband still scares me."

She shook her head.

"Were you ever scared of him?"

Mia's lips quirked. "Not scared. I thought he was an asshole."

A laugh came from deep in my chest. "I wasn't expecting that."

"At the time, I was right." Her smile softened and her eyes shone. "Since then, he's proved me wrong."

"For the first time since Papà told me that I was coming, I'm glad to be here."

DAYS TURNED INTO A WEEK.

One week turned into two.

Even though I was living in the same house, I rarely saw *el Patrón*. The first time I did after Mia's and my conversation, he and I passed ways in the kitchen. It was after I'd thought everyone had gone to bed, and the house was mostly dark. The light of the pool allowed enough illumination for me to search for a late-night snack. When I stepped from the pantry, he was there. All six feet-plus of muscle and tension. My first instinct was to scream or maybe run. In what order I didn't know.

Instead, I remembered Mia's words. When she first met him, she thought he was an asshole. Involuntarily, my cheeks rose, and my lips curled into a smile. "*El patrón.*"

"*Me puedes llamar de* Jano." His features mellowed. "*Gracias, chiquita.* Thank you for staying with Mia and helping her out at the apartments. It means a lot to her."

"I'm glad I can be of assistance."

"You are. It's one thing off my mind." He nodded.

With that he was gone, out the door to the garage. I heard the garage door open. The time on the microwave was nearly midnight. I wondered how he knew the way Mia felt. It seemed like he was always working.

Since that night, I have been less nervous around him. It wasn't like I would be calling him by his first name, but I no longer hyperventilated in his presence. I was also becoming more comfortable at the apartments with the tenants. I found that I no longer dwelled on their profession. It was a small step, but a step nonetheless.

I didn't know what was happening with the war—only that we were still restricted in our ability to be anywhere but at the apartments or home.

When I arrived at the office exactly two weeks after my first day, I was surprised to find Em sitting at my desk. He'd been by almost every day to check on things. It was wishful thinking that he was there because of me. The sight of him made my mouth go dry, my pulse race, and parts of my body twist. I found myself thinking about him as I lay in bed. I'd relive the sight of his toned abs and imagine tracing the snake's tail higher over his muscular arm and wide shoulders. While he was always nice to me, except for the one thing he said about inappropriate thoughts, he had been a gentleman—nothing like my father said men in the cartel would be.

I was suffering from a schoolgirl crush. That was all this was. Em was the first unrelated man I'd ever spent time with. A woman would have to be dead inside not to be affected by his handsome exterior and his kindness.

Currently, he was staring intently at the computer screens.

"Hey," I said as I entered. "You're sitting at my desk."

His dark stare came my direction. For a moment, my skin warmed as if he were seeing beneath my slacks and blouse. By the time his gaze met mine, my nipples were hard, and I prayed my padded bra was doing its job.

"Our system was hacked last night."

"What? The network here?"

He nodded. "Rei is working on it from Sacramento."

"Reinaldo knows networking and computers?"

"He's one of the best."

I'd heard the same about his interrogation skills. I shrugged. "Apparently, a man of many talents."

Em smiled. "We're all talented in an array of subjects." His eyebrows danced. "I'd be happy to show you sometime."

I didn't know how to respond. Instead, I went around the desk to see the screen and asked, "How did Rei find out about the hack?" There were rows and rows of data moving faster than I could read. Instead of his usual fresh scent, Em emanated a spicy tobacco aroma.

"He watches over all the cartel's networks. The good news is that the apartments weren't connected to any of our other networks."

"Mia can access this from home."

"Yeah, that's through a separate server and

multiple firewalls. I've already been in contact with Silas. He's running a check, but so far that seems clear."

"What about all the women's data?"

"Fucking compromised."

I thought of something else. "What about the computers in the computer center? They have accounts and personal information like their bank accounts."

"Rei had everything well protected. We're not sure yet what they got."

I placed my purse in the side drawer of the desk, where Liliana had shown me on the first day. I inhaled. "Do you smoke?"

He sniffed his shirt. "Not regularly. Sorry if I smell. It's been a long night."

A smile came to my lips. "No, I like it. My Uncle Vincent sometimes smoked a pipe. I didn't like him much, but I liked the smell of his pipe."

"I'll remember to not shower every day."

"That might be carrying it a bit too far."

The processing data on the screen stopped. Em reached for the mouse. Many boxes popped up. He was clicking faster than I could read. Finally, he closed them all out.

"The data is restored. I think." He stood. "You know the program as well as anyone, and you know what you've added. Can you check to see if it's accurate?"

Nodding, I sat. The chair was warm from his body heat. For the next few minutes, I opened different files and checked the running spreadsheets. When I came to the one where the tenants added appointments and requests for leaving, I stopped. "How long will this lock-down continue?"

"Tension is still high."

"You know, when I conceded to the idea that I was coming out west, I imagined seeing more of San Diego and southern California than Mia's house and these apartments."

Em pressed his lips together and stretched his arms in the air. The snake on his right arm caught my attention.

"Why a snake?"

He grinned. "Have we now moved on to more personal information?"

"Maybe."

"You get one question, and I get one question. We both must answer honestly. Deal?"

"Why am I suddenly worried about what you'll ask?"

His dark eyebrows arched.

"Deal. Why a snake?"

"What I do—we do—can be dark and dangerous. A snake is a symbol of rebirth because of the way it sheds its skin. Each day is a new one with more possibilities than we can ever fathom."

"I thought a snake was evil, like the serpent who offered Eve the apple."

"I told you; I'm the bad guy." He leaned his firm ass against the edge of the desk and crossed his arms over his wide chest. "My turn."

I lifted my hands to my face. "I'm scared."

Em prized my fingers away until my hands were engulfed by his. His nose was millimeters from mine. His dark brown eyes shone as his stare intensified. It was as if he could see beyond my gaze. His deep tenor reverberated through me from my ears to my toes and everywhere in between.

"You're not scared, Isabella. I watched you transform right here in this office two weeks ago. The girl back at the capo's wouldn't have made it through that day. You did. And you've been back every day since. We live in an evil world and yet, since you've arrived, you've blossomed. You're fucking fascinating to watch."

I swallowed. That was a lot to process. I inhaled and pulled my hands from his. I immediately missed their warmth. "Go ahead. Ask."

"I'd like to take you out after work tonight. Show you around San Diego."

"A date?"

EIGHTEEN

Emiliano

My lips quirked. "Would you like it to be a date?" The thought of having this stunning, strong woman on my arm brought life back to my tired body.

Isabella nibbled on her plump lower lip. "Is it safe?"

I nodded. "You're safe with me, Isabella."

"My parents wouldn't approve."

"Then we'll call it a tour. You just said you wanted to see more places. I'm simply at your service."

"Horace will come?"

"I think you've exceeded your one question.

She stood, pushing back the chair. "I can't go unsupervised. My father was furious when you and Rei snuck Jasmine out."

She was so fucking close that I could smell her sweet scent. I stood straight and squared my shoulders. "I learned my lesson. We won't sneak. I'll get Jano's approval."

"*El Patrón?* But I'm not cartel."

"You're under our protection. That makes you cartel."

The way she nibbled on her lower lip when she was unsure was the sexiest thing I'd ever seen. My circulation warmed as I imagined leaning down and kissing her. Every fiber in my body wanted me to take one step closer, wrap my arm around her slender waist, and pull her softness toward my hardening body.

My curiosity of Isabella took root back at Cat's house. Those feelings had changed drastically over the last couple of weeks. Since her first day here, Isabella has been a bright fucking beacon, singing a siren's song that I heard even in my slumber. It was as I'd said: she'd blossomed outside of the suffocating watch of her father, a flower finally allowed sunshine.

When she looked up, her milk-chocolate stare met mine. "I'd like that."

Fuck.

The longer it took her to answer, the more afraid I was that I'd blown the connection we'd been developing throughout the past weeks.

My smile grew. "I'll pick you up here."

Isabella looked down at her clothes. "I should go to Mia's and change."

"Not a date, remember. You're perfect for your first tour."

Her smile grew. "Where are we going?"

"That's my surprise." Slowly, I backed away, possibilities running through my thoughts. "I'll see you tonight."

Isabella nodded. "Tonight."

On my way out, I started to tell Horace I'd take care of Isabella after she was done with work, but I stopped, telling myself I should ask Jano first. Speak of the devil, my phone buzzed with a text message.

It seemed that going home, showering, and getting some shut-eye was going to have to wait. Jano's orders had me driving from the Marina neighborhood to Del Mar Heights. It wasn't good enough to have emailed reports from our chiefs on the streets. Jano wanted each army chief to be questioned in person by a lieutenant. The personal touch was to let them know we were watching and monitoring their businesses as well as our stakes in those businesses. It was fucking tedious, but I had to admit, it was getting the attention of the street soldiers.

The new *el Patrón* wasn't going to put up with shit. Do your job and do it right. Roríguez will reward you. Don't do your job or do it poorly, and you're fired. In the cartel, *fired* was meant literally not figuratively—a bullet *fired* into the back of your head.

It was nearly four in the afternoon before I made it back to Jano's office.

He looked up from his desk as I entered, looking even more tired than I felt. "*Qué pasa?*" He motioned toward the chairs across his desk from him.

I took a seat. "No problems from the chiefs I met with

today. Business is hot, and there haven't been any sightings of Herrera's soldiers."

"Did every chief show?"

"They did."

Jano pushed back against his chair, stretching his neck. "Kozlov's men, the ones from the club, they've opened up a whole new world of intel for us." He nodded. "So far, their information has checked out. The charred bodies were identified as Kozlov's soldiers. We've gotten Volkov's attention."

"Isabella asked when the lockdown would end."

Jano slapped the top of his desk and deepened his tone. "When I have Herrera's and Volkov's heads right here, fucking soaking this desk in their blood."

I leaned forward. I'd given this some thought throughout the day. I could ask to take Isabella out for a tour or a date, or I could go big and ask for her hand. She'd only been out west for two weeks, and she was thriving. This was where she was meant to be. "Have you talked to the capo lately?"

Jano narrowed his gaze. "Have you heard something?"

"No. I was wondering about Isabella."

Jano stood, sending his chair rolling backwards. "Fuck. *Hay algún problema?* I thought Mia said things were—"

I stood and lifted my hand. "No problem. I want to know if the capo will allow me to marry her. If you will."

His lips came together, and his nostrils flared. "You asked that in the wrong order. Try again."

Fuck. Not the best start.

"*El patrón*, I would appreciate your permission to marry Isabella Luciano."

"Fuck, Em. We have more important things to think about." When I didn't speak, he asked, "How old is she?"

"Eighteen."

Exhaling, he retook his seat. "Mia thinks we should do away with arranged marriages." He gestured with his hand. "Consent of the woman…blah blah…"

"I believe she'd consent."

"Why her? She's a frightened child."

I started to speak.

Jano lifted his hand. "She lives here. I know what she is. What about someone older? Mia's cousin Giorgia should be past her mourning period after the death of her husband." He grinned. "I'd recommend marrying a widow over a frightened child."

"Eighteen is an adult. She isn't frightened around me."

"Remember Liliana?"

"With all due respect, I'm not my uncle, the asshole Gerardo Ruiz."

Jano shook his head. "I can't think about this right now." He inhaled. "I'll speak to the capo on your behalf. Candidly, I don't anticipate Carmine Luciano accepting your offer. Giorgia's father, on the other hand… He wants her out of the house."

"Isabella is an adult. She doesn't need his permission."

"We can't fuck with the alliance. We're getting close

to Volkov, especially now with the help of Ivanov's man. Once we get Volkov, we'll be a step closer to Herrera."

"There have been two marriages since yours. They've strengthened the alliance, not fucked with it."

He lifted his hand again. "I'll speak to the capo. For now, this is tabled."

"She asked to see San Diego. She's been on lockdown since she arrived. I'd like to take her for a tour."

"A date? In the middle of a fucking war?"

"I was on the streets today. Tension is high, but the threat level is down. Volkov is evaluating his strategies with the uniforms patrolling around since the car bomb. The bomb was ingenious. It's his calling card, and the uniforms fell for it."

"You're a lieutenant. You don't need my permission to give a tour. Don't you fucking get her killed or injured."

"*Gracias*. I'll return her safe and sound."

"By ten o'clock. No fucking tour goes on that long."

A smile came to my lips. "*Sí, jefe.*"

He ran his hand through his ruffled hair. "Fuck, it's like I'm her *padre*."

"She's under the protection of the Roríguez cartel. That means you."

He shook his head. "If I ever have a daughter, she's on lockdown until she's twenty-five."

A look at my watch told me I had enough time to hurry home, shower, and get to the apartments. Once I was back in my Mercedes-Benz, I sent a text message to Horace.

. . .

"I'M TAKING Isabella on a tour of San Diego after work. Stay with her until I arrive. I'll return her to el Patrón's house before ten."

HE TEXTED BACK.

"HAS this been cleared with el Patrón?"

MY RESPONSE.

"YES."

MY NEXT TEXT message was to Isabella.

"I'LL BE THERE AS SOON as I can. Your tour awaits."

SHE REPLIED.

"IT'S okay if we have to postpone it. I know you're working hard."

. . .

Oʜ, fuck no. We weren't postponing this.

"Dᴏɴ'ᴛ ʟᴇᴀᴠᴇ *the apartments without me.*"

Hᴇʀ ʀᴇᴘʟʏ ᴄᴀᴜsᴇᴅ my dick to move.

"Yᴇs, ᴊᴇꜰᴇ."

CHAPTER

NINETEEN

Isabella

It was around four thirty when Horace knocked on the doorframe to my office. "Miss Izzy."

I smiled at his use of my first name. "Yes, come on in."

He stepped inside. "I received word from Emiliano Ruiz that he is taking you home tonight."

Warmth filled my cheeks. "I told him I wanted to see more of San Diego, and with the lockdown" —I shrugged — "he was nice and offered me a tour."

"You're my responsibility."

"Should I not trust Em?"

He took a step closer to my desk. "That's not what I'm saying."

"Em said he'd get *el Patrón's* approval. He must have."

"*Sí*, I asked Lieutenant Ruiz that same question."

"Then it's settled."

"Miss, I'm asking you if you'd like me to accompany you and him on this *tour*?"

The way he emphasized the last word made me think he thought tonight was about more than a tour. "Horace, take the night off or do whatever it is you're supposed to do when you don't have to babysit me. I mean, you leave every night after you take me to Mia's. You must have someplace to go."

"You have my number. Your phone has a GPS tracker. If you need me at any time, call. I can find you."

A GPS tracker. When did that happen?

Instead of asking, I simply replied, "Thank you. I will."

I'd been staring at a grant application for most of the afternoon. The process was more complicated and exhausting than I'd anticipated. I made a mental note to talk to Mia about it tonight or in the morning. I couldn't stop my smile from growing as I thought about spending time with Em away from here or even Mia's.

As if tipped off about my plans by an angel or the devil himself, my mother's name appeared on my phone. We'd only spoken twice since my arrival. With my newfound knowledge about Papà and well, everyone, I wasn't certain what to say. I answered on the second ring. "Mom."

"I miss you, Izzy."

"I miss you too, Mom. How are Noemi and Tony?"

"We're all well, but the house seems empty without you. I'm so worried about you out there all alone."

"I'm not alone."

"Are you safe? Are you well? Is Mia helping you? What are the whores like?"

"I'm safe and Mia has been great. As for the residents, they're women, Mom. Just like you and me. They simply chose another profession."

"They use their bodies to please men and make money."

A thought occurred to me. "How do you make money?"

"What?" she asked, aghast.

"You, Aunt Giulia, Mia, and Aunt Arianna. Your work is to please your husbands and that includes sex."

"Isabella Louisa. What has happened to you? How dare you speak that way to me."

"It was a question." I stood and walked to the window. Traffic was almost nonexistent on the street beyond. "You and Papà sent me out here to learn about life and about helping people. That's what's happened to me. I'm not perfect by any means, but I'm expanding my world and learning the truth about people who before, I never would've even questioned."

When I turned, Isla was standing at my door.

"Mom, I need to go. I'm still at work."

"I'm going to speak to your father. I think you need to come home immediately."

"Goodbye." I disconnected the call. "Isla, please come in."

"I'm sorry to bother you, *Señorita* Izzy."

"You can just call me Izzy." I gestured toward the

table. "Would you like to sit with me? I have water bottles if you'd like one."

"Sit, *sí*." She walked slowly to the table. "No water. I'm fine."

"Would you like me to close the door or leave it open?"

"Close," she said at a barely audible level.

I closed the door and walked toward her. "Are you fine?"

Isla held her hands in her lap, staring at them. "I was looking for Liliana, but Celeste said she was somewhere else in the building."

"Is there something I can help you with?"

She peered upward with a hooded stare. "Can you talk to Mia for us please?"

"I can. I live with her."

She sat taller. "I didn't know that."

"I guess it's not common knowledge. I see her every day. What is it that you'd like me to talk to her about?"

"It's about something at Wanderland—someone. He just started. He's a new guard."

"Who?" I asked.

"*Su nombre es* Efrain."

"Has Efrain done something?"

"He comes into our dressing rooms and our showers. He just stands and watches. We've told him to leave, but he just laughs."

I questioned, "You said he's new. Who's his boss?"

"Lieutenant Ruiz, Nicolas."

That was the name Celeste and Reina mentioned on my first day. "Have you told Nicolas?"

Her eyes opened wide. "No, Izzy. Nicolas doesn't like us to complain. If we do, he would punish us not Efrain."

"Physically?" I asked, shuddering inside, afraid of her response.

She was back to looking at her hands. "Sometimes but in other ways. Nicolas determines our customers and if we're in VIP or not." She looked up. "VIP is where we want to work, but Nicolas only assigns girls there who he likes. No one wants on his bad side."

"I'll talk to Mia about Efrain. Maybe he just needs to be reminded of the club rules."

"Before Mia, the rules were different. I was thinking that if she knew…"

I sat taller and leaned forward. "Isla, thank you for trusting me. I promise I'll speak to Mia."

"Please tell her not to use my name."

"I'm sure she knows."

We both turned to a knock on the door. Isla stepped quickly down from the chair. "I should go. If … please don't tell anyone but Mia about what I said."

"We were just chatting. I have a lot to learn."

"*Gracias*, Izzy."

Walking toward the door, I gave Isla one last reassuring smile and opened the door.

Emiliano was standing there. Gone was the spicy tobacco aroma and back was the clean, fresh scent. It was as if he'd recently stepped from the shower. His dark hair was damp and combed back. The usual beard growth running over his chiseled jaw was gone, leaving what I could only imagine would be smooth cheeks. I wanted to reach up and feel them for myself. In place of his blue jeans and black t-shirt, he was wearing a white button-down with the sleeves rolled to his elbows. Only the tip of the snake's tail was visible. His black denim jeans fit his ass and long legs to perfection. When he flashed his panty-melting smile, I had to remind myself that this was a tour.

Nothing else.

I tried to temper the excitement about our tour in my voice. "Hi, Em."

"*Adios*, Izzy," Isla said as she hurried away.

"Thank you for your help," I called after her.

My heart fluttered as Em lifted his arm to the door-frame and stared down at me.

"You showered."

"I do that on a regular basis."

"I should have changed clothes."

He scoffed. "Your job is a lot cleaner than mine."

I led him inside, leaving the door open. "How many people did you have to kill today?"

"It was a slow day." He touched his thumb against his fingers as if he were counting.

"You're teasing me."

His grin grew. "I am. Zero kills. Wait, does maiming count?"

Shaking my head, I leaned my behind against the edge of the white lacquer desk and crossed my arms over my breasts. "I think I should have accepted Horace's invitation to have him join us. You sound dangerous."

Em took a step or two, his long legs bringing him right in front of me. So close, I needed to look up to see his eyes.

"I am dangerous."

The deep tenor of his voice sent a chill over my flesh, leaving goose bumps in its wake. While my increased pulse and twisting stomach could be physical reactions to fear, by the twisting between my legs, I knew it was something else. "You spoke to *el Patrón*. He knows I'll be on a tour with you tonight?"

"I did."

Something from my earlier conversation with Horace came to mind. "Why did Horace call you Lieutenant Ruiz? Isn't that your father?"

"I've recently been promoted."

My eyes opened wide. "That's good. Or...is it? Is it more dangerous?"

His lips quirked. "It's good. The danger level varies by the day, not by the title."

He was so close. I cleared my throat, mentally reminding myself that this wasn't a date. "Let me freshen up and then we can go." I was halfway to the bathroom when I stopped and spun toward him. "Where are we going to go?"

"It's a surprise."

TWENTY

Isabella

I'd never been on a date.

Never.

Not even a school dance.

Attending an all-girls Catholic school didn't give me much exposure to men in general. If this was a date, I wouldn't know how to act. Maybe it was better for it to simply be a tour.

Em and I walked together through the security doors and said goodbye to Horace and the guard on duty. I reassured Horace that I was good.

High in the sky, the sun shone brightly, warming my cheeks. A gentle breeze blew strands of my hair as we exited the building and entered the parking lot. Once outside, Em placed his hand in the small of my back. I unintentionally stiffened.

He leaned down, his deep voice echoing in my ear. "Protecting you. Without Horace, that's my job."

I turned. The sight of his handsome face allowed me to relax. "My personal protection from a lieutenant. I should be honored."

"No, I'm honored." He led us to a sleek two-door black Mercedes. Compared to the SUV's and sedans I'd been driven in, this car looked like it belonged on a race-track. Em opened the passenger's door. A luxurious ivory leather interior glistened in the sunlight, the new-car smell filling my senses.

"When José or Horace drives, I sit in the back seat."

"Not today." He motioned toward the front seat.

While the softness of the leather and the contour of the seat supported me as I sat down, I already missed the presence of Em's touch on my lower back. I was trying to recall the last time I'd sat in a front seat. It was such a simplistic act and yet, as I stared at the elaborate dash-board, large screen, and windshield, I couldn't come up with a time.

Em's long legs bent as he sat in the driver's seat. The fresh scent of his cologne mixed with the leather aroma as he started the car. The soft rumble of the engine told me that while this vehicle may look like a race car, it was all luxury.

My heart beat faster as the gate to the parking lot moved, we turned the opposite direction from Mia's house, and we entered the city of San Diego. Being here with Em was nothing like riding with bodyguards. Even the view from the front seat was exciting and new.

I turned to my tour guide. "Thank you. I've been

excited about this since you asked." I leaned back as he guided us through traffic. "But being here now..." I hummed. "This is exhilarating."

"If fighting five o'clock traffic is your idea of fun, I can't wait to see what you think of where we're headed."

"Where are we headed?"

He reached over, laying his hand on my thigh. "If I told you, it wouldn't be a surprise."

My breath caught. Swallowing, I stared at his hand. When it didn't move, I shifted my gaze to his profile. "This isn't a date, right?" My voice came out less confident than I would have liked.

Instead of moving his hand, he gently squeezed my thigh. For a brief moment, he turned toward me, his dark gaze drinking me in. "If it's all right with you, I'd rather not define whatever this is until the evening is over."

This wasn't real.

"Okay." I let out a breath and leaned back, taking in the surroundings.

"Are you hungry?" he asked.

"If the tour includes food, I wouldn't complain."

His lips curled. "Good, because we have reservations at one of my favorite restaurants. I hope you like Italian."

I pushed against his muscular arm. "You don't ask an Italian if they like Italian. It's like me asking if you like Mexican food."

"I do." He peered my way. "The spicier, the better. I also like Italian."

He peered over, looking at my feet.

"What?" I asked.

"The restaurant has valet parking. I was checking to

see if you had walking shoes or non-walking shoes. The self-parking is about a seven-minute walk."

"I don't mind walking." I looked down at the ballet flats I'd put on this morning. I wasn't much for high heels. "My shoes are comfortable."

"Good," he said. "I don't like strangers having access to my car, and walking will give me a chance to show you around."

After parking in a garage, Em opened my door and offered me his hand. I stared at his large palm and long fingers before placing my hand in his. His fingers encased mine as I stood. When we made it back to street level, my first clue to where we were was the numerous Italian flags flying from the buildings.

I turned to him. "Is this Little Italy?"

"It is."

My body vibrated with excitement at seeing all the people on the sidewalks and seated in outdoor dining areas. The crowd was eclectic. "Thank you. This was a great choice." I spun around, letting my hair flow in the breeze as I looked down the street. When I stilled, Em reached for my shoulders.

"You are so fucking full of life."

I smiled. "This feels like I've been let out of prison."

"You're free, Isabella. This is only the beginning." He reached for my hand.

I didn't protest or stiffen as our fingers intertwined.

We headed north. With sunshine and fresh air on our faces and my hand in his, I marveled at the people, casually sitting, drinking cocktails, and eating delicacies. Out of the corner of my eye, I caught our reflection in large plate glass windows.

Do we look like a couple?

I pushed that thought away and took in the surroundings. Barricades separated the street from the numerous restaurants. Strings of lights and pots overflowing with flowers added to the unique beauty. I leaned against his arm and whispered. "After the last couple of weeks, I expected gun battles in the streets and boarded-up windows."

"Wars aren't new. Most people don't realize what's happening right under their noses. They're like you. They want to see the best of people. That pureness of heart isn't shared by everyone."

I gripped his hand tighter. "Are there bad things here that I don't see?"

He looked down at me. "Yes, but I see them. I won't allow it to darken your view."

Sighing, I leaned my head against his arm. "I feel safe with you."

"I'd fucking kill for you without hesitation."

A grin curled my lips. "Trying to up that kill count for the day."

To my shock, Em leaned down and kissed the top of my head.

In the middle of the sidewalk, I stopped walking and let go of his hand. Nibbling on my lip, I looked up and asked, "What's happening?"

Em inhaled and moved us closer to a building and out of foot traffic. "I want you, Isabella. I thought I did at Ariadna

Gia's birthday." He shook his head. "That day, it was your exquisite beauty that drew me to you. Now, it's more. It's your fucking perseverance. It's watching you come alive at the apartments and with the tenants." His lips quirked. "In a car in fucking horrible traffic and now here on the street in Little Italy. Over the past two weeks, I came up with any excuse to go to the apartments even when my schedule said I shouldn't. I can't get enough of you. I'm mesmerized. I know —or I can imagine—what you've been told from your family about us, the cartel. I've been trying to show you that while we aren't the good guys, we aren't the bad ones either."

With each word, I watched the way his lips moved, feeling warmth brought on by the closeness of our bodies. Without thinking, I pushed up on my tiptoes and brought my lips to his.

My first kiss.

His large palms framed my cheeks as he held me close to him. His lips pushed back. Fireworks exploded behind my closed eyes, as shock waves reverberated through my nervous system. My hands landed on top of his as I stepped back, gasping for breath.

Slowly, the world around us reappeared. The people passing by. Sounds of talking and traffic. The scents from the various restaurants. The warmth of the sunshine.

I pressed my tingling lips together and lowered my forehead to his chest. "I don't know why I did that," I mumbled, looking down and listening to the rapid drumming of Em's heart.

With a finger and thumb, he lifted my chin. "You can do that" —his words rumbled in his chest— "whenever the urge hits. You're going to be mine. Fuck that. You are mine, Isabella."

I shook my head. "My father will never…"

Steadying my chin, he lowered his firm lips to mine. I pushed back, wanting the amazing sensation one more time. When our lips separated, his deep timbre filled my ears. "I'm not fucking letting you go, not back to Kansas City, not anywhere without my ring on your finger and me at your side."

Tears prickled the back of my eyes. "That was my first kiss and my second. I was so wrong about you. My parents were wrong—about so much. But if I get my hopes up, I'm afraid you won't only be my first kiss. You'll be my first heartbreak."

"That's not going to happen. But there will be many more firsts." His intense stare gleamed as his devilish smile made my core twist. "How many dates have you been on?"

It was my turn to smile. "This is my first one."

He reached for my hand and tugged. "Come on, we have reservations. I want to make this first date something you'll never forget."

It already was.

TWENTY-ONE

Emiliano

I liked the feeling of the way Isabella's hand fit perfectly in mine. Spending these few weeks with her has opened a floodgate of feelings I'd never before considered. While my mind was constantly on the war we fought and the business we ran, at unexpected times, Isabella would come to mind. I wondered if she would like this or if she'd prefer that. I worried about her safety at the apartments and even at *el Patrón's* home. Since the afternoon when she melted down and came back to life—a stunning phoenix—I had the overwhelming desire to protect her while at the same time, to make her happy.

Those instincts roared to life in me like they never had before. I'd been attracted to women in the past. Dated here and there. But the life I led in the cartel wasn't conducive to organic relationships. The women I saw the most were the whores from Wanderland. Since Mia's apartments opened, I'd stopped using their services. If I examined the reason, it would probably be that knowing them at the apartments transformed them in my mind, taking away the anonymity from before.

Isabella's soft brown eyes peered about as if she was seeing life for the first time. Perhaps there was such a thing as fated loves. I wasn't ready to care for someone else until now. And now, that someone was here, holding my hand and leaning against my arm.

Isabella chatted with excitement as we passed different businesses on our way north toward the restaurant. With the life I led, it was too easy to see the dark side of every situation. That was a survival technique that Isabella didn't possess. She saw the world as a shining star filled with happiness and possibilities. Being in her presence reminded me that the other side existed. It had to, because the qualities radiated from her being.

The bad was here too.

Not shootings on the street. Although that was possible. I personally had two guns, and two knives concealed beneath my clothing. I wasn't the only one. The holsters and bulges were easy to spot when you knew what to look for.

Some of the bad was benign, such as the kid who pickpocketed an elderly man walking the opposite direction. The street venders who doubled their prices for tourists. The levels increased, such as the woman we just passed. The misery in her expression as the man at her side grasped her arm and hurried her along was a warning of worse to come. If not for Isabella, I would have intervened.

Scanning my surroundings was something I constantly did. It wasn't a conscious effort but the way I'd been taught to survive. Isabella, on the other hand, lived a life of protection, bodyguards, Mafia soldiers, and her family. They watched for the darkness, allowing her to bask in the light.

"Oh," she exclaimed. "There's the Little Italy sign."

I squeezed her hand. "Our restaurant is just up ahead."

She peered upward. "It's such a beautiful evening; are we going to sit outside?" Almost every restaurant along India Street had outdoor dining.

I wouldn't scare her by telling her that we wouldn't because of the dangers lurking about. Instead, I smiled and said, "This is one of my favorite restaurants, and they have my favorite table waiting."

"You have a favorite table?"

"I do."

"How many women have you brought here?"

My lips landed on the top of her head, kissing her hair. "The only woman who matters is the one with me right now. The last time I was here, I was with Nick and two cartel chiefs."

"Sounds romantic," she quipped.

"It can be."

Stepping through the glass doors, I let go of Isabella's hand and placed my hand in the small of her back. Once inside, the delicious aroma of garlic awakened my hunger. We came to a stop in front of the hostess stand.

Evelyn, the hostess, opened her eyes wide with recognition. "Mr. Ruiz. Welcome back." She smiled at Isabella. "Is this your first visit with us?"

"It is. Yes."

Evelyn's gaze was back to me. "We have your table waiting." She picked up three leather-bound folders and said, "Follow me please."

We passed by tables filled with customers on our way to the back of the large room. My table was a semi-circular booth on the back wall. From my seat, I could see the front door and the door to the kitchen. No one would have the opportunity to sneak up on me.

Evelyn laid the menus on the table.

Isabella scooted in and I followed.

Evelyn picked up the top leather-bound folder. "Here is our drink menu. We've added a few cocktails since your last visit."

I took the menu. "Thank you."

"Antonio will be your waiter. He'll be over shortly."

"Thank you," Isabella said.

When Evelyn walked away, Isabella leaned closer. "She was flirting with you."

Her observation caught me off guard. "She wasn't. That's how she acts around all the customers."

She laughed. "For an observant man, you can be unaware."

Under the table, I laid my hand on Isabella's thigh. "I'm not unaware. I just have eyes for one woman."

A beautiful rosy hue filled her cheeks. "Is this real, Em?"

"Fucking feels real to me."

Antonio appeared in front of us. "Good evening. May I get the two of you something from the bar. A bottle of wine perhaps?"

Isabella stiffened at my side.

"I believe we will begin with water."

"Very well. I'll be back with your water."

Once he was gone, Isabella leaned closer. "You don't have to not drink alcohol just because I can't."

I lifted my brow. "You can't? Do you have a physical reaction to alcohol, an allergy?"

She grinned. "I'm not old enough."

My smile grew. "But say in the privacy of your home…"

"My family serves wine with dinner." She scrunched her nose. "I'm not a big fan."

"Then you've had the wrong wine. My father owns a winery here in Southern California. If you're interested, we can find you the right wine. I'm not much of a drinker, but I know my mother and sisters have their favorites. When you could be called on at any hour of the day or night, alcohol consumption is at a minimum."

Isabella's pink lips curled. "Good. I'm glad you're not abstaining because of me."

"Oh, it is because of you. If anyone thought they could steal my girl, I plan to be sober so as to not miss my mark."

She laughed as if it were a joke.

It wasn't.

Antonio arrived with our water in a tall glass bottle. He proceeded to pour it into our goblets as he explained the specials of the day. We ordered our meals. After the waiter walked away, I said, "Some say it's bad luck to toast to water." I winked. "I can't associate you with bad. So here goes." I lifted my glass of water and Isabella did the same. "To us."

Our glasses clinked and we both took a sip.

"I mean it, Isabella. It might seem fast, but I want to marry you. I've asked Jano to talk to Dario."

She pressed her lips together and blinked her eyes. "You asked?"

"I did."

"My father will never approve."

"I won't give up."

From soup to salads to entrees, the food kept coming. When Antonio questioned us about dessert, Isabella placed a hand over her stomach. "I couldn't eat another bite."

Nodding to Antonio, I said, "Our check please."

I sent a text message.

With my hand in the small of Isabella's back, we walked back out onto the sidewalk. The number of people had doubled as the dinner hour attracted more customers. I led us south, the way that we'd come. "We can continue to walk around this neighborhood, or we have enough time to make it to Imperial Beach for the sunset."

"Oh, I've heard of that place. Isn't there a long pier?"

"Almost 1500 feet."

She reached for my arm. "My tour continues." Lifting her face to the sky, she closed her eyes and hummed. "I love being outside."

She was so fucking vibrant and beautiful. I wanted to

wrap her in my arms and repeat our kiss from earlier. No, I wanted more than a kiss. The thought of holding her soft curves against my hard body had my circulation rerouting as we walked.

"This way." I tugged her to turn left on Cedar Street."

"Isn't the parking garage that way?"

"It is. One more surprise."

When we came to a stop in front of a bakery with a line out the door, Isabella groaned. "I can't eat more food. Besides, if we stand in this line, we'll miss sunset."

"It would be criminal to bring you to Little Italy without getting the best cannoli you've ever tasted."

I tugged her past the line.

"What are you doing? Em, we can't cut."

We came to a stop at the counter. As soon as Beatrice, one of the owners, saw us, her smile widened. "Emiliano." She reached for a small white paper bag. "For you."

She'd obviously gotten my text message.

"Beatrice, you're the best." I reached for the bag and handed it to Isabella before reaching for my wallet.

"No. Go." She shooed us with a brush of her hand. "Can't you see I'm busy."

"I can't—"

She smiled. "Next time you can pay." Her gaze went to Isabella at my side. "I'm sure you two have plans. Go."

"*Gracias.*"

"*Prego.* Go."

"Does everyone flirt with you?" Isabella asked as we stepped outside.

"Beatrice is sixty years old if she's a day."

"That doesn't mean she can't flirt." She opened the white bag. "Oh, those smell delicious."

By the time we reached the parking garage, my willpower was failing. I opened Isabella's car door but before she could sit, I pinned her against the car, my left arm caging her. She tipped her face upward, soft suede irises meeting mine as she nibbled on her lower lip.

With my other hand, I reached for her chin, freeing her lip. "Whenever I see you do that, it makes me want to bite your luscious lip to see how good it tastes."

Her smile returned. "No biting."

My grin quirked. "You don't know. You might like it."

She dropped the cannoli to the seat and lifted her arms around my neck. "I know I like your kisses."

Fuck yeah.

Cupping her neck, I pulled her toward me until our lips met. She tasted of sunshine and garlic. When a soft moan came from her throat, I was ready to blow a wad.

Beyond our bubble, I heard the distinctive click of a cocking gun.

"In the car now." My timbre changed. "Lock the doors." Isabella looked confused. I shoved her into the car. In less than a second I shut the car door, hit the thumb safety on my Beretta, and then pointed my loaded gun toward the shadows. Twenty feet away, standing near a large concrete pylon, I saw the culprit. "Drop your gun, motherfucker." With my arms straight, I walked toward him. Step by step, my boots echoed on the concrete as he remained in my sights.

The asshole couldn't be over fifteen years old. He was shaking like a leaf. If he wasn't careful, he'd shoot himself or possibly me. Even though I was his target, I had better things to do than take a bullet.

"Drop the gun now." I was less than ten feet away.

Fuck. The darkening of his sweatpants let me know he pissed himself.

"Put the gun on the ground, fucker. I'm not going to say it again."

He did as I said and stood straight, looking as if he might get sick.

"Now kick it toward me."

"*No hablo ingles,*" he said with his hands in the air.

"Te v*oy a matarte.*"

He kicked the gun and fell to his knees. "I was supposed to rob you." Praise God. He miraculously learned the English language.

I walked closer, my barrel pointed at his head. "What's your name?"

"Daniel. Don't kill me."

Fucker wasn't in the position to make demands.

"Who told you to rob me?"

"The man on the street. He offered me a hundred dollars. I was supposed to bring your wallet and the girl's purse back to him."

"More specific, asshole. What's the man's name?"

"I don't know."

I took another step.

"I can't say."

"This Beretta is already cocked. All I need to do is pull the trigger and your brain will be splattered all over this garage."

He closed his eyes as a tear ran down his cheek. "He goes by Manuel. Manual Lopez."

Fucking common name.

"Where was he on the street?"

"We watched you walk out of the bakery on Cedar."

The barrel of my gun made contact with his temple. "Daniel, tell Manuel Lopez that if I find him, he's a dead man. If he tries to fuck with me again, he's a dead man. Can you do that?"

"*Sí*. I'll tell him."

"If I see you again, you're dead. Now get up and get the fuck out of here."

I carefully picked up the Glock he'd kicked by pinching the barrel. Turning around, I saw my car and like a punch to the gut, remembered that Isabella was inside. Hurrying back, I popped the trunk and threw the Glock inside.

When I came around to the driver's side door and peered in, Isabella was staring my direction, wide-eyed. I opened the door. "Are you all right?"

"Are you?"

I got in, closed the door, and reached for her hands. "I'm sorry if that scared you."

"You went toward him."

"That's what I do."

A smile slowly curled her lips as she reached down to the floor and lifted the paper bag. "I smashed the cannoli when I accidentally sat on them."

Relief flooded my nervous system as I grinned. "You're amazing. And the idea of eating them after your ass smashed them..." I wiggled my eyebrows.

A faint pink hue filled her cheeks. "I'm not the one who went after a shooter. Did you...? I didn't hear a gunshot."

I shook my head. "He's alive. He was a kid, probably not even fifteen. Someone paid him to rob us. I sent a strong message back with him to his boss."

She leaned her head back against the seat. "Maybe I should leave this part out of the tour when I talk to Mia."

"Do you want to go back to her house or to Imperial Beach?"

"My tour isn't over yet." Her smile grew and glistened in her eyes.

"Then onto the sunset."

TWENTY-TWO

Isabella

Despite what had just happened, Em seemed calm as we headed south from Little Italy. He reached over and splayed his long fingers over my thigh. "I'm sorry if that scared you."

"I think I was too unsure of what was happening to be scared." I looked down at the white bag from the bakery. "The cannoli though...they're smashed."

Em smiled. "They'll still taste great."

"Why would some young kid try to rob you?"

"According to him, it wasn't his idea. Someone offered him a hundred dollars."

"It seems like the price should have been higher."

He scoffed. "Much higher. That means one of two things. One, it was some kind of initiation, and they had no idea who I am, or two, if they offered more, the kid would figure I was someone important and push for even more."

I shook my head and stared out the wide windshield. The sky had already begun its transformation. Colors changed. Blues faded into red and orange. The vibrant hues radiated under the few clouds such as flames searing their underside.

My thoughts went back to earlier. Em said he'd asked *el Patrón* for my hand. Does that mean we're engaged, or do we have to wait for Dario's approval?

Em found a parking space not far from the large sign reading Imperial Beach. Hand in hand, we hurried toward the pier. I stopped near the sandy beach as waves crashed against the tall pilings holding the wooden pier. "Is that safe?"

He squeezed my hand. "I'm not sure how long it's been here. But I know it's popular for walking, fishing, and sunsets." His lips curled in a smile. "Come on. The view is stunning."

Our shoes clipped over the wood planks. Even though he'd told me the length, the pier was much longer than I imagined. As the sun continued to lower, the water began to glow. Tall lampposts on the right of the pier were illuminated, creating small circles of light. Up ahead I saw the silhouette of a building. "What's up there?"

"That's the Tin Fish. It's a little restaurant. They have picnic tables and live music. During the day, this place is filled with fishermen."

The walkway swayed with the incoming waves. And the evening air felt suddenly chillier.

Em let go of my hand to wrap his arm behind my back and around my waist.

I nestled against his side. His warmth shielded me from the cool breeze.

We reached the end of the pier as the sun kissed the horizon. The people present watched in awe at Mother Nature's beautiful exhibition. Even the music we'd heard as we approached stopped, everyone paying reverence to the spectacular display. As the orange ball disappeared, the horizon glowed with crimson hues.

Em leaned down. As I turned to him, his lips met mine.

I wrapped my arms around his torso as his arms encircled me.

This was more than I dared to hope for—ever.

Around us, the music resumed, and the people began to talk amongst themselves.

"That was spectacular," I said.

"It was nice," he replied, staring down at me. "I prefer this view."

I sucked in a breath. "I'm afraid I'll wake up tomorrow and this will all have been a dream."

He shook his head.

"What time is it?"

Em looked at his watch. "We still have over an hour to safely get you back to *el Patrón*." He pointed to the north. "From here you can see San Diego."

"It looks so pretty from here."

"I always want you to see it that way. Don't let the

darkness I see overshadow the light you see." He turned us to the left. "See those lights down there?"

I nodded.

"Plaza Monumental de Tijuana. Or some people call it the Bullring by the Sea."

"What is that?"

"It's a stadium in Tijuana."

"In Mexico?" My neck stiffened. "How far are we from the border?"

"Five miles."

Suddenly, the air felt cooler as I looked around at the crowd. "How can we be that close and it be calm?"

"It just is. Most realities are different than the way we're told to believe."

That was the truth. I was still reeling from the difference in what I thought it would be like with the cartel to the way it actually was.

Em tilted his chin toward the Tin Fish. "Ice cream?"

"No." I shook my head. "I may never eat again."

"Then how about a walk on the beach?"

"I'd like that."

I took off my shoes and wiggled my toes in the soft white sand. Carrying my shoes in one hand, my other hand was securely in Em's grasp. The sound of the surf and the salt-filled air created a peaceful setting. We were a few minutes into our stroll when I asked, "What does this mean for tonight or tomorrow?"

"This?"

"You and I. Honestly, I'm afraid if we tell others that my mother or father will find out and send one of their guards to take me home."

Em stopped walking and turned to me. "That won't happen."

"You don't know them. I was talking to my mother earlier today, and she said that I've changed. She said she was going to talk to Papà and wanted me to go back to Kansas City right away."

By the light of the moon, I saw Em's jaw clench. He brought his thumb to my cheek, stroking my face. "I'd marry you tonight. That wouldn't be good for you, me, or the alliance. We need to give Jano and Dario a chance to make this work."

"What if they don't?"

"Do you want to marry me?"

I sighed with a grin. "It scares me. I mean, I woke up this morning not in a relationship and this evening I might be engaged."

He lifted my hand. "There's no ring. And I'm not certain you said yes."

"It's so fast."

To my shock, Em dropped to one knee on the sandy beach. Holding my hand, he looked up at me, the moonlight shining in his dark brown orbs. "Isabella Luciano, this is an official proposal. You know how I feel about you. If marrying me is something you want, I'll fight for it to happen. If it's not, please tell me now because I'm damn sure I've fallen in love with you."

"In love?"

He nodded. "That day in your office when I first touched you, your arms, and held your freezing cold hands? I knew I wanted to spend the rest of my life taking care of you, watching you blossom, touching you, and encouraging you to push your own boundaries. Dario may have sent you out here to fail. If that's the case, he underestimated you. I think nothing is beyond your ability."

Tears filled my eyes as I fell to my knees. "You love me?"

"I do."

As I palmed his cheeks, I dove deep within myself.

Do I love Emiliano?

I loved the way he made me feel. I loved his encouragement and belief in me. I loved the way he kissed and touched me. I wasn't sure if I loved him, but I believed I could. Every moment with him took me closer to that conclusion. I nodded. "I want to marry you."

His lips crashed with mine. Forceful and tender. Possessive and giving. My lips parted as his tongue sought entrance. Moans and whimpers escaped my throat as his tongue slid over mine, dancing to a melody that was only ours. He wove his fingers into my long hair, tugging my head backward and sending shock waves to my core.

When we finally pulled apart, my nipples were hard and for the first time, I understood what was meant in books. Because I was certain my panties were damp.

"I think you're right," he said as I still panted for air.

"About?"

"I'm going to fucking hate not touching you and kissing you, but we should keep this between us right now. Have faith in Jano and Dario." He grinned. "That doesn't mean we can't steal a kiss here and there."

I nodded. "Okay. I'll try to have faith."

Em stood and taking my hand, helped me stand.

My slacks were covered with sand. As I tried to brush it away, I said, "How will I explain this to Mia?"

"You were on a tour, remember. I took you to Imperial Beach."

"Yeah, a tour. I remember now." I looked up at him. "For the record, it's been the best tour of my life."

He wrapped his arm around my waist. "I don't want to do it, but it's time to get you back before we break your curfew."

"Back to prison."

"No, back to being protected."

"I'm free for another tour sometime."

We chatted about places to go. When Em mentioned the zoo, I remembered that I'd heard good things about the San Diego Zoo. I'd forgotten about the incident in the parking garage until we were back in the car.

"Are you going to tell *el Patrón* about what happened earlier with that kid?"

"I will. I have the kid's gun and the name of the man who hired him. More than likely the gun is stolen, but we can run the serial number. It might tell us something."

"I thought only the police could do that."

Em scoffed. "I could do it by the time I was your brother's age. Wouldn't be surprised if he can do it too."

"Tony and Noemi," I said with a tug in my chest. "I don't want to leave them."

His fingers splayed on my thigh. "When we marry, you can always go visit or they can visit us. We need to do our part, the cartel and famiglia, to eradicate our greatest threats, and then you'll be safe to travel."

"You wouldn't mind if they came out here?" I thought about our walk. "They'd love to see the ocean."

"Isabella, I'd never try to separate you from your family."

I laid my hand over his and stared at the highway as we headed north back to Mia's home.

TWENTY-THREE

Emiliano

We didn't kiss again after we passed the first gate to *el Patrón's* home. With Silas's security and surveillance as well as the guards standing by, it couldn't have happened without some detection. Instead, before getting out of the car, I squeezed her hand. "I love you, Isabella. We're going to make this work."

"I'm so scared that this will all fall apart."

"You're mine to have and to hold. I can honestly say I've never felt something this strong. It seems I've been waiting for you to come into my life. They can't stop what's meant to be."

Before we could say any more, the door next to Isabella opened.

"Welcome back, Miss Luciano," Silas said with a bow before offering his hand.

"Thank you, Silas."

I watched as she stepped from the car. The white bakery bag remained on the seat.

Silas leaned down, making eye contact. "Lieutenant Ruiz, *el Patrón* would like to see you."

I shut off the car and grabbed the bag. "I'll be right in." Looking inside, I saw the flattened cannoli, and the scent of sugary goodness filled my senses. As I walked behind my vehicle, I remembered the kid's gun.

Inside the trunk, I pulled two rubber gloves from the box in my supplies and picked up the Glock 45. With the popularity of this model, I doubted we'd learn anything, but we should try. Silas waited for me by the door. When I nodded, he opened the front door. While I could hear Isabella's and Mia's voices from the living room, I went directly to Jano's office.

He looked up from the monitors in front of him. "How was the tour?"

"Good," I replied, keeping my voice even.

His dark gaze went to the gun in my hand. "Tell me about that. Since you're wearing gloves, I assume it isn't yours."

"It's not mine. Although I did touch it. So, my prints will be on it."

"The trigger?"

I shook my head as I laid the Glock on Jano's desk. "The tour started in Little Italy." That put a smile on Jano's face if only for a moment. "Yeah, that seemed like a good idea to me too. Anyway, we had dinner. On the way back we stopped at a bakery." I put the white bag by the gun. "I parked in the parking garage on Ash."

Jano nodded.

"As we got to my car, I heard the distinctive click of a weapon cocking."

"Fuck, Em. I told you not to get her killed or injured."

"I didn't. I secured her in the car and took off after the asshole." I shook my head. "He was a kid. Latino. Scared shitless. He said he and his boss saw us coming out of the bakery. His boss, someone named Manuel Lopez, offered him a C-note to rob us."

Jano leaned back against his chair and templed his fingers. "Did you believe him?"

"If I'd been alone, I would have taken him to Wanderland or the warehouse for more questioning." I shook my head. "I wasn't doing that with Isabella. I took his gun and told him to give Lopez a message. If I find him, he's dead."

"Kid?" Jano asked. "How old do you guess?"

"No more than fifteen. He pissed himself. My guess is that it was an initiation. Question is, one of our crews or one of Herrera's? If it's one of ours, someone was fucking with him to send him after me. If it is Herrera's, they were hoping to get lucky."

He shook his head. "If it was Herrera's, why wouldn't the chief do the job himself and kill you? You'd be a fucking big prize." He scanned me from my head to my boots. "Unless they didn't recognize you clean-shaven. The fuck? For a *tour*."

If Jano wasn't *el Patrón*, I'd tell him to shut the fuck

up. However, it was in my best interest to keep that thought to myself.

Jano stood and stretched, reminding me of a cat. If he was a cat, he would be a black-footed cat. Based on kill counts, the deadliest cat in the world. After retrieving a plastic bag from his desk, Jano walked around and looked at the weapon. Using a pen in the trigger guard, he picked it up. "Your prints are on this weapon."

"*Sí*. On the barrel. I carried it to my car and threw it in the trunk."

He dropped the Glock in the bag. "Take it to Nick. Tell him to run prints and the serial number. We'll see if anything comes up." His gaze met mine. "What about this Lopez? Couldn't have come up with a more generic name."

I nodded as I removed the rubber gloves and threw them in a trash can near Jano's desk. "When I get home, I plan to run his name through the known databases. The kid said they spotted us coming out of Pappalecco. I'm going to check traffic cams and neighboring businesses' security for a visual of the kid and who he's with. I thought I'd loop Rei in on it too."

Jano nodded before stifling a yawn. "There were two reasons I told Silas to have you come in. The first was to let you know I spoke directly to Andros Ivanov."

I nodded. He was the pakhan in Detroit.

"He's accepting Kozlov's men. They and their wives will be sent to Detroit in the morning. He's also sending more soldiers to us. We're going to make a move on Volkov as soon as next week."

"What kind of move?"

"Like what he did to Kozlov and *mi padre*. I want his fucking head."

"Herrera?" I asked.

"Fucking coward is paying others to do his dirty work. We get rid of his minions, and he'll come out of hiding."

"I'm here, *jefe*. Whatever you need."

"I need you to give me an honest assessment of the chiefs you spoke to today." He lifted his hand. "Not now. Tomorrow. Bring me every name and swear to me that you have no suspicions. If you so much as have or have had a passing thought to their fidelity, let me know. This mission will be done with only our best and most loyal."

My mind was already going through the list of names. "*Sí*, I'll work on that right after I take the gun to Nick." I started to pick up the plastic bag.

"Not yet," Jano said. "There's one more thing."

I squared my shoulders and held my hands in front of me, standing to attention.

"Before I had a chance to speak to the capo on your behalf, he called Mia."

My heart sank. "About Isabella?"

"*Sí*. It was like they call a fucking game of telephone. It goes something like Isabella's mother spoke to her and was very upset. She then spoke to her husband who took the matter to the capo." He moved his hands as he spoke.

"What—?" His raised hand stopped my question.

"Mia adamantly defended her cousin to her brother. The problem came when Aurora Luciano later called Mia, saying she couldn't reach Isabella and demanded to speak to her."

"Fuck."

"Fuck is accurate. My wife told her that Isabella and Liliana were together watching a movie at Liliana's apartment. Mia assured her that the two girls were safe and guarded. She suggested that probably Isabella had her phone off for the movie."

I let out a long breath. "I need to thank Mia, but why did she lie?"

He took a step toward me, and his volume rose. "You didn't ask if you could take Isabella on a *tour* without Horace. She's too young and too virginal to be unescorted—by famiglia standards and ours."

"She's still a virgin."

"And you know, how?"

"Fuck, Jano. We went to Little Italy, ate dinner, and walked around. Then I took her to Imperial Beach. We walked the pier to watch the sunset. I didn't defile her." When he didn't speak, I added, "You said I could take her around San Diego. That's what I did."

Jano threw his head back. "Fucking women. It's always about a woman."

"Did you talk to Dario about my request?"

"No," he shouted. "I didn't talk to him about your request. I took the phone from Mia because she was obviously upset. He said Carmine wanted Isabella back in Kansas City. She's to leave Saturday morning."

"Fuck no."

Isabella
A little while earlier

I found Mia sitting at the kitchen island looking at her laptop. "Hey," I said.

Mia spun around and scanned me from head to toe. "Tell me you're okay."

My smile couldn't be hidden. "I'm good. Why?"

She got down from the stool. "You shouldn't be with Em unaccompanied."

"I was safe. Heck, he's deadlier than anyone else out there."

"Come" —she motioned toward the counter and stools— "sit down and tell me what happened. What made you want to do something so reckless?"

I went to the refrigerator and got myself a bottle of water. Sitting with a stool between us, I unscrewed the cap, trying to compose my response. Finally, I laid my hands out on the counter. "I'm sorry if you thought Em showing me around San Diego was reckless. I went because he asked. He even asked your husband first."

"He didn't ask Jano to take you without Horace. You have a bodyguard for a reason."

I scoffed. "I'm certain that Em is as capable of protecting me as Horace."

She lowered her voice. "Do you know what your mother and father would say if they knew you spent the evening unaccompanied with Catalina's brother—a member of the cartel?"

"I wasn't planning on mentioning it to them."

"Then you should have answered your phone when she called you."

My phone.

Shit.

I pulled my purse from where I'd draped the strap over the kitchen stool. Opening the zipper, I removed my phone. After entering the passcode, my stomach sank at the sight of eight missed calls. "Oh no. Mom called me this afternoon, and after that call, I turned off the volume. With it being in my purse, I must not have felt it vibrate." I met Mia's stare. "Should I call them?" I looked at the clock. Nine thirty in California meant eleven thirty in Kansas City.

"Yes, but wait a minute. The whole ordeal was a shit show. Apparently, Aunt Aurora was upset about her call with you earlier. Then the more she consequently tried to call you and you didn't answer, the more upset she became. She told Uncle Carmine that she wanted you back in Missouri. I guess I'm a bad influence." She shrugged. "Anyway, Uncle Carmine called Dario."

With my elbows on the counter, I held my head in my hands. "This is ridiculous." I looked up. "Papà called the capo. Then what happened?"

"Dario called me, asking me what I was doing with you, exposing you to…basically saying that working in the apartments has corrupted you in only two weeks."

Tears prickled the back of my eyes. "Mia, I'm sorry. You haven't corrupted me." I gestured toward *el Patrón's* office. "Em hasn't corrupted me or done anything reckless. I told him I wished the lockdown was over and I could see San Diego. This is my first time here without my family, and all I've seen is your house and the apartments."

"Jano told me. A *tour*?" She wiggled her eyebrows.

"A tour. First, he took me to Little Italy."

"Oh, I love that neighborhood."

My smile returned. "We had a fabulous dinner that was way too much food. And then we bought cannoli." I looked around. "Shoot. I must have left those in his car." I met her gaze. "And then he took me to Imperial Beach."

"The pier?"

I nodded.

"Did you see the sunset?"

"Yeah, it was magnificent. I guess I haven't been paying that close of attention to the setting sun from your pool deck or my bedroom window. Being out there with all those people. It was spectacular."

"Your tour sounds very much like a date."

I let my forehead drop to the counter. "I -I." I looked up. "I'm sorry. I'm sorry the capo was upset with you."

"Don't worry about Dario and me. We have a love-hate sibling thing going on. But...." Her smile lessened. "It was when Aunt Aurora called that I made a decision."

"Mom called you, too. Jeez."

"I decided to lie. When you call them, you can tell them the truth, or you can stick with my story. You were at Liliana's apartment watching a movie. You had the volume to your phone off."

I opened my eyes wide. That was a good alibi. "Why would you lie for me?"

Her nose scrunched. "I was you. I was eighteen, sheltered, and scared."

"You were scared?"

Mia nodded. "I already knew I was marrying Rocco, and I'd accepted that. We'd known each other for most of our childhood. It wasn't really a fall-in-love thing. More like a get-used-to-each-other thing. My father was mostly concerned about Dario and Dante, but when his attention did come my way, it was stifling. Every decision was made for me. My mother didn't intervene because my life had been hers when she was eighteen. It's a fucking vicious circle, and it needs to stop."

"What were you scared about? Getting married?"

Mia let out a long breath. "I don't think so. I was too young to have any idea about marriage except what I'd seen from my parents. Their marriage wasn't the best example, and I was naïve to think Rocco's and mine would be different. What I feared more than anything was a future in which I had no say. I'd always thought I might want to go to college. My dad and then Rocco said no. I watched movies and read books and dreamed about traveling the world." She leaned closer. "Here's a secret. Except for a trip to New York for a big celebration involving famiglias from all over the country, and moving here, I'd never ventured far from Kansas City."

"I'm sorry that none of your dreams have come true."

Her smile was back. "Don't be. Currently, my dream is to continue what Jano and I have built. He's ten—no, one hundred—times the man my first husband was. Jano can be a strong man to the world and a kind, loving man with Jorge and me. That's what a real man is. He's not someone who bullies you into his way of thinking."

"Like my papà."

Mia nodded. "I lied to your mom because if I had told the truth, your papà would have had Piero or another of the famiglia's guards on a plane to come out here and take you home. You've experienced a taste of freedom, even in lockdown. That is an opportunity I never had. Ever. When I called Liliana tonight, she raved about the way you're interacting with the tenants."

"Oh, that reminds me of something."

She laid her hand on the counter. "Your father still wants to send someone to take you back. He said they would be here this Saturday."

My eyes filled with tears. "Please, I don't want to go back. I don't want to go back to their rules and ..." My thoughts were scattered. "Did you know that tonight with Em was the first time I can recall sitting in the front seat of a car? How fucked is that?"

Mia's eyes opened wide. "I am a bad influence."

"Is there anything you or *el Patrón* can do to change his mind?"

Mia pressed her lips together.

"I'm scared of things too. I'm scared of going back. I asked to go to college. I even spoke to Catalina about it. My grades were good." I sighed. "Papà said no. The whole story about wanting me to help Mom with her philanthropic endeavors was her blowing smoke because she didn't want to admit to Catalina that they'd denied my request. I suppose I would have helped Mom if I were back in Kansas City. But she sits on committees, drinks coffee and then wine. What you've done at the apartments is real help. That's what I want to do. I want to do more than raise money and gossip. You're changing the tenants' lives."

"I'll talk to Jano. I can even call my brother. Ultimately, the decision is his."

"Thank you." I took a breath. "Today one of the tenants came to my office." I smiled. "She confided in me, and it felt good and bad."

"Why bad?"

"Because she asked me to talk to you, and I want to help her. I don't know how." I went on to tell Mia what Isla had confided in me about Efrain, the new guard at Wanderland. I also mentioned what she'd said about punishment from Lieutenant Nicolas Ruiz. "He holds their assignments over their heads. If they don't do what he says, they find themselves with the less desirable clients."

Mia nodded as she listened. "I'll do what I can."

"Can you help?"

"I have a thin line to walk without the soldiers believing Jano can't control his wife."

I lifted my eyebrows. "Can he?"

She grinned. "He'll listen to me. He's also knowledgeable regarding the club and the workings within the cartel. I'll ask his advice. He may choose to talk to Nicolas himself, or he could bring his son, Nick, in on it. One way or the other, it will be dealt with. I'm glad Isla told you. If you ask me, the men at the club know I'm currently on maternity leave and are trying to take advantage of my absence." She reached out for my hand. "This is why I truly need you here."

"I want to stay here. Maybe even longer than a month."

"I have to ask," Mia said softly. "Are the tenants and the apartments the only reason you want to stay in San Diego?"

Warmth filled my cheeks.

Before I could verbally reply, we turned to the sound of men's voices and the opening of *el Patrón's* office door. Mia's husband was speaking to Em very loudly in Spanish. Em appeared in the arch of the hallway, visibly agitated.

"What is it?" Mia and I asked in unison.

The room became quiet, like the flipping of a switch. Em's jaw clenched and the muscles in the side of his face pulsated. "Your parents," Em said, looking at me. "They're sending a bodyguard Saturday to take you back to your home."

I stood. "Mia told me. She said she'd try to stop them."

El Patrón ran his hand through his hair and made a growling noise.

Mia moved her gaze from Em to me and back. Then she turned to her husband. "Jano, has Emiliano come to you about something you haven't mentioned?"

"I have a fucking war—"

Mia smiled. "Of course. Why didn't I see this?" She slapped her palms against her thighs. "Well, this changes everything."

I watched in stunned silence as Mia walked to her husband and laid her hands on his shoulders. Something Liliana said to me came back. She'd said that all Mia had to do was smile and she would get her way. The two of them spoke low in a mixture of English and Spanish. Em stood at the other end of the kitchen island, staring at me as if he wanted to take me from this house this minute.

"Faith" I mouthed.

Em swallowed, his Adam's apple bobbing as we both waited quietly. *El Patrón's* head shook from side to side as Mia continued speaking. She pushed up on her tiptoes and kissed his cheek.

"Fuck. I'll make the damn call." His voice was strong and more measured than a moment ago. He ran his hand over his hair and stared directly at me. The intensity was intimidating. "Do you want to marry Emiliano?"

"I'm afraid my papà—"

"No," he said, cutting me off. "That was not what I asked. Do *you* want to marry Emiliano?"

Swallowing the dryness in my throat, I turned my gaze on Emiliano. I was young and naive, the same as Mia described; however, in the short time I'd gotten to know this man, I didn't fear a future without choices if I became his wife. That future would come if I returned to Missouri. I stood taller as new tears streamed down my cheeks. "Yes, I want to marry Emiliano."

"Fuck," *el Patròn* growled. "I'll call the capo soon." He pointed at me and at Em. "This won't be a repeat of Camila and Dante. You must have the consent of the *famiglia* and the cartel." He exhaled. "I need you here in San Diego, Em. That's not debatable. I give my permission. The final decision rests with Dario." He turned to Em. "Go. You have work to do."

Em nodded. "Thank you, Mia."

Her husband shook his head. "You're not very good at knowing who you should ask or thank."

Em's lips curled. "Thank you, *el Patròn*." He turned to me and winked.

TWENTY-FIVE

Isabella

It shouldn't be a surprise that I had a difficult time falling asleep. Once I was upstairs in my room, I called my mother. It was nearly midnight in Kansas City, and the call went to voice mail. I told her I loved her. I stared up at the ceiling. Between the memories of Em's and my first date and complete shock over the way my world has been turned upside down in the course of a few weeks, sleep was elusive.

This morning, after I showered and dressed for work, I went downstairs. Mia was sitting at an umbrella table and drinking coffee out by the pool. Jorge was content and babbling in that colorful fence thingy. I stepped into the sunshine. "Thank you for what you did last night."

She turned toward me and wrapped her fingers

around the warm cup. Her expression was sober. "Have a seat."

My heart fell as I sat across the table from her. "Dario said no."

Mia shook her head. "Jano kept his word. He called last night. My brother didn't commit one way or the other. I would expect he'll be in discussions with Uncle Carmine. Honestly, you could hear in five minutes or at midnight tonight. There will be a decision made today especially since they want you home tomorrow." She lifted her eyebrows. "You know, if you go back home, I'm sure they'll find you an Italian husband."

My eyes fell to the table. "They already have." I looked up. "I wasn't looking for a husband. I wanted to go to school."

"Wait. They've found you a husband. Is it official?"

I shook my head. "Papà said it would be when I went back to Kansas City."

"But you didn't want to marry, and you do now. What changed?"

A smile curled my lips. "Emiliano. The apartments. The realization of the lies I've been told my entire life. I feel like a heavy veil has been ripped away from my eyes. I'm seeing the sky for the first time."

"Concentrate on the first one. Emiliano Ruiz. Did you know that he's thirty years old?"

I looked down and back up. "No. I guessed somewhere around there. There's a lot about him I don't know."

"Then why do you want to marry him?"

I sighed with a grin. "Because of what you said about

a good man. Em is a good man. He listens when I talk. He helped me with the different programs for the apartments but didn't smother me. He guided me and sat back, like he knew I was capable. I remember my father getting frustrated with Mom. When she was having difficulties with something, he didn't offer to help her achieve the task—he'd just take it from her." I lowered my voice. "I remember the first time I heard him tell her she was stupid." I met Mia's gaze. "I couldn't believe he'd say that to her. I think what made the memory lasting was Mom's response."

"What was it?"

"Nothing. Acceptance. Submission. I don't want a husband like that."

"There are probably good men closer to your age."

I shook my head. "Do you really think Papà will let me wait five or six years to marry?"

Mia pinched her lips together. "Probably not. But that isn't a reason to jump into—"

"I love him," I blurted out. "I don't know if it's love or lust or infatuation, but I know that when I'm with him, I feel special, valued. I want to see him happy. I like when he touches me."

Mia's eyebrows jumped. "He touched you?"

"He held my hand and wrapped his arm around me. I know what he does, but that doesn't mean I'm frightened of him." I sighed. "His job scares me *for* him. Last night I lay awake wondering about our future, fearful that one day he'd be a casualty of the war."

"I know that feeling."

"When I'm at his side, I feel safe. Isn't that the way

it's supposed to be? I mean this is unquestionably fast, but the thought of being separated from him forever frightens me more."

"There's also the matter of Lieutenant Andrés Ruiz."

"Em's father."

Mia nodded. "He's married both of his daughters to Lucianos. I can't see him arguing with Jano, especially when Em wants you, but at this point he's still an unknown." She leaned back with her coffee mug. "I helped Camila marry because I believe in the woman's right to have a voice in her future. I like your answers, and I know Em. He is a good man. I'm here to help all I can. There's a chance with the war that a big wedding will be out of the question."

"I don't care about a big wedding." I shrugged. "I've never dreamed of my wedding day."

"I've had two." She grinned. "Other than the gunshots, I preferred Camila's."

I blinked. "Did you say gunshots?"

"Machine guns." Mia smiled and shook her head. "If Isla comes to you again today, tell her I'm working her problem, and no, I didn't use her name."

My cheeks rose and my lips curled. "Thank you, Mia, for everything."

I stayed at Mia's as long as I could. After no word from Kansas City, I left with Horace. It was past time to get to the apartments. Liliana was already there when I arrived. I said good morning to José, Reina, and Celeste as I entered.

Before I could get my purse put away, Liliana came to my office, closed the door, and leaned against it. "Spill. I want all the details. I can't believe you went on a date with Em."

For a moment, I stood with my lips agape.

"Don't look so scared. Mia told me. Well, she didn't tell me it was a *date*. She said Em was giving you a tour of San Diego. But I can read between the lines."

My head was shaking. "When did she tell you that?"

"Last night. She told me that if anyone asked, you came to my apartment to watch a movie."

Sitting in my desk chair, I leaned down until my forehead hit the desk. "This is ridiculously out of control."

Liliana came forward and sat at a chair across from my desk. When I looked up, she was intently staring my direction. "Tell me what it was like. I've never been on a date."

"How is that possible? You were married."

She wobbled her head. "We never dated. I only knew him as Sofia's father. *El Patrón* said we were to be wed. That was it. My parents bought me a dress and there was a wedding." She shrugged. "No dates."

"That makes me sad."

"It's not uncommon. It happens."

"Mia said she wants that to end. She thinks the women should have a say in the matter."

Liliana sat back in the chair. "It could be romantic. Or not." Her eyes lit up. "Tell me about last night."

A smile curled my lips. For something Em and I agreed to keep secret, the word was spreading fast. "He took me to Little Italy. We had a delicious dinner. We stopped at a bakery and got cannoli. And then he drove to Imperial Beach. We watched the sunset."

Liliana rubbed her hands together. "That sounds like what a date should sound like. Did Horace keep his distance?"

"Horace wasn't there."

Her eyes widened. "Just the two of you? Oh, how scandalous. Do you like him?"

"Horace is fine."

"No." She shook her head. "Do you like Em? It was pretty obvious that he's been hanging out here more than normal."

I didn't know that. Of course, I didn't know what normal was either. I thought about her question. "I do." I remembered something. "Your husband was older. Was that an issue for you?"

"Yes, but I had a lot of issues with Gerardo. Em is different. I know that about him. He's just always been kind. He's a good man."

Good man.

My smile returned as I sat up straight. "I agree. The problems are my parents and the capo."

"Do you mean Em's asked to marry you?"

My body tingled. It was unreal to be discussing this with a friend. "He did. He proposed on the beach last night." I wiggled my fingers. "No ring until we have both the cartel's and famiglia's approval."

"You live with *el Patrón*. Has he given the cartel's approval?"

I nodded.

Her smile grew. "Hey, if you need another alibi, I'm your go-to."

"Thank you."

Liliana stood and walked to the door. "I'm one hundred percent in favor of this marriage."

"You are? Why?"

"Because if you marry Em, you'll move to San Diego permanently, and we won't lose you here at the apartments."

"I like it here more than I could have imagined."

The rest of the day moved slowly. I watched YouTube videos about filing grant applications. That was enthralling. I worked on the program and ate lunch with Liliana and other tenants in the cafeteria. I was beginning to know all the tenants' names and faces. The spreadsheet helped. I guessed I was a visual learner. Seeing their names spelled out helped me retain the information.

It was after four when my phone rang. It was my mother.

TWENTY-SIX

Emiliano

It was near five o'clock on the West Coast, and I still hadn't received an answer from the capo.

Since Isabella's and my secret relationship wasn't a secret, after a day of assessing our chiefs, I decided to detour to the apartments, hoping to catch Isabella before she left. The image of her beautiful face mouthing 'faith' played on repeat in my thoughts.

As I neared my exit, the alarms began to sound. The blaring wasn't cautioning me of an incoming tsunami, rapidly growing wildfire, or any other natural disaster. The sound was my phone exploding with messages.

Andros Ivanov's men are here.

Volkov knows they're in San Diego.

Volkov is in San Diego
We have to move NOW.

Fuck.

Taking the first exit I came to, I reentered the interstate, changing directions and heading south toward the large warehouse.

As I fought traffic on the 5, new concerns filled my mind. We weren't ready. Moving now was too early. The raid was scheduled for Monday on the bratva hideout we'd learned about through Adrian—Andros Ivanov's man. We needed time to strategize with our Detroit bratva counterparts. My thoughts raced back to Isabella.

I called Horace.

He answered on the second ring. "Lieutenant?"

"Have you seen the messages?"

"*Sí*. I'm waiting on word what to do with Miss Luciano."

Rage boiled within me. If anything happened to her...

She wouldn't be top of mind to anyone but me. I gripped my phone tighter. "Don't leave the apartments. You and José spend the night, increasing the guards. Call trusted soldiers. Don't tell them what's happening. Just get more outside coverage."

"*Sí, jefe.*"

"I'm also closing Wanderland for the night."

"Miss Izzy, what should I tell her?"

Almost every fiber of my being wanted to pacify her and not increase her fright. One small voice reminded me that we'd promised to always be honest. "Tell her the truth. Emphasize that she cannot tell a soul."

"*Sí*. I'll talk to her. I'll also inform Señora Ruiz about the change in schedule regarding Wanderland. She'll let the whores know."

Another call was ringing in. A glance at my screen told me it was *el Patrón*.

Without another word, I disconnected the call with Horace and answered the incoming call. "*Jefe.*"

"Meet us at the distribution center in Midtown."

"Midtown?" I questioned, looking for another exit so I could turn around again. "The warehouse south is bigger."

"Midtown," Jano repeated forcibly. "This operation is only a need-to-know basis. I'm not trusting this job to fucking soldiers and very few chiefs. Nick's on his way. There's a stockpile of weapons, vests, and whatever we'll need in Midtown. Adrian will arrive shortly with Ivanov's men. Three of the famiglia's men are there as well. We don't need any more."

Shit was getting real.

"I called Horace," I volunteered. "He's keeping Isabella and Liliana at the apartments. I'm also about to close Wanderland."

"No. If Wanderland doesn't operate as usual, the uniforms will come to us first when Volkov is found. The *chiquitas* can stay in the apartments. They're not on Volkov's radar. That also leaves José and Horace there to help guard the tenants."

Fuck.

He was right about Wanderland.

"Has my father been notified?"

"No," he answered definitively. "Don't call him or your uncle. Understand?"

Well, that didn't bode well for my father or Uncle Nicolas. "Jano, my father isn't a traitor."

"His fighting days are behind him. Tonight, we need the best. That's not old men."

"I understand. Is there anyone else to contact?" I asked as I again took an exit off of the 5. Fucking traffic."

"Silas is on it," Jano said. "Rei is en route, but we need to move fast before Volkov has a chance to organize or hide."

"Are we hitting their hideout?"

"We'll discuss in Midtown."

"I'm on my way." As soon as the damn light turns green. I pounded the base of my palm against the steering wheel. Reaching for the glove compartment, I pulled out my stash of cigarettes and a lighter.

I had just enough time to light it and take a soothing drag before the light changed.

As soon as I began moving again, I called Horace back. "*El patrón* wants business as usual at Wanderland. Liliana and Isabella are to stay—"

"I will not move them."

"You have my authority to bring in extra security at Wanderland, tell them there's a VIP guest coming. No more information on the streets."

"*Sí, Teniente.*"

The Midtown distribution center was near the airport in a sea of warehouses and shipping containers coming from the port. I pulled my Mercedes into one of the loading docks. When I opened the door to the interior, I heard the echoes of things being moved in the back. Throwing the butt of the cigarette on the cement, I smashed it with my boot.

Unholstering my gun and releasing the thumb safety, I made my way through a series of hallways and doors. Nick, Piero and Lorenzo from the famiglia, Adrian, and two other Russians from Ivanov's bratva were opening wooden crates of weapons. I holstered the Beretta.

Nick met me at the doorway. "*El Patrón* wants to lead this mission."

My eyes opened wide. "Fuck no. He and Silas can stay here and monitor us through cameras and headsets."

My cousin shook his head. "No cameras. Jano won't take a chance of the video falling into the wrong hands."

"He still shouldn't go." I inhaled. "We won't survive if we lose him. It's not worth the risk."

Nick clenched his jaw and the tendons in his neck pulled taut. "I tried to reason with him. It's fucking impossible. He's spent the last six months planning his revenge on Volkov and Herrera. He's not going to sit back and watch." Nick went on. "Intelligence came in earlier today. Volkov was spotted going into an abandoned building in East Village."

"Why would he be in an abandoned building? What about their hideout?"

"Adrian heard chatter. Sounds like they're storing weapons, drugs, and possibly human cargo. It's a big operation. Volkov was personally checking out the merchandise."

"The guns, the drugs, or the women?"

Nick shook his head. "No way of knowing. Possibly all three."

"Fuck, it feels like a setup. Is that where we're going?"

Nick shook his head. "Not to the hideout either. After leaving the abandoned building, he was followed back to The Legend."

I blew out a gust of air. "High rent—by Petco Park."

"Rei got into their security. Volkov is staying in a $1.5-million-dollar condo on the second floor."

Fuck.

"Jano thinks we're going to barge in there...it's a fucking setup. Volkov knows Jano's obsession, and he's going to bring us all down with it."

Nick lifted his phone. "The target is Volkov, not his men. Rei found the building's schematics, courtesy of the government and building permits. There's a service elevator near the loading dock. For the serenity of the high-paying residents, no deliveries are made after hours. All other building personnel including cleaning staff and executives must leave the building by six. That leaves The Legend down to three security guards by seven—one at the front desk, one monitoring the elevators in the front lobby, and the last one monitoring the security dock. Of course, the residents can employee private security."

I was thinking about the timeline. "The building is basically cleared by seven and the sun sets around seven thirty."

Nick nodded. "If we can't convince *el Patrón* to stay

back, there will be eight of us. If Rei makes it, that will be nine."

Nine fucking people performing a swat operation in one of the high-rent buildings in downtown San Diego. "How far out is Rei?"

Nick looked down at his phone. "Touching down in twenty-five."

Piero used a crowbar to open another crate. He started throwing out bulletproof vests, military grade.

I looked at the message on my phone and called out, "*El Patrón* is here." That meant everyone for the mission was present except Rei. We still had a couple hours before go time.

Jano strode in looking as if he was about to explode. "We have a location." He lifted his fist and volume. "Are we ready to fight?"

A cheer came from the men.

Jano turned to Nick and me and lowered his tone. "You see how many cartel we have here tonight?"

The three of us and Silas—who had just entered—replied in unison, "*Sí.*"

"Diego and Felipe are with Mia and Jorge. José and Horace know what's going down. That's all." His jaw clenched. "The fewer people, the more deniability." He patted me on the shoulder. "Live through this assignment, Em. The capo called on the way here. Your request has been approved."

Shock and excitement collided with the gravity of tonight's operation. "Fuck."

His lips quirked. "Not until you're married."

I couldn't believe we were approved. "Carmine didn't protest?"

"I didn't have time for details. The capo gave you permission. That's all that you need to know."

Isabella was mine or would be soon. However, if I didn't keep my mind in this fight, she would be right about her first heartbreak. Straightening my shoulders, I vowed not to let that happen.

An hour later, Rei and Sebastián, Rei's number-two up north, arrived with a slew of computers.

"No cameras," Jano repeated.

"*No te preocupes, hermano,*" Rei replied. "Once I have all of this set up, *el Patrón* and Sebastián will watch the building's surveillance from here and relay to us where to go."

"I'm with my men."

"Hermano," Rei said.

Jano sent him a piercing glare.

Rei shook his head and continued. "Once we're on our way out of The Legend, Sebastián will replace the footage of us entering and exiting with still footage we've collected."

"How much time do we have?" Jano asked.

"In and out in eight minutes or less." Rei continued, speaking to everyone. "It's confirmed that Volkov is in the condo. It's believed he's there with his mistress."

"Do we have an ID on her?" I asked.

Rei's nostrils flared as he let out a breath. "We do."

"Is there a problem?" Nick asked.

"Just one." Rei reached for the mouse and projected a picture of a thin dark-haired woman, dressed in a long evening gown. Her clothing was expensive. Her face was youthified by Botox or surgery—maybe both. However, if anyone asked me, she looked as if she'd been ridden hard and put away wet. My guess was that she was somewhere in her fifties.

"That's his mistress?" Piero asked. "Apparently, he doesn't like them young."

"No," Rei replied. "Volkov chose her for another reason." He showed another picture of the woman with an older man. While I couldn't place him, I knew it wasn't Volkov. "Two months ago, she married Dmitri Makarova."

That name rang a bell. "He was with Myshkin's bratva in Kansas City."

Rei nodded. "He's now with Volkov. Worked his way up the ladder fast. I don't trust him or the woman."

I shook my head.

"Wait a minute," Lorenzo said. "Volkov is sleeping with the wife of one of his men—one of his top men?"

"Who the fuck is this woman?" I asked.

"Rei's mother-in-law," Jano answered.

The room went silent.

Rei planted his feet shoulder-width apart and nodded. He took us back to the picture of her in the long evening gown. "This is Leah Renner, Jasmine's biological mother. History includes manslaughter. Twenty years ago, she sold drugs to a college boy, and he died. She served her sentence in the Women's Eastern Reception, Diagnostic and Correctional Center. From what we can determine, Dmitri worked a deal with the parole board. She was released earlier this year before her sentence was complete. It appears she wasn't going to let her imprisonment or Myshkin's death stop her pursuit of fortune. She's now Leah Makarova—Mrs. Dmitri Makarova."

Nick and I exchanged glances.

Rei went on. "If she's there, she's to meet the same fate as Volkov."

"You're authorizing a hit on Jasmine's mother?" I asked.

"I'm authorizing a hit on the woman married to one of Volkov's newest officers, who is also sleeping with Volkov. It's a fucking perfect setup. We get in and get out. Who will be the number-one suspect?"

It all made sense. "Fuck, Leah's husband—Makarova."

Adrian spoke in his heavy Russian accent, "Fucking Dmitri tried to kiss Andros's ass. Pakhan didn't trust him. That's why the leech sucked up to Volkov. I wish they were having a fucking three-way. I'd gladly take them all out."

"Volkov is mine," Jano said. "I want to see his fucking face as he takes his last breath."

"What about guards?"

Rei brought a video feed up on the screen. "There's usually two outside the door and one near the elevator. We're going to have to utilize the element of surprise and take them out—collateral damage. In and out in eight or less," he repeated.

"Fucking let's do this," Jano said.

As Sebastián continued setting up the technology,

Rei came to Nick and me. "I don't like the idea of Jano on this mission."

"I tried to stop him," Nick said. "It's impossible."

Rei continued, "Whatever the fuck happens tonight, Jano makes it out of there alive."

Nick and I nodded.

"I fucking mean it," he growled. "We swore an oath to the Roríguez cartel. Any one of us before him."

"*Sí*," we replied in unison.

Isabella
Earlier

"Mom," I said, answering my phone and closing the office door. I walked back to my desk. "I tried to call you last night." I sat in the white leather chair.

Her sobs came through the phone.

"I can't understand what you're saying." Panic rose within me. "Are you hurt?" I stood, gripping my phone tighter. "Is it Noemi? Tony?"

"Isabella…" She struggled for breath. "Dario wants to do…He's a vile, awful man…. He wants your father to…" She continued to struggle. "It's awful."

Letting out a long breath, I sat back in my chair. "It's not terrible."

"I needed to let you know that Catalina's brother

asked for your hand. It's unfathomable. I want to plead directly to the capo, but your father won't allow it. He says this is men's dealings. I don't know what kind of deal they made, but Isabella, I will not sleep until we have you back where you belong."

I looked around Mia's office. "I think I've found where I belong."

"Here with your family, with your sister and brother—that's where you belong. I haven't told them. Poor Noemi. She was happy to hear you were coming home early. And..." She gasped. "Tony will be heartbroken. Izzy, I'm heartbroken. Never did I imagine. Honey, I'm so sorry we agreed to send you out there among those horrible people—"

"They're not horrible. They're not anything like you and Papà assume. You were both wrong."

"Catalina's brother..."

"His name is Emiliano." I held my breath. "Has the capo made a decision?" Tension seized my body, making the space-time continuum slow. As I waited for a response, it was as if the second hand on the clock refused to tick.

"He gave his permission."

Tears of relief flooded my eyes, streaming down my cheeks. "That's wonderful."

"No. The opposite of wonderful. What is wrong with you, Izzy. I think that somehow, they brainwashed you. I don't know how Arianna can handle both her boys and her daughter being married into that family, but it's going to stop."

Boys?

The capo dei capi and his consigliere.

Sure, Mom, boys.

Mia was the happiest I could remember.

I shook my head.

"I don't want it to stop, Mom. I want to marry Em. I'm in love with him."

Mom gasped. "Isabella, I hate to be the one to tell you this, but you're too young to know what love is. You're simply infatuated. He's an older man who is paying attention to you. You're enchanted by the idea of love. You know nothing about the reality of marriage."

My neck stiffened. "I'm not going to argue my age. I will ask you to remember how old you were when you and Papà married."

"That's irrelevant. Things have changed."

"Did Papà propose?" I asked.

"Your grandfather Vincent spoke to my father."

I repeated the question.

"We had a family dinner where Carmine presented me with an engagement ring. Tradition."

"Em asked me. He got down on one knee and asked me." When Mom didn't respond, I went on. "There wasn't a ring because we both knew we needed Dario's and *el Patrón's* approval."

"He asked you?" she said quietly.

"He did. And I accepted."

"That's not your choice."

"Why? Didn't you say things have changed?"

"Your father barely tolerates Catalina. We've never invited the capo and his wife to our home. You can't marry this...Emiliano."

"Why, Mom?" My voice got louder. "Are you saying that if I do marry Em, my husband will not be welcome in my childhood home, or are you saying that neither of us will be? Because if you or Papà bans Em, you're also banning me."

The crying on the other end of the call began again. "I don't want to lose my daughter."

"It's rather simple. Welcome my husband and you still have me as a daughter. That also goes for his sisters and parents."

"Do you realize what you're doing to us?"

"What am I doing to *you*?"

"You're beautiful, Isabella, a true treasure. Your father has entered into discussions with the Esposito famiglia in St. Louis. They're very respected."

I shook my head. "I don't know them."

"Yes, dear, you met them when we went to St. Louis for the wedding of their capo dei capi's daughter, Emilia. Francesco Ricci is the Esposito famiglia consigliere. You and his son Aldo were friendly."

That was who Papà mentioned. I recalled the wedding. "I was nine."

"You're eighteen now. He never forgot you."

Inhaling, I decided to put a stop to this conversation. "I forgot him."

"Do you realize what it would do for your father to be connected to the Esposito famiglia? It would give him clout—leverage over the capo."

My mouth fell open. "Seriously, my marriage to a man I don't know would be better for Papà. If we have Dario's approval, Em and I are getting married."

"Fine," she pacified. "Honey, it will take months for me to plan a wedding—maybe we should think Christmas or better yet springtime in the Ozarks. Yes, that time of the year, Arianna's place would be beautiful."

Seriously, it was early September.

She went on, "We must consider the guest list. Remember the tension at Dario and Catalina's ceremony?"

"I don't want to wait months. I also don't need a big wedding to outdo Aunt Arianna." I had an idea. "If we chose to marry out here in San Diego, will you come?"

"Izzy," she cried.

"The choice will be yours. Do you want me as a daughter or not?" I hit the red icon and tossed my phone on the desk. My attention quickly went to a knock on the door.

I'd told everyone my door would be open.

A quick look at the bottom of the monitor told me it was time to head to Mia's. I rubbed my temples. After that conversation, I could use not only Mia's advice but a few laps in her pool.

"Come in."

The door opened. "Miss Izzy," Horace said as he entered. "May we talk?"

My smile blossomed at the news my mother had shared. "Horace, *el Patrón* and the capo have both approved of Em and I being married."

His eyes opened wide. "The lieutenant...I didn't realize." Pressing his lips together, he nodded. "That makes sense."

"It's quick, but that doesn't mean it's not real."

"Congratulations, Miss Izzy."

I stood and pulled the desk drawer out to retrieve my purse. "I can't wait to tell Mia—unless she already knows. And Em." I continued that thought. "He can't know. If he did, he would have called me." I picked up my phone to see if I'd missed his call.

No calls from him.

"Maybe he doesn't know." I met Horace's gaze. "I'm going to call him."

"No, please don't call him."

The joy of a second ago evaporated with the tone of his voice. "Why? Don't scare me."

He gestured toward my chair. "Please sit down. There have been developments today, developments that must stay confidential."

"Is Em injured?"

"No, miss. José is speaking to Señora Ruiz. No one else must know what I'm about to tell you. None of the tenants. If any rumors start, you must deny all knowledge."

My hands began to tremble. "Why are you telling me?"

"Because you're engaged to Lieutenant Emiliano Ruiz, and he told me to be completely honest with you."

I feigned a smile at the memory of us agreeing to those terms. "Did he tell you we were engaged?"

"No, miss. He told me to be truthful. You told me you are engaged."

I gripped the arms of my chair, tightening my hold until my knuckles blanched. "What is happening?"

"I can tell you what I know."

My fingers didn't loosen as I listened to Horace share what details he could share about the war. Tonight, there will be a significant clandestine operation against Volkov. With each word, I told myself to breathe. I concentrated on the air entering and exiting my lungs. This information wouldn't send me into shock. I was past that reaction.

My brain understood my pep talk, but my body was on the verge of another breakdown. The room cooled and at times Horace spoke in slow motion as if his words were distorted.

He spoke of a dangerous life-or-death operation. For me to feel Em's touch again, his lips on mine, or see his smile, I had to hope for the death of a man I never met. One whose name was a mystery to me a few weeks ago —Volkov.

I reached for my bottle of water and took a sip, trying to fight the sudden dryness. "Will Em be safe?"

"There are no guarantees. *El Patrón* made him a lieutenant. That means he has faith in him."

I started thinking of others, like Em's cousin Nick and even *el Patrón* himself. "Could they be killed?"

"Our lives are in danger every day."

Was this the life I wanted to live?

Did Mafia wives have the same stifling worry?

Horace went on, "It's not always guns and wars. Danger comes in all forms. Tripping and falling, a traffic accident, a plane crash."

Letting go of the arms of the chair, I sat forward and

rubbed my temples. "I don't worry about losing people I care about in a fall."

He nodded. "Doing so would make it impossible to live."

I looked up. "What are you saying?"

"I'm saying that the lieutenant wanted you to know, not so you will worry but so that you will understand if he can't reach out to you for a while. I won't lie. Tonight's operation is dangerous. Honestly, every day in the life of the cartel carries danger. That's why I'm staying here with you, Miss Izzy, until we get the all clear."

"We have to stay here? Surely, it's safe at Mia's."

"*Sí*. You and Señora Ruiz will stay here. We can't risk the drive."

Señora Ruiz—Liliana.

"It's only twenty or thirty minutes."

"Miss, Lieutenant Ruiz knows you're here, safe and secure. Do you want him to worry about you on the streets of San Diego or to concentrate on his mission?"

Nodding, my stomach twisted. "His mission. Liliana knows what you're telling me?"

Horace nodded. "*El patrón* wants Wanderland to function as usual tonight. No deviations that could set off suspicions."

"We can't tell them about the escalation in the war so they'll be prepared?"

Horace shook his head. "You may not."

The temperature around me rose. "Being uninformed and vulnerable. That could be dangerous for the tenants."

"There will be extra protection."

Names and faces flashed like a slide show through my mind. "Maybe it would be better to close it for the night. I don't know, maybe we make up a story. We could say there's a problem with the air conditioning."

Horace shook his head. "Lieutenant Ruiz recommended that. *El Patrón* made the decisions."

Em had thought of that.

He's a good man.

I tugged on my lip with my teeth. *"El Patrón* could be making the wrong decision, and it could cost these women their lives."

"That isn't for either of us to decide."

"What about Mia? Is she aware of what's happening?"

His nostrils flared. "I don't know what she's been told. You are to be trusted to keep this information here between you and Señora Ruiz."

"Where will Liliana and I sleep?"

"There are unoccupied apartments. Down hallway five, there is a furnished unit with three bedrooms. You two can each have your own bedroom. José and I will take shifts in the other. You'll be watched over all the time."

"Did Em set that up?"

"He told me to keep you safe. I'm doing my job."

I swallowed "Thank you, Horace."

TWENTY-EIGHT

Isabella

It was after midnight as I sat alone on a twin-sized bed in a room that was big enough for the bed, a dresser, and a desk. The light fixture above was new but plain, giving off a harsh white illumination. With my knees to my chest, and my back against the wall where a headboard should be, I stared at the four corners, not willing to turn off the only source of light.

My head and jaw ached from the stress. My stomach was twisted in knots.

I couldn't stop worrying about Em. How could it be that he finally tells me his feelings and I admit mine, and then he could be taken away from me? I was afraid my heartbreak would come from my father's refusal or maybe Dario's. Instead, it could be so much worse.

Closing my eyes, I asked the God I'd been taught

about all my life to spare Emiliano, pleading his case. He wasn't a perfect man. He'd admitted to murder. But that didn't mean he wasn't a good man. He'd asked *el Patrón* to close Wanderland. I also asked the same for others, not even knowing for sure who was part of the operation or—if it was too late—if anyone was already injured or dead.

My teeth clenched as I imagined crime scenes from movies, wondering how accurate they truly were. Em never lied about what he did, telling me over and over that it was dangerous. What he didn't tell me was that giving my heart to a handsome, strong, protective, and yes, good man would cause this much fear.

Throwing back the covers, I stood barefoot on the cool vinyl floor. Goose bumps peppered my arms and legs.

What was happening at Wanderland?

Were the tenants safe?

Is Volkov dead?

Have his men retaliated?

I paced next to the bed, back and forth, the questions multiplying in my head. There was no source of news. I didn't even have my phone. Horace had it. I don't know if that was his doing or Em's, and at the moment, all I wanted was word of my fiancé.

Word that Em was safe and alive.

My fiancé.

The knots in my stomach multiplied.

Horace promised he'd bring me the phone if I received news. What he didn't want was for me to freak out and call someone I shouldn't share the information with. He didn't want me scrolling for news stories or listening to rumors.

"Gah," I called out, the pressure within me mounting. I felt like a lioness trapped in a cage.

Looking down, I assessed the clothes I wore, wondering if they were appropriate enough for José and Horace. One of our bodyguards would be in the common area while the other one slept.

Liliana found each of us a pair of shorts and over-sized men's t-shirts from donations the apartments received. The clothes had been washed, dried, and cate-gorized by size. The shirt she handed me was clean with a faded LA Lakers logo on the front. It fell to my knees. The shorts were soft with an elastic waistband. We utilized hygiene supplies that Mia kept on hand for new arrivals.

Biting my lip, I went to the door and opened it a crack. I saw Horace sitting in a chair near the closed door to the hallway. "Any word?" I asked.

He shook his head.

"Are you telling me all you know or are you trying to protect me? Because not knowing is unbearable."

"The mission is complete. That's all I know."

"Casualties?"

My eyes flooded with tears and my throat constricted when he nodded.

"Names?"

Again, he shook his head.

I turned toward the opening of Liliana's door. She peeked her head out. "What do you know?"

My nostrils flared as I tried to form words. "Not

much." I wiped my runny nose on the back of my hand. "The operation is over. There are casualties. No names."

Liliana came out and reached for my hand. "Come in my room. I can't sleep and neither of us should be alone." With my hand in hers, she looked at Horace. "What about Wanderland?"

"No word, ma'am. Business as usual."

She exhaled. "The club closes at three. Wake me up if I'm asleep when the tenants return."

"Señora Ruiz, they can't know what is happening. If they know you're here all night, there will be questions."

I replied to him, my voice an octave higher than before. "What are we supposed to do, show up tomorrow in the same clothes and act like we went home?"

"Yes, miss. That is exactly what you will do."

"Come on," Liliana said, tugging my hand.

I'd never officially shared a bed. There were times throughout our childhood that I'd sneak into Noemi's room, or she'd sneak into mine. That was different. We were sisters and we each had queen-sized beds for as long as I can remember.

Liliana peeled the top blanket from the bed and handed it to me. Next, she peeled the top sheet and wrapped it around herself like a big cape. "Let's sit here."

We both sat on the small bed with our backs against the wall on the long side and faced straight ahead.

"Have you ever done this before?" I asked. "Been made to stay here overnight?"

"No. There's been times I wasn't taken to my apartment. I've slept at Valentina's or Mia's before."

I held my knees to my chest. Breaking down, I laid

my face on my knees and cried. My shoulders heaved as I gasped for breath. Lifting my head, I turned to my new friend. "What if I lose him? We haven't had enough time together."

"How much time do you want?"

Her question caught me off guard. "I want forever."

She inhaled and nodded.

"Oh shit." I wiped my eyes on the blanket. "Liliana, I'm sorry. I'm such an idiot."

Her eyes opened wide. "What are you sorry about?"

I closed my eyes, feeling the pounding in my head. "I'm crying and carrying on about the unknown fate of Em and you lost your husband."

She shook her head.

"Do you mind me asking what happened to him? Was it an operation or battle?"

With her lips pressed together, she shook her head. "No, he was killed, but not in service to the cartel."

I reached out to her raised, sheet-covered knees. "Killed? The Russians? The other cartel?"

"Herrera? No, I believe he was killed by *el Patrón* himself."

What?

My thoughts went to Mia's husband. "Why would Aléjandro kill your husband?"

Her voice was monotone, almost robotic. "Not Aléjandro. Jorge, his father. My husband betrayed the Roríguez cartel."

I couldn't comprehend.

She turned to me. "You say you want more time with Em. Are you praying for him?"

I nodded.

"I used to pray." A tear slid down her cheek. "I thought God was punishing me—for what, I didn't know." She took a ragged breath. "I prayed every day for *no más tiempo*—no more time—with Gerardo." Her timbre changed, becoming stronger. "Every morning, he'd swim laps in our pool. I'd slip into the shower, get down on my knees, and pray that he'd be stricken down. A heart attack or drowning—I didn't care. I even considered poisoning him." Her lips curled upward. "Did you know you can make poison out of crushed cherry pits?"

I shook my head.

She went on. "I didn't know that he was betraying the Roríguez cartel. When Valentina came to tell me that he was gone, I felt the greatest sense of relief. Not Sofia. She cried." Liliana shook her head. "I never shed a tear."

I rubbed her knee with my hand. "I don't know what to say."

"*El Patrón* himself questioned me. I truly didn't know what Gerardo was doing. He let me live." She took a breath. "I enjoy working with the tenants because while I never worked at a place like Wanderland, my parents sold me into hell—a slave to Gerardo's sick, abusive…" She shook her head and took a breath. "My parents didn't think twice, all because *el Patrón* told them to do it." She feigned a smile. "The funny thing is that I've never told any of the tenants that story. And yet, it is as if they know we share an understanding."

"You're amazing with them. I told Mia that the first day I worked."

She lifted her brow. "You told her that?"

"I did. I meant it." I inhaled. "I'm sorry for..."

Liliana shook her head. "Because of Mia, I wasn't made to remarry right away. Allowing me to live alone was unheard of. My parents think I should be back with them or remarried." She turned her attention to the door. "I'm praying too, Izzy. Aléjandro and Mia are good for the cartel. If we lose *el Patrón*, I don't know what will happen to us." She shrugged. "We could go to Herrera. And then what?"

We reached for each other's hand.

I closed my eyes. The words weren't audible, yet they came from my heart. "Please watch over Emiliano, Aléjandro, and everyone who was with them." I remembered what Horace said about casualties. "Please don't let anyone suffer. Bring Emiliano back to me so I can spend the rest of my life showing him how wrong I was before. And please, let Liliana find happiness."

I opened my eyes at the knock and opening of Liliana's door. I sprang to my feet at the sight of Horace. "Have you heard?"

"*Sí.*"

TWENTY-NINE

Emiliano
Earlier: 7:56 pm

The sound of voices was nonexistent, intensifying the rumble of the engine and hum of tires on the streets. Tension permeated from every occupant in the panel van. No doubt, everyone was deep in thought as we traveled toward The Legend. We'd planned our operation down to the second, aiming to get in and out in under seven minutes. That would be a minute faster than the eight Rei gave us. I gritted my teeth as I maneuvered the vehicle through San Diego traffic. Since I'd lived here all my life, Nick or I would be the most experienced drivers. This wasn't the time to be pulled over for some stupid move.

Nick was in the back, his mind set on protecting *el Patrón*. Piero was at my side, riding shotgun. The other seven occupants were in the back, weapons, vests, and helmets in place. While we would all be armed with multiple guns, knives were our weapon of choice—less noise.

Back in Midtown, Sebastián was able to communicate with us through earpieces, but his only visual was through deviated security. In a matter of four minutes, the security guard at the front desk would see earlier recorded video, not what was happening in real time. As soon as we were out of the building, Sebastián would delete any footage of us, replacing it with what the security guard viewed—if he was paying attention at all. The San Diego Chargers were playing their final preseason game against the Saints. Kickoff was at eight p.m. Surely that was more exciting than a luxury building's hallways and doors.

Neither of the security guards in the front of the building should be an issue. If things went as planned, they'd both live to see another day.

It would be Rei's job to enter the shipping dock, take out the first guard, and then call for us to enter. The plan was to go up the service elevator, surprise Volkov's two guards, and enter the condo.

This mission didn't need nine people.

The possibility of us being caught off guard was why we had the extra men. It seemed unlikely that Volkov would feel the need for extra bodyguards while he was fucking his mistress, but we couldn't be too sure. We could be walking into a setup.

"Loading dock cameras are diverted," Sebastián said through our earpieces.

The area near the loading dock had tall lights, brightening the parking lot. My heartbeat pounded in my ears as the lights slowly dimmed, darkening the area. "Fuck yeah," I whispered to Sebastián. Between him and Silas, they knew their way around this technology.

"Eight o'clock," Jano said.

Rei opened the side door. Wearing all black with his military-grade gear, he stayed in the shadows, making his way up the side ramp.

I held my breath as he picked the lock. The door opened. "Under ten seconds," I relayed as Rei disappeared into the loading area.

We all waited until Rei gave the all clear.

The next seven minutes lasted years, or at least they felt that way.

Rei's voice came through the earpieces. "Clear."

We exited the van, moving in tandem. In our black gear, from the air, we'd appear like worker ants following a trail. Once inside, I saw that the guard was dead, his throat slit. We were following the plan.

There wouldn't be a cleanup crew following this mission. The point was to leave clues leading to Makarova. Rei had the service elevator waiting as all nine of us piled in. The grate doors would expose us when we reached the floor of the condo. However, there shouldn't be a guard at the service elevator.

We all held our long guns, pointed at the entrance as we moved higher in the skyline.

A collective gasp filled the air as we were met with no guards or guns.

"*Volara,*" Jano whispered.

"Quiet," I repeated for our Russian friends.

The blueprint of the floor was etched into our brains. With Rei in the lead, we moved stealthily through the back hallways, created for workers to remain invisible. Cracking open the door from the janitor's closet, we had visual of the guard outside Volkov's door. The fucker was looking down at his phone with an earpiece in his ear.

Shouldering my gun, I approached quietly. The Chargers' score was zero to zero as he realized I was there. My eight-inch blade sliced his neck, letting blood spurt from his carotid as he slumped into the chair. Piero hurried past me, on his way to his mission: the guard at the elevator.

I couldn't see what happened, but as soon as Piero returned, we were joined by the other seven.

"I'm going in first," Nick said, looking at *el Patrón*. "He's your kill, but you're not meeting a gun upon entry."

Jano nodded.

Rei picked the lock and a second later, Nick pushed his way in. We scanned from left to right. Luxurious furniture and expensive décor could be found in every room. Music filled the air. There were dishes on the dining room table as if a meal had recently been consumed. Nick led with Jano on his tail. The sweep of the first few rooms had me worried that Volkov had been tipped off.

Nick pushed open the primary bedroom door.

No one.

The bed sheets were tousled, but there was no one.

We all stilled at the sound of voices.

Jano motioned with his head toward what I assumed was the bathroom door. He kicked the door in. Volkov and Leah were submerged in a long bathtub. Leah screamed and dropped her glass of wine. The glass shattered, splattering red wine on the tile floor. Volkov jumped to his feet, his face beet red and his shriveling dick disappearing.

Jano stepped forward. "*Esta noche mueres.*"

Rei turned to Volkov, translating Jano's warning. "Tonight, you die."

Looking confused, Adrian translated the warning again for Volkov in Russian.

Volkov's eyes bulged as he called for his guards.

Jano lowered his gun and unsheathed his long blade. "*Por mí padre.*" He slit Volkov's abdomen from right to the left. Rei pulled the naked woman from the tub by her arm as Volkov's intestines fell to the water. Blood bubbled from his lips as the horror settled in his dark stare. For a split second, Volkov reached for the bloody organs as if to hold them in place. Using the same blade, Jano sliced left to right across Volkov's neck, the realization of his ultimate death prevalent in Volkov's expression. A millisecond later, he crumpled into the tub. The red water sloshed against the white-tile backsplash as his head and one arm dangled over the side.

I stepped back from the growing pool of crimson.

Leah stared at Volkov's open, lifeless eyes as his lips were agape.

Rei held his hand over Leah's mouth. "Your turn."

She shook her head wildly.

He lifted her as she kicked her legs. "Fuck," he cursed as she bit his hand.

"I won't tell. Please don't kill me," she pleaded.

Jano walked toward her. "You won't tell because you will die." He nodded to Rei.

Rei grabbed her hair. "This is for what you did to your daughters." He slit her throat the same as he had done to the guard in the loading dock. As her eyes fluttered, he added, "You have a grandchild coming who you will never see."

She gurgled as he let her go, her head hitting the tile with a thud. Dark red blood pooled around her.

I didn't know what she'd done to her daughters, but the shock and recognition in Leah's eyes as death came for her told me she knew what she'd done.

By the time we left the bloodied bath, Piero and Lorenzo had carried the guards' bodies into the condo, leaving them on the marble floor. We slipped out the same way we entered—through the back hallways, accessible only to staff, and down the service elevator. Nick ran lead as we slowed by the service door.

Had anyone found our van?

Cracking the door, Nick surveyed the loading dock and the parking lot beyond.

At 8:07 p.m. we drove away, relief flooding my circulation.

"Send the soldiers to the abandoned building," Jano said.

Sebastián replied, "*Sí, jefe.*"

"Back to Midtown," Rei said, patting me on the shoulder.

HOURS LATER, the Midtown DC was clean as a whistle. The crates of weapons were hidden, and the technology Sebastián and Rei had brought with them was packed and ready to fly north to Sacramento.

Wanderland had operated without any unusual instances. There were still hours to go before it closed. I called Horace and told him to keep the extra guards vigilant.

The cartel chiefs I'd vouched for carried out the raid at the abandoned building. The hideout would need to wait. After the intel Adrian heard, the abandoned building was our target. If human trafficking was involved, it couldn't wait until Monday, not with the Volkov bratva's leader dead in a tub of blood and human waste. The nine of us waited for word from the chiefs regarding the soldiers' progress.

I received the call a little before midnight. Eight sets of eyes were upon me as I answered the phone.

"*Esta hecho.*"

"It is done," I relayed to the men around me.

"What did they find?" Jano asked.

"*El patrón* is with me," I said. "I'm putting you on speaker. He has questions."

"Did you find Herrera?" Jano asked.

"No, *jefe*. Weapons and ten women. We lost two soldiers. They lost all six that were here."

That would be eight of Volkov's men, his mistress, and the big prize himself.

"Fuck," Jano roared. "I want Herrera." His nostrils flared. "Tell me about the women."

"They're pretty beat up and scared. Doesn't seem as if they've eaten recently."

"Where are the women?" I asked.

"Took them down to the south warehouse. They're getting medical attention, but communication is a problem."

Adrian stepped forward. "Russian?"

"*Sí.*"

I nodded.

"I'll go down," Adrian volunteered. "I'll be able to get their information. Then what do you want done with them?" he asked Jano.

"Their choice. They go back to where they came from, or they make us money at Wanderland."

Adrian looked at Jano, his eyes narrowing. "Could we have a word?"

The two walked away.

"The weapons?" I asked the chief on the phone.

"We confiscated them and brought them down here too."

Adrian and Jano returned.

Jano spoke, "The women can either go back to where they came from or go to work for Andros Ivanov. Adrian had a point. Suddenly having Russian whores at Wanderland would be a beacon to not only the uniforms but also smaller bratvas. Ivanov will take credit for the raid at the abandoned house."

There was something reassuring in a boss who was

willing to listen. I never felt that way around Jorge. That doesn't mean he didn't take advice. We all nodded.

"We're on our way," I told the chief before disconnecting the call.

"No," Jano said, placing his hand on my shoulder. "Go clean up and tell your woman that you have permission."

My lips curled for the first time in hours.

My woman.

"You don't need me down at the warehouse?"

He shook his head. "I'm headed home to blow off some steam and get some sleep. We're halfway to our goal. Get this marriage over with, Em. I need your head in the game."

"Lockdown?" I asked.

Jano nodded. "No change until the dust of tonight settles."

"We just made Herrera weaker."

"We're cornering him." His eyes opened wide. "What is the saying? Scared animals return home, regardless of whether home is safe or frightening."

"You think he'll go back to Mexico?"

"We'll talk tomorrow."

CHAPTER

THIRTY

Isabella

Horace opened the door, and I leapt forward. My body crashed against Em's. I wrapped my arms around his shoulders and buried my face against his chest. The sound of his beating heart and the sensation of his arms holding my body against his calmed my spiked blood pressure. "You're alive," I managed to say through a new shower of tears.

Em cupped my cheeks and brought our lips together. Warmth radiated through my body from my head to my toes. It was the sensation I needed, an addiction I had only begun. Without thinking, I climbed higher, wrapping my legs around his torso and holding on to his broad shoulders. Em's hand went to my behind, holding me in place.

I leaned back, ending our kiss as I palmed his smooth cheeks. "You're alive."

He teased stray strands of hair away from my face. "*Sí*, my love. I am alive."

My heart melted as I stared into his dark brown orbs. "I've been so scared. I love you, Emiliano. Don't leave me."

Horace cleared his throat.

Em's grin quirked as he set me back on my feet. He held tightly to my hand. "Horace, I'm relieving you of your duty to Miss Luciano. You may pick her up Monday morning at *el Patrón's*, unless you're advised of another location." He looked down at the LA Lakers t-shirt. "Where are your clothes?"

"They're in the room where I was supposed to sleep."

"Lieutenant," Horace said. "I must urge you to reconsider. Miss Luciano's family...the famiglia...this is unprecedented."

"I promise you, Horace, I will take care of my fiancée. On Monday, if you pick her up, she will be Señora Ruiz."

My breath caught and my eyes opened wide. "This weekend?"

"Unless you object."

Holy shit.

I quickly shook my head. "I don't object." I squeezed Em's hand. "Come with me to get my clothes. I don't want to let you out of my sight."

He followed me into the tiny bedroom, closed the door and crossed his arms over his wide chest. The fresh scent of his cologne and bodywash filled my senses. His smile grew as his gaze lingered, devouring me inch by inch. "Had you been told we had permission to marry?"

"I found out this afternoon. My mother called."

He quirked an eyebrow. "I imagine that she's thrilled."

"I wouldn't exactly use that word."

"My parents are happy."

"They are?" I asked.

He nodded. "My mom wants me happy and has thought I should have married a long time ago. My father has accepted two of his daughters marrying into the famiglia. He worries less about the alliance than anyone else."

"Why didn't you—marry a long time ago?"

"Because I was waiting for you."

Warmth radiated through my circulation as I gathered my clothes. "Are you taking me to Mia's?"

He reached out.

Leaving the clothes on the bed, I went to him, placing my hands in his.

His deep timbre was slow. "Isabella, tonight was intense."

I nodded.

"I don't want to wait another minute to marry you."

"It's after midnight."

"I spoke with my mother and father when I went home to shower." He grinned. "Yes, I still live with my parents. Once the dangers are calmed, we can get our own house. In the meantime, they're happy to have you live with me in their home."

My eyes blinked as I tried to comprehend. Thoughts

of my conversation with my mother returned. "Your parents will accept me in their home?"

"Of course. What parent wouldn't accept the person their child loves?" He squeezed my hands. "They have one condition. A condition that I'm sure the famiglia would also agree to."

"What is that condition?"

"We must be married by a priest."

Inhaling, I sighed. "I want that too."

"Papá can have a priest to our house tonight. We will have a quick ceremony with his blessing. Then, Sunday, giving your family time to travel, we can have a real ceremony, a full mass. It won't be as big as Jano and Mia's, but it will satisfy the critics, and we'll also have a license by then."

I lifted my hands to his wide chest and peered up at him. "We could be married tonight?"

"With only my parents present. The cartel needs to lie low to see what tomorrow brings."

What tomorrow brings.

My gaze met his. "I want to marry you tonight. If tomorrow brings a day like today, I want to know that we've spent as much time together as we could. I want you to know how much I love you. If carrying that love into battle keeps you safe, I want you to have it."

Cupping my neck, he pulled my lips to his. Fireworks flashed and warmth flooded my circulation, yet the beating drum of my heart wasn't rapid. I wasn't frightened or unsure. In every fiber of my body, I knew this decision was the right decision.

He looked again at my attire and jutted his chin

toward the bed. "You should probably change back into those clothes, unless you want to be married in a Laker's t-shirt."

"You're right." When he didn't move, I shook my head. "We're not married yet." I shooed him with my hand. "Go. Keep guard at the door. I'll be right out."

Without turning, he opened the door, backed out, step by step while his devilish gaze stayed locked on mine. Without saying a word, I felt the heat of his laser stare. He didn't break eye contact until the door was fully closed. My nipples were taut as if the temperature had dropped and there was a twisting between my legs.

I'm getting married.

I'm getting married tonight.

A wave of realization swept over me. My fingers trembled as I buttoned my blouse. However, by the time I slipped my feet into the ballet flats, my onset of the shakes was gone. My heart rate was normal. Taking a deep breath, I opened the door. Em was right there. "Are you ready?"

"More than ready."

I took the clothes I'd worn to bed to Liliana. "Thank you for these. They should stay here for the tenants."

"You won't be in tomorrow?" she asked.

I glanced at Em and back. "I think I'm taking the weekend off."

Liliana grinned. "I hope one day I look as happy as you do right now."

"Keep your calendar open for Sunday." I stepped forward, wrapped her in a hug, and whispered, "One day, you will. I prayed for that too."

As I backed away, I saw the glimmer of hope in Liliana's eyes.

Em took my hand and led me from the apartment.

"Hey?" I asked as we stepped into the quiet hallway. "How did you get to this room?"

"I walked."

"But you're not allowed."

He nodded. "Only in the case of emergencies." He squeezed my hand. "Retrieving my fiancée was an emergency."

I scoffed and laid my head against his arm. "Do you get to determine emergencies?"

"Yeah, that's what lieutenants do."

Once I was seated in his front seat and he was behind the wheel, I asked the question burning in my mind. "Horace said there was a casualty or more than one. Were they from the cartel?"

Em nodded, starting the engine. "There were more casualties in the bratva." He pulled his car out onto the quiet streets.

"Is Volkov dead?"

He again nodded. "We can't talk about anything that happened tonight in front of anyone, even my parents."

"Even your parents?"

His hand came to my thigh. "I'll always be honest with you. Sometimes I might not be able to answer, but I'll never lie. The lieutenants who were not involved will be briefed tomorrow."

"Your father wasn't involved."

Em turned my way.

"One more question." When he didn't respond, I asked, "Who in the cartel was killed? Not *el Patrón*."

"Valuable soldiers. They'll be missed. But *el Patrón*, Nick, and Rei are safe."

A sigh of relief came as I laid my head against the seat. "It's crazy."

"What's crazy?"

"I was worried about all of you. Ten days ago, I barely knew any of you."

Em turned my way with a grin. "It's not crazy. Isabella, you have a pure heart. You're naturally kind. The women in the apartments see that. You're also empathic. I would guess you're worried about more than those of us on the mission."

I nodded. "I'm still worried about the tenants that reported to Wanderland tonight. Have you heard anything?"

"I've heard that it has been business as usual. No incidents."

I dropped my hand over his, the one on my thigh. Em turned his palm up. Our fingers intertwined. "Is tonight what it will be like being your wife. Will I constantly be scared you might not come home?"

"Not constantly. Tonight was unusually dangerous." When he turned my way, I saw a gleam in his eyes. "And when we're married, I'll watch you undress, not wait outside."

My cheeks warmed.

"And we won't have to wait for a priest to take the edge off."

"The edge off?"

"Sex, Isabella. The best way to calm the beast inside of men like me after a dangerous operation is to fuck."

I opened my eyes wide. "Oh, good to know." I looked up, taking in his handsome profile. "I suppose this is a tested theory?"

"I'd be lying if I said no."

Of course he'd been with other women.

Em added, "I guarantee that is what everyone else is doing right now."

A chuckle came from my chest. "Poor Emiliano."

"Don't feel sorry for me. My time is coming" —he winked at me— "and so is yours."

Beneath my bra and blouse, my nipples hardened. "You know I've never…"

"I didn't know, but since yesterday was your first kiss and first date, I kind of guessed." He squeezed my hand. "Trust me, Izzy."

It was the first time he'd used my nickname. My gaze went down to where our hands were linked. "I do."

"That's what you need to tell Father Gallo."

"When is he going to arrive?"

"He's already there."

Em drove us beyond a locked gate. Looking up at the house, I remembered attending Mia's wedding here. As I recalled, similar to Mia's house, the other side of the house was situated high on a cliff overlooking the ocean.

Not once during Mia's wedding had I imagined coming back to this location, and definitely not as Emiliano's intended wife. The clock on the dashboard read nearly one in the morning. "How did your mother get a priest here at this hour?"

"Father Gallo has been on call for the Roríguez cartel for many years. He performed Jano's and Camila's weddings. Now he'll perform ours."

My parents wanted tradition.

This was tradition—just not theirs.

Em parked the car on a large brick driveway. Opening my door, he extended his hand. "Come, Miss Luciano. Forever more, you will be Mrs. Isabella Ruiz."

I stepped out into the cool night air.

THIRTY-ONE

Isabella

Em led me to the front step with his steady hand in the small of my back. The door opened and his mother welcomed me at the front door with tears in her green eyes. She wrapped her arms around me and tugged me into the house. "*Eres un ángel enviado del Cielo.*"

While I couldn't understand her words, her welcoming intent was evident.

"Mama," Em said, "this is Isabella."

"Beautiful name for a beautiful girl. I was afraid Emiliano would never marry." She clasped her hands together. "And tonight, he comes home, and my prayers are answered."

"Isabella," Em said, "my mother, Valentina."

"Nice to meet you, formally." I nibbled on my lower lip. "This is rather sudden."

"Love doesn't live by clocks." She smiled. "You're a good girl. I can see that. For the two of you to wed, you need a priest's blessing."

I nodded. "My parents would agree."

"We will let them know your marriage is blessed. Sunday, if *el Patrón* agrees, we will host a small wedding, so your parents won't miss out."

"If he doesn't agree?" I asked, suddenly worried.

"Then it will be smaller, a full ceremony with a license nevertheless."

I feigned a smile. "Thank you."

"Come," she looped her arm around mine. "Meet Emiliano's father, Andrés, and Father Gallo."

As we approached, moving farther into the house, it seemed as though Em and his father were in an intense discussion.

"Andrés," Valentina said, getting his attention. "Meet Emiliano's soon-to-be wife, Isabella."

Andrés Ruiz dramatically bowed at the waist. When he stood erect, his dark gaze, similar to his son's, met mine. "Isabella, welcome to our family."

"Thank you."

A man with a collar appeared. "Hello, Miss Luciano. I'm Father Gallo. May I speak to you and Emiliano for a few minutes?"

I turned to Em, who nodded.

"Yes," I answered, unsure what this was about.

Em took my hand, and we followed Father Gallo

deeper into their home. When I'd been here for Mia's wedding, the house was decorated and filled with tables and chairs. Without all that clutter, it was stunning. Room after room of opulent décor. As we approached the back room, it extended the width of the first floor with a wall of windows looking out to the pool deck. In an abyss of darkness, the pool water glowed with changing colored lights. Beyond the deck, the sky was black and dotted with a million stars. The sound of crashing waves from the ocean below could be heard through the open glass door.

The large room had a fireplace at one end and multiple groupings of couches and soft chairs. Father Gallo motioned to one grouping.

Em and I sat on one couch and the priest sat on another facing us.

"Is everything all right?" Em asked.

Father Gallo smiled. "Of course. I'm not unaccustomed to being called in the middle of the night to marry members of your family." He sat back. "When Mia called for Camila, I was satisfied with Camila's desire to wed. I'd known Camila since she was young—her first communion—I believe." He brought his stare to me. "Isabella, I don't know you." He turned to Em. "I do know you, Emiliano." Back to me. "Isabella, before we proceed, I'd like to talk about you."

I held tight to Em's hand and replied, "Okay."

"Please reassure me of your faith, your virtue, and your willingness to commit to Emiliano to be his wife."

Inhaling, I sat tall. "Father, my faith is without question. I attended Saint Mary's of the Woods throughout my twelve years of schooling." I lifted Em's hand and looked up at his handsome face. "I love Emiliano. It happened fast, but I believe it was meant to happen." I turned back to Father Gallo. "I want to be his wife, tonight and until forever."

The priest nodded. "Good answers. As the word of God tells us, a virtuous woman is worth more than rubies. The heart of the husband does safely trust in her, so that he shall have no need for spoil. She will do him good and not evil all the days of her life. Are you this woman for Emiliano."

Before I could answer, Em spoke up. "Father, I assume your next question will be about my virtue. I assume you will ask me if I am a virgin, if I've committed any sins..."

Father Gallo sat taller. "I'm doing what is right."

"What is right," Em said, "is to have faith that Isabella and I have had this conversation. If you're so inclined to be told the answer, I suggest that as you say your bedtime prayers, you present the question to God. For he is all knowing."

Father Gallo swallowed and nodded. "Emiliano, what are your intentions regarding Isabella?"

"I love Isabella with all of my heart." His dark brown eyes shone down at me as he grinned. "She's beautiful."

"*Sí*," said the priest.

"But she's much more than that. I can't explain the way she makes me feel. My mother was right. I'd never thought much about marriage. It's different with Isabella. I want to protect her, love her, and make her every wish come true."

Father Gallo stood. "Then I think I have a marriage to perform."

"Will you be doing the ceremony on Sunday afternoon as well?" I asked.

"Yes, unless either of you have an objection."

Em let go of my hand and stood. "I think we've cleared the air."

Father Gallo held his hands together and bowed his head toward me. "I did not mean to offend, Miss Luciano."

"As Em said, the air is cleared."

"The marriage license?" Em enquired.

"I have a contact with the county clerk. The license will have today's date—Saturday. It is tomorrow already."

Valentina and Andrés joined the three of us. "Out on the pool deck?" Valentina said. "It's a beautiful night."

Em furrowed his brow. "Maybe on Sunday. Tonight, we can stand near the open doors."

Valentina didn't question. I suspected his answer was because of all that had happened last night. His mother handed me a bouquet of fresh flowers, their stems wrapped in white ribbon. "They're from my garden. Sunday, you may have whatever you'd like."

Inhaling their sweet scent, I smiled. "Thank you. They're beautiful."

She went to Em and placed something in his hand. When he shook his head, she closed his fingers. "It's symbolic."

"Are we ready?" Father Gallo asked.

Em took my hand, and we turned toward one another.

The priest's voice echoed through the cavernous room. "Isabella Luciano and Emiliano Ruiz, have you come here to enter into marriage without coercion, freely and wholeheartedly?"

I stared up at Em's handsome face.

"Yes," he replied.

My throat tightened. "Yes."

"Are you prepared, as you follow the path of marriage, to love and honor each other as long as you both shall live?"

Em squeezed my hand as we both answered affirmatively.

"Since it is your intention to enter into the covenant of Holy Matrimony, keep your right hands joined and declare your consent before God and His Church."

We repeated Father Gallo's declarations.

Em was first. "I, Emiliano Ruiz, take you, Isabella Luciano, to be my wife. I promise to be faithful to you in good times and in bad, in sickness and in health, to love you, cherish you, and honor you all the days of my life."

Next, it was my turn to commit to the vows.

"I, Isabella Luciano, take you, Emiliano Ruiz, to be my husband. I promise to be faithful to you in good times and in bad, in sickness and in health, to love you, cherish you, and honor you all the days of my life."

I concentrated on the man before me, not on the absence of my family.

Father Gallo spread his arms to his sides. "May the Lord in his kindness strengthen the consent you have declared before these witnesses and graciously bring to fulfillment his blessings within you. What God has joined, let no one put asunder." He turned to Em. "This is the time for the giving and receiving of rings, but that can wait until Sunday."

I looked down. "I'm sorry, I don't have a ring."

"I have one," Em said.

The priest looked at me. "The ring is symbolic. The marriage is still covered by God's blessing."

I nodded and handed the bouquet to Valentina.

Em retrieved from his pocket the band that his mother had given him and reached for my left hand. It may have been the ocean breeze or my ongoing swings in emotion. Whatever the cause, my hand trembled.

I concentrated on Em's calming gaze as he lifted my left hand, gently turned it, and kissed my palm. "Breathe."

It was like the first day at the apartments. I was staring into the same hauntingly beautiful dark brown eyes. I inhaled and exhaled. He turned my hand back over and slid a golden band over my fourth finger. To both of our astonishment, it slid easily over my knuckle and fit almost perfectly.

"Isabella, receive this ring as a sign of my love and fidelity. In the name of the Father, and the Son, and the Holy Spirit."

I held on to his left hand. "Emiliano, I don't have a ring. All I have is me."

His Adam's apple bobbed.

"Receive me, my body and my soul, my future and

my past. I give you all of me as a sign of my love and fidelity. In the name…"

Father Gallo lifted his hands. "In the sight of God and these witnesses, I now pronounce you husband and wife. Emiliano, you may now kiss your bride."

His warm palm cupped my cheek as our lips came together.

"May I be the first to introduce to you, Señor and Señora Ruiz."

"My wife," he whispered.

My heart fluttered within my chest. "My husband."

"Go in peace," Father Gallo said.

Valentina hugged me again. "You and Em decide what you want about wedding rings." She lifted my left hand. This ring belonged to my abuela. When she and my grandfather married, they couldn't afford rings. They made rings out of string. Many years later, my grandfather surprised her with this band. She treasured it all of her life." She touched the band. "The filigree is worn. And inside, in the right light you can see the inscription." Her smile grew. "You will not hurt my feelings if you want Em to get you something new and shiny. I've had it in my jewelry box. I don't ask that you wear it forever, only that you treasure it."

I nodded. "I will. Thank you."

"It's late," she said to both Em and me. "Andrés and I will walk Father Gallo out to his car. We will see you both in the morning."

I looked up at Em.

This was real.

I am Isabella Ruiz.

Emiliano

With Isabella's hand in mine, I led her up the stairs. With each step, her grip of my hand intensified and her breathing shallowed. When we reached the top, I stopped walking and took both of her hands in mine. "You can trust me."

"I do."

"This door is my father's office."

She turned her soft gaze to the door.

"That direction" —I motioned to the left— "is my parents' suite. Tradition states we're supposed to spend our wedding night in their bedroom."

Isabella's eyes opened wider, and her lips parted.

I lifted her knuckles to my lips. "I informed Mom that we wouldn't be following that tradition."

She let out a long breath and color returned to her cheeks. "That would just be weird."

"Since I've lived here as long as I can remember, I agree." I tugged her hand. "Come, let me show you the other wing. I had it all to myself until my parents brought Cat home and then Camila. It seems that my days of having it alone are over."

She chuckled. "The same thing happened to me with Noemi and Tony." She shook her head. "I'm afraid my family won't come for Sunday's ceremony."

What the fuck?

"Of course they'll come."

She leaned against the wall in the hallway and looked up at me. "I told my mother if she and my papà didn't accept you, they'd lose me."

"I'll talk to Dario. After all, he's my brother-in-law. He and Cat and Dante and Camila will come. He'll make sure your family is here too."

Isabella shook her head. "No." She reached her hand to my cheek as her gaze met mine. "I love that you want to make me happy, Em." She dropped her hand. "But I don't want my parents to be forced to attend their daughter's wedding. When my call with Mom ended, I made peace with the possibility of stepping away from them for good." A tear teetered on her eyelid. "It's Noemi and Tony that make me sad. They won't have their own choice. It will be whatever Papà decrees."

I lifted both arms to the wall above her shoulders, caging this gorgeous creature. It wasn't a move to contain her, more of my burning desire to shield her from the unhappiness in the world around us. I kissed her nose. "We are a family now." I kissed her lips. "You and I." I trailed my lips down her slender neck. "Together, we will move mountains." She leaned her head, allowing me to take my kisses lower, over her collarbone. "I love you, Izzy."

Her breathing was labored as her breasts heaved against her blouse.

My low timbre and kisses had goose bumps scattered over her beautiful skin. I reached for her chin. "Tell me what you want."

She looked up, opening her eyes. "I don't know. After yesterday, I want to feel safe and loved."

Isabella shrieked as I swept her into my arms. "You are safe, and you are loved."

She brought her arms around my neck as I opened the door to my bedroom suite. I flipped on the light and set her feet back on the floor. She turned a complete circle, taking in my suite.

A bouquet of flowers sat on the table near the balcony with a bottle of champagne and slender crystal glasses. My quick scan confirmed that my suite appeared cleaner than usual, no clothes strewn around. That meant that Mom had spoken to our house manager, Lola. The linens on the large bed were fresh with the blankets pulled down, revealing black satin sheets.

There wouldn't be discussion of blood like the famiglia did after Cat's wedding.

"This is your room?"

"No. It's now *ours* until we have a home of our own."

She walked from one piece of furniture to the next, running her fingers over the surfaces. Isabella stopped at the glass French doors. "There's a balcony. At Mia's I had a window that looked out to the ocean."

I walked up behind her and opened the door. The salty sea breeze tousled her long locks. We both took a step out onto the concrete. Isabella held tight to the iron railing and lifted her face to the wind.

"I've lived my entire life in Missouri. The ocean fascinates me."

I wrapped my arms around her waist, bringing her back to my front. "You fascinate me."

She spun in my arms. With our proximity, there was no way she couldn't feel the erection pinned beneath my jeans. Isabella lifted her chin and stared upward. "You fascinate me, Em. You're such a contradiction. You're the fierce man who scared me at the birthday party. At the same time, you're gentle and caring."

"Tell me again what you want."

"I want you."

I tugged her into the bedroom, leaving the balcony door open. With the house's placement over the cliff, leaving it open wasn't a danger. Once inside, I removed the holster from my waistband, my boots, and the two ankle holsters, laying the weapons on the table near the flowers.

"Any more?" Isabella asked.

"Earlier I had a shoulder holster, but I didn't put it back on after I showered." I walked to the bed, sat on the edge with my legs spread and motioned with my finger for her to follow.

With only a millisecond of hesitation, she came closer until she was standing between my legs. I tugged her across my lap with her round ass on one leg and her legs over the other. I reached for her shoes, removing them one by one.

This was far from my first sexual encounter—about fifteen years far. However, it was the first encounter with my wife, the first first-encounter that I truly wanted to make perfect. I stroked her gorgeous golden hair away from her beautiful face. "You're mine."

With a smile curling her lips, she nodded. "I am. Forever." She looked down at the ring on her left hand. "This is beautiful." Her eyes came to mine. "What was your mother's grandmother like?"

"I don't know. She passed before I was born."

"Her husband, your great-grandfather?"

I shook my head and lifted her hand. "I heard Mom telling you the story. It sounds like they loved one another their entire lives."

Isabella nodded. "I don't want another wedding ring."

"In case you wondered, money isn't an object."

"I didn't marry you, Emiliano Ruiz, for your money. I married you because of the way you make me feel."

"Fuck, Isabella, I want to make you feel right now. I also don't want to frighten you or turn you against sex. I'm like a man walking the plank right now. I don't know if I should jump in or if I should walk slowly backward onto the ship."

She angled her face, bringing her lips to mine. There was nothing timid in her approach as her soft palm came to my cheek and her tongue prompted my lips to open.

Fuck.

This woman in my arms tasted like springtime, the first clear day after rain. She was sunshine after a long winter. Such as that ray of sun, her lips scorched mine as our hunger for one another grew. The sweet scent of her cum filled my senses as she squirmed in my lap and our kiss deepened. Soft moans filled the air. The closeness of her soft body caused my blood to change circulation.

Shifting, she wrapped her legs around my waist, bringing her covered pussy over my hardening cock. Our faces moved and turned. Our noses bumped as we filled the suite with the sounds of lovers through the centuries. It was when she began to rub her pussy over my erection that I lifted her and moved her until her head was on the pillow and I was leaning over her.

Her large suede stare was questioning. "Did I do something wrong?"

"Fuck no," I said, kissing her lips. "You surprised me was all."

Isabella brought her hands up to my shoulders and rubbed them over my arms. "I won't break, Em. I'm young and inexperienced, but I know what sex is. I know I like it when you kiss me. I love it when you touch me." She rubbed her palms up and down my bare arms. "I want to touch you too. I want to know what it means to be yours."

If I didn't move fast, I'd fucking come in my blue jeans.

I inhaled and began with the top button of her blouse. "I will make you feel. I want to see my wife." My smile quirked. "What she hid from me earlier tonight."

Her smile grew. "We weren't married yet."

Another button and I saw the white lace of her bra. I leaned down, covering her collarbone and between her breasts with kisses. Another button and another. I tugged the hem of her shirt out from her slacks.

Isabella twisted, helping me remove her blouse. With skill that comes with practice, I unsnapped her bra. Again, she wiggled as I prized the straps from one arm and then the other.

My cock doubled in size as I took in her pert tits. The olive of her complexion accentuated the deep red of her areolas and her nipples stood erect, perfect tight buds. I leaned down, sucking one nipple and then the other. Isabella's back arched as she called out.

"Oh God, Em."

My lips moved lower, down the flat plane of her stomach.

It was as I reached for the button to unfasten her slacks that she reached for my hand. Our gazes met. While I expected fright, in the depths of her irises, I found an unabashed twinkle. "Mrs. Ruiz?"

"Take off your shirt. I want to see all of your tattoo."

Standing, I pulled my t-shirt from my back and lifted it over my head.

Her pink tongue darted to her lips.

"I hope you like what you see."

THIRTY-THREE

Isabella

L*ike?*

I sat up, lost in the sculptured contour of Em's abdomen. Moving to my knees, I ran the pads of my fingers over his toned, muscular torso. His tawny skin was marred by various scars, appearing silver against his flesh. I leaned forward, bringing my lips and a kiss to each one.

"Fuck, Isabella."

My attention went to the snake. While I'd only seen its tail, I could now follow the creature wrapped around Em's arm over his muscular bicep and over his shoulder. The face on the front of his pectoral muscles had beady, dark black eyes. Its mouth was open, fangs visible, and tongue striking. My gaze met Em's. "That seems more dangerous than rebirth."

He lifted my chin. "To be reborn, you must die. It's dangerous."

"Don't die, Em." Despite the menacing tattoo, I leaned forward and licked the fangs and tongue. When I looked up at Em, I grinned. "I've tasted the venom. I'm now immune."

He reached for my chin. "I'm jumping into the ocean. If you don't want that, tell me now."

I reached for the button on my slacks and unfastened it before lowering the zipper. As I shimmied out of my slacks, I watched in fascination as Em unbuttoned his blue jeans. The sound of his zipper lowering caused my breath to hitch.

However, it was the sight of his hips and the way his torso slimmed into a V that caused me to forget to take the next breath. A trail of dark hair led below the band of his boxer briefs that contained what romance books had told me was a penis—considering the size of the bulge beneath the silk, a very large penis.

My slacks, his blue jeans, and most of our clothing found its way to the floor below. Without thought, I nibbled on my lower lip. Em's smile turned devilish as his gaze zeroed in on my lower lip.

"I told you what I would do if you continued to bite that lip."

Before I could respond, he came toward me, pushing me against the soft mattress, and I yelped.

"You bit me."

His dark gaze shimmered. "I did. That lip tastes pretty good. I wonder how the rest of you tastes."

My mind and body disconnected in some sort of out-of-body experience as Em moved his lips down my body. A nip here and a kiss there. The sensations were too many and too unfamiliar. Pleasure grew like the increasing pressure beneath a volcano. Words were uttered and others shouted as I gave in to the control Em had taken of my body.

By the time he looped his long fingers under the waistband of my panties, my mind was melted goo. As he brought his mouth to my core, the pressure exceeded anything I'd ever felt. Like the volcano, I erupted. Nerve endings sparked throughout my nervous system. I dug my fingernails into the satin sheets as my body shuddered and moisture filled my core.

Thoughts weren't processing as every touch was magnified. The lightest kiss was electrified. I lifted my head, wondering why we'd left the lights on. As my properly trained mind tried to tell me this was wrong—too intimate—I became engrossed at the sight of my husband lapping at my core. From my angle, I could only see his jet-black hair. The sensations and sounds filled the blanks in my imagination.

As the pressure returned, I reached for his face, pulling him toward me. "Em, take me."

His brown eyes turned black with desire as his lips captured mine. I realized the new taste on his tongue was me. It was different, but not in a bad way. Our tongues danced as he shimmied out of his boxer briefs.

For a second, I froze at the length of the hardened cock against my stomach.

With his elbows on each side of my face, Em kissed my nose. "Look at me, Isabella."

I brought my gaze to his.

"Do you want to see my cock? Do you want to touch it?"

I shook my head. "I mean, I do. But not right now. If I see it, I'm afraid I'll worry it won't fit."

His smile lifted his cheeks. "It will fit."

"Okay." Lifting my knees, I braced myself.

Em's thumb came to my cheek, rubbing and caressing. He stared deep into my eyes. "Breathe, beautiful."

I inhaled as his instructions reminded me of that first day at the apartments.

"Keep breathing."

A whimper escaped me as my core constricted at the invasion. My body stiffened.

"Do you want to stop?" Em asked.

I shook my head. I didn't want him to stop. I wanted it to be over.

"I love you, Izzy. I want this to be good between us." He pushed deeper and resumed the caressing of my cheek. "I'm so damn lucky that you came to San Diego. You're the woman I've waited for. I didn't even know I was waiting, but I was."

I gasped as he pushed deeper.

His soothing, comforting words never stopped. "I want to spend the rest of my life showing you how much I love you."

He pushed deeper and this time a sharp pain radiated through my body. I turned my head, unsuccessfully muffling a scream. A tear floated down my cheek.

"Isabella."

"I should have asked questions of the tenants. How do they do this every night?"

His wide chest vibrated with laughter. "That was the worst of it. I promise."

I wanted to believe him. He promised not to lie.

We lay still for a minute. As I relaxed, my core found a way to accommodate the massive cock inside me. In reality, I had no way of knowing if Em's penis was big or not. I had no comparison, but from my viewpoint, I imagined something giant.

Finally, I nodded. "I'm better."

Slowly he began pistoning his hips. His cock moved in and out, in and out. I lifted my hands to his shoulders, feeling the indentations of his muscles. I focused on his breathing. As his breaths came faster, his hips increased in speed. With my eyes open, I watched as his handsome face contorted, he stretched his neck, and a beastly roar filled the room. One. Two. Three more deep penetrations and his hard body fell over me.

Within my core, his penis continued to throb.

Em lifted his face, taking in my expression. "Are you all right?"

I nodded.

"Talk to me."

"The first part was amazing. I've never felt anything like that, like my body was being wound up."

He rolled, disconnecting us.

Moisture spilled between my legs.

Em had his head lifted on his fist with his elbow near my face. "The second part?"

I pressed my lips together. "I want to lie."

His lips curled. "We don't lie."

"If I tell you the truth, you'll think I don't want to do this—have sex. I do want to."

"But...?"

"It hurt."

"It will get better."

"If it didn't, I don't care how much money I made, I could never do what they do."

Em's laugh filled the room. "You're never going to do what they do. There's only one man's cock who will ever be in that tight, perfect pussy, and that man is me." He kissed my lips. "I'll be right back."

Back?

Where is he going?

I pulled myself up, sitting with my back against his headboard. As my muscles protested, I pulled the sheets over my breasts and looked around his bedroom. I'd been too nervous to take in my surroundings when we first entered. It was a nice-sized room, bigger than the one I had at Mia's and maybe bigger than my one at home.

A smile came to my lips. *This is now my home.*

My lip disappeared beneath my teeth at the sight of my new husband walking from the bathroom, completely nude. My focus went to the appendage bobbing from his pelvis. "That was inside me?"

"Yes, my love."

His endearment made me smile as I moved my eyes to his. It was then that I noticed he was carrying a washcloth.

"Let me help you."

"Help me?"

"Clean you. This washcloth is warm. It will help."

I lifted my hand. "I mean, I can do it." It was one thing that we'd just had sex. But to clean me...?

His tone dropped an octave. "It's my job to take care of you."

Again, I tugged on my lip.

"What did I say about that sexy, plump lip?"

My cheeks rose as I released my lip. "Seriously, Em. That" —I looked at the washcloth— "seems...intimate."

More laughter. "That first part that you liked?"

I nodded.

"I had my face buried in your pussy. When you came, you gushed the sweetest cum until it was dripping down my chin."

I lifted my arm over my eyes. "I'm embarrassed."

Em moved my arm. "Never be embarrassed for the way your body reacts to me. My body has been reacting to you since the first day at the apartments."

"Really?"

He nodded.

Acquiescing, I lowered the satin sheet. To my horror, my inner thighs were red with the combination of blood and semen. "That's normal." I met his eyes. "Right?"

"It is. But tomorrow morning, no one will be talking about the blood on our sheets. That's why I requested Lola put black sheets on the bed."

The warm washcloth did feel comforting.

When Em was satisfied with his work, he took the washcloth back into the bathroom. Entering the bedroom, he turned off the lights and climbed back under the sheets. Rolling toward one another, our noses touched. "I love you, Isabella Ruiz. You're mine to have and to hold forever."

I nodded. "I love you, too. Will you hold me now?"

He moved his arm around me as I curled next to his warm body. "Forever."

It was the last thing I remembered as I drifted to sleep."

THIRTY-FOUR

Emiliano

Men in the cartel didn't take women home to spend the night. That wasn't only because I lived with my parents and my father was a lieutenant. It was because truly no one could be trusted. As I woke to sunlight streaming through the open curtains and the glass doors opened, a primitive and unexpected feeling filled my chest.

It was trust.

Pure, unadulterated trust.

Isabella trusted me, and I trusted her.

As I turned to my side, Isabella's beautiful face was inches away, her eyes closed, golden hair a tangled mess over the pillow, and her lips slightly parted. For a moment, I simply stared in awe that she was mine. Memories of the night before flooded my thoughts.

There was no question that the timid girl back at the capo's was no longer a caterpillar. She was a beautiful butterfly, no longer caught in her cocoon. While I'd watched Isabella spread her wings at the apartments, I didn't know what to expect on our wedding night. I'd heard stories of couples who didn't consummate their marriage until further down the road. If my wife had asked for us to wait, I would have complied. I might be a monster when it came to running our streets and dealing with our enemies, but I wasn't and never would be with the woman I wanted at my side for the rest of my life.

Not only did my wife willingly participate, but she also initiated. The idea of spending fifty more years with her in my bed brought a smile to my face.

Battling with myself about whether to wake her or not, I gently teased strands of her hair from her cheek. Her long eyelashes fluttered, yet she didn't move.

A check of the clock told me it was nearly seven thirty, Saturday morning. That was much later than I usually slept. No doubt, Jano would want to meet soon with the lieutenants. Hopefully, everyone had a late night—taking the edge off.

Isabella and I hadn't closed our eyes until after two. I leaned closer, hearing her even breathing and gently kissed her cheek. Again, she didn't move. If it wasn't for seeing her eyelashes flutter and hearing her breathing, I might panic.

Quietly, I eased out of bed.

Walking nude to the glass doors, I closed them and shut the curtains, giving Isabella darkness to continue her slumber.

Once in the bathroom, I closed the door. The bloody washcloth on the vanity satisfied an animalistic need in me. I hadn't set out to marry a virgin, but now that I had, I couldn't deny the knowledge that no other man had ever been near her moist pink pussy satisfied me. My fingers were the first. My tongue was the first, and my cock will be the last. As I ran the cloth under warm water, rinsing away the blood, I recalled Father Gallo's question.

Fuck him for asking Isabella and not asking me. Her virginity wasn't what she pledged to me, although she had given it to me. She pledged her complete self. That was what I wanted—all of her.

After a quick shower, I entered the bedroom. My wife was still sleeping in the exact position she was when I woke. Going into the closet, I scanned the clothes racks. I would need to move my things around to make room for Isabella's things. Dressing in clean jeans and a different black t-shirt, I picked up my socks and shoes.

While I hated to leave with Isabella asleep, I also couldn't bring myself to wake her. The flowers on the table caught my eye. I found a piece of paper in my desk and wrote a note. Plucking a yellow and white daisy from the bouquet, I left the flower and note on my pillow before stealthily making my way out of the bedroom, closing the door behind me.

In the kitchen, I poured myself a cup of coffee and turned to the stares of both Mom and Lola. Mom's eyebrow quirked, and Lola smiled. "Good morning."

"Good morning," Mom said. "How is Isabella?"

"She's asleep."

"Did everything go well?"

I shook my head. "Not a conversation I'm having with my mom." I had a thought. "Are there any of Cat's or Camila's clothes still here?"

"*Sí*," Lola said. "There were things Camila didn't want anymore. I was supposed to donate them." She turned to Mom. "*Lo siento*. I haven't."

"No, that's a good thing," I said.

Both women looked at me. "Isabella came here last night with literally only the clothes on her back. Could you take her a few things" —I shook my head— "I don't know. Whatever women need. Later today, she can retrieve her belongings from *el Patrón's* home. And we can send for her things from Kansas City. Fuck, she can buy a whole new wardrobe. I don't give a shit."

"Emiliano," Mom scolded.

I pressed my lips together. "She just needs something for this morning."

"Do you have a minute?" Lola asked me.

"I need to get to Jano's. A minute for what?"

She hurried toward the back staircase. "Come with me. I know there are some items your wife might want. You could take them to her now so we're not disturbing her."

My wife.

Leaving my coffee, I followed Lola up the back stairs past the door to Isabella's and my room and into what used to be Camila's room.

Lola first went to the dresser. "I only saw your wife from a distance last night."

"Oh, I'm sorry. You should have joined us."

Lola shook her head. "It was family."

"On Sunday, you'll be a guest."

Pink filled her cheeks. "*Gracias*, Emiliano." She opened the top drawer of the dresser and removed a pair of my sister's panties and a bra.

"Whoa." I lifted my hands and turned.

"Señor Emiliano, you are a husband. Husbands know about things like their wives' underclothes."

"But those aren't Isabella's. They're Camila's."

Lola nodded her chin. "Once you give them to Señora Isabella, they'll be hers."

I inhaled. "You're right, Lola, as usual."

Opening Camila's closet, she came out with a soft long robe and slippers. She also had a sundress and sandals.

"I've never seen her wear a dress." And then I remembered. "Oh, she did have a dress on at the birthday party."

"You take these to her, so she'll find them when she wakes. Once she comes downstairs, I'll offer her anything else she would like from Camila's things. If your sister wanted these things, they would be in Missouri."

"Thank you, Lola."

I took the items and headed across the hallway. Turning the doorknob, I opened the door quietly. To my surprise, the bed was empty. Laying the clothes on the bed, I looked out on the balcony. It was also empty. That was when I heard the water from the shower running.

The bathroom door was closed.

A flimsy doorhandle lock wouldn't keep me out.

Then again, if she wanted privacy, kicking in the bathroom door wasn't a wise move. I debated before trying to turn the knob. To my relief, it turned. I pushed the door inward.

Steam floated out of the glass enclosure. Through the foggy panes, I stared at the sexy silhouette of my wife. Isabella was stunning—a goddess. She tipped her face up to the spray allowing it to saturate her long golden hair. I reached for the glass door and opened it a little.

Isabella startled, jumped, and covered her breasts.

"Too late," I said with a grin. "I've already seen them, licked them, sucked them, and even bitten them."

She shook her head. "You scared me. I thought you were gone."

My gaze scanned from her painted toenails, up her shapely legs, to the V between her legs, covered by a small patch of golden curls, up the hollows of her stomach, and the roundness of her breasts. By the time I was looking into her milk-chocolate gaze, my cock had doubled in size. "It's taking all of my fucking willpower for me to not step into this shower and run my soapy hands over every inch of that gorgeous body."

Isabella ran liquid soap over a loofah and wiped it over her breasts. "Like this."

"Fuck."

I kicked off my boots and threw my wallet, keys, and phone on the vanity.

Isabella giggled as I stepped under the spray wearing the rest of my clothes. "You're crazy."

"Crazy for you." I put out my hand. "Give me that loofah."

"Don't you need to go to work?"

The water soaked my hair, plastered my t-shirt to my chest and added another ten pounds to my jeans. I pressed my lips together and shook my head. "Be a good girl and give me the loofah, and tonight, I'll let you come again, with my mouth."

"You'll let me?"

I nodded.

With suspicious eyes, she handed me the loofah.

I added more soap. "Turn around."

"Em."

My timbre slowed. "Turn around."

She did.

"Put your hands on the wall." When she didn't move, I lowered my face to the crook of her neck and kissed her sensitive skin. "Good girls get to come."

Her nipples beaded as she obeyed.

I glided the soapy sponge over her shoulders, down her back, and over her sexy round ass. Then I reached around, washing her arms, breasts, and down to her pussy. "Are you sore?"

Isabella nodded.

"Let me know when you're not. Because right now, my cock wants out of these jeans."

She craned her neck and flashed me a smile. "Maybe tonight."

"No rush, my love." Using my soapy fingers, I gently massaged her clit. Isabella's lips opened, and her forehead fell against the tile as moans and whimpers filled the stall. Her body quivered as she laid her head back against my chest. With one arm around her waist, I kept her from falling as she bounced with my touch. While I was careful not to penetrate, I didn't stop until Isabella called my name and shuddered in my grasp. She looked up at me and smiled. "I must be a good girl."

"You're very good."

"I feel like a ragdoll."

I kissed her hair. "Sorry?"

Isabella shook her head. "I like it."

I helped her to the corner bench. As she sat, I gently added shampoo to her long hair. Removing the detachable showerhead, I rinsed as the suds flowed down her perfect body and down to the drain.

"Conditioner?"

I shook my head. "Sorry, that's not something I use. Make a list and we'll get whatever you want."

"My things are at Mia's."

I turned off the water and unbuttoned my jeans.

Isabella's eyes opened wide.

"No, Izzy. You're not ready for more fucking. I don't want to get the bathroom wet." She watched as I stripped out of my clothes. Despite my mind knowing she wasn't ready for more, my dick was ready to go. And the look of desire in her eyes as she fixated on my bobbing cock wasn't calming the beast.

Once out of the shower, I wrapped a towel around my waist and began drying my wife from her beautiful face down to her toes.

"You do know I can wash and dry myself."

I lowered my lips to hers. "My job to take care of you, remember." We kissed. Once we separated, I lifted my phone. It was now almost nine, and I had two messages and a missed call from Jano. "Fuck. I do need to go."

"Don't tell *el Patrón* that it's my fault you're late."

"It was your fault." I kissed her again. "But I'll take the blame." I remembered why I'd returned to the bedroom. "We will get your things from Jano's today. In the meantime, Lola found some things Camila left here." I shrugged. "If you want clean clothes."

Isabella sighed. "Oh, I do. Lola?"

"Our house manager. My father is probably already where I am supposed to be. It's just Mom, Lola, and Miguel downstairs. They'll take good care of you."

"Miguel?"

"Mom's bodyguard. He won't bother you."

Her expression radiated happiness and contentment in a way I'd never seen before. "I'll be fine. I'm home."

"I fucking love you."

Isabella blew me a kiss as I grabbed my things from the vanity, walked out of the bathroom, and entered the closet to dress for the second time today.

THIRTY-FIVE

Isabella

My investigation of Em's bathroom discovered more things lacking than present. Some crucial items were MIA:

Blow dryer.

Curling iron.

Makeup of any kind.

Luckily, I had mascara and lip balm in my purse.

I couldn't make myself wear someone else's panties. I also didn't want to wear the ones from yesterday, the ones lost somewhere to the floor. Pushing my own boundaries a little more, I chose to go commando. After I slipped on the bright green sundress and plaited my hair into a braid that fell forward on my shoulder, I tried on the sandals. While I could squeeze my feet into them, they weren't comfortable. Instead, I found my flats.

As I was about to leave the bedroom, I looked at the bed.

A few minutes later, I made my way down the back stairs to what I hoped was the kitchen, with the balled-up set of sheets in my arms.

"Isabella," a woman I didn't recognize said as I reached the first floor. "*Qué estás buscando?*"

I lowered the wad of black sheets and peered at her over the top. "Hi, you must be Lola."

Her brow furrowed. "*Sí*, let me take those."

Pivoting, I blocked her reach. "Um, it's okay. I was wondering where the laundry room was located. I can put them in the washer."

"No. No." She pulled them from my arms. "You don't do your own laundry here."

Warmth tingled my cheeks. "It's that...you shouldn't have to...they're..."

Her stern expression melted into an understanding smile. "I've washed many sheets after a wedding night. Don't be embarrassed."

I lifted my palms to my cheeks. "I am."

"No, Mrs. Isabella. You're now a Ruiz. I'll take care of everything." She walked away with the sheets as I tried to make sense of my life. I scanned my new surroundings. This was the first time I'd been in the kitchen, and by the sound of my rumbling stomach, it had been a while since I'd eaten. The room was large and stylish. In the center was a large island with a sink on one side and a counter with multiple stools on the other.

Lola returned from the secret laundry room with a

satisfied smile. "What can I get you for breakfast? Coffee?"

"No coffee, but juice would be good." I laid my hand over my stomach. "I don't think I ate much dinner last night." I'd been too nervous about Em's mission.

"Tell me what I can make you."

"Toast and fruit would be great."

As I sat on one of the tall stools at the big island, Lola went to work. She talked the entire time. My guess was that it was a ploy to distract me because she created a feast of more than I'd requested. By the time she was finished, I not only had a bowl of fruit but also a plate with eggs, bacon, and toast. I also had glasses of orange juice and water. The water was the first to go. Apparently, I was thirsty too.

My stomach wasn't upset about the amount of food—on the contrary. I was famished.

Valentina entered as I took the last bite of the sourdough toast drowning in butter, dressed as if she had plans. "Good morning."

I swallowed. "Good morning."

She scanned my dress. "You look pretty in Camila's dress."

"Um, thank you. I have clothes at Mia's house."

"We'll send for your things later today. When you're done eating, Miguel is going to drive us to a bridal boutique in Del Mar. Catalina and I looked there for her wedding dress. They had some beautiful off-the-rack dresses."

I blinked. "We're going to get a wedding dress?"

"Of course. If we had more time, we could have one

made. But with the ceremony tomorrow, I'm afraid we'll have to see what we can find. I called *Satin Serenade* and spoke with the owner. She's thrilled to fit you in. The earlier the better as they will most likely also need to make some alterations."

Satin Serenade in Del Mar.

I took a deep breath. "Did *el Patrón* lift the lockdown?"

Valentina waved her hand at me. "Miguel will be with us. It's a private boutique, by appointment only."

"I don't need a bridal gown. I'm already married."

Valentina sighed. "This is your choice, but if you don't mind some advice from an old lady…?"

"You're not old."

"An older lady."

I nodded.

She sat at the tall stool at my side. "Weddings are for a lot of reasons. The couple is far down the list. After last night, you and Em are wed. Father Gallo said he'd bring the license over today. Tomorrow's ceremony is about the Luciano famiglia and the Roríguez cartel." She shook her head. "I know about both families because both of my daughters now have Luciano as their last name. I've become familiar with your famiglia. Weddings bring two families together. I spoke to Mia who spoke to your mother." She smiled. "Your family will be here tomorrow. A wedding gown will help your parents understand that you are a married woman."

My mind was stuck on the fact that my family was coming. "My parents and siblings are coming?"

"And others, I believe."

"Okay. Who else will be here?"

"As many as *el Patrón* will allow." She winked. "We have Mia on our side, so don't worry." She tapped the counter of the island. "Let me know when you're done eating and we'll go."

After finishing the breakfast, I made my way up to our bedroom. The bed I stripped was made. I flipped back the blankets and smiled at another set of black sheets. In the bathroom, Em's clothes that he'd left in the shower were gone. Fresh towels replaced the ones we'd used. As I turned to the vanity and opened the medicine cabinet, I thought about the toothbrush I left at the apartments.

Running my tongue over my teeth, I decided that after what Em and I did last night, using his toothbrush wasn't as weird as it sounded. As I rinsed, my phone rang. The name on the screen read *Your Husband*.

I smiled, wondering when he'd changed his name.

I answered, "Hi, husband."

"Hey, wife. I'm over at Jano's. Mia is collecting your things. She also mentioned you were going dress shopping with Mom."

"It was news to me too."

"Lockdown."

"I told her. She said that bodyguard you mentioned named Miguel would be with us."

Em paused. "There is too much happening to argue with Mom."

My forehead creased with concern. "What's happening?"

He lowered his voice. "No secrets, just not a good time."

My lip disappeared behind my teeth. "I understand."

"I'm not taking any chances. Horace is on his way to the house. Don't leave until you have both bodyguards with you."

"Is the dust settling?"

He sighed. "Some."

"Your mom said my family is coming for tomorrow. Will *el Patrón* allow us to have the ceremony?"

"No matter what happens, we're married."

"It seems silly to get a dress."

"You deserve a real ceremony. Just don't leave the house until Horace is with you."

"*Sí, jefe.*"

Em lowered his voice. "You know what that does to me?"

Memories of last night flashed through my mind. "Now I do."

"Stay safe."

"You, too," I said. "I love you."

The call disconnected.

I experimented with different routes to and from the first level, trying to learn my way around this giant house. It wasn't quite as huge as Aunt Arianna's in the Ozarks, but it was close. Walking down the front staircase, I watched as a man opened the front door. Horace entered. "Horace," I called.

He looked up. "Miss Izzy." He bowed his head. "*Mrs. Izzy.*"

"That's me."

His smile widened. "It's very good to see you today. You look…"

What is he going to say…fucked?

"You look happy."

I made it to the bottom of the stairs and walked toward my bodyguard. "I am."

He lifted a brow. "I hear we're wedding dress shopping. I also heard there was already a wedding."

"You seem to be in on all the gossip. There was a wedding, but tomorrow is the full ceremony."

"Very well."

The man who opened the door returned. "Señora Ruiz, I am Miguel."

I nodded. "Miguel, I am Isabella or Izzy."

He grinned. "Señora Valentina is ready to go."

I looked at Horace. "Let's go shopping."

THIRTY-SIX

Emiliano

Jano sat behind his desk with Rei and Silas at his side. The rest of the men in the office were the famiglia men on the mission; Adrian, Andros Ivanov's second-in-command; and our local lieutenants. My father and my uncle were among most lieutenants hearing about last night's operation for the first time. While there was an undertone of grumbling, most likely because they weren't notified earlier, the news of Volkov's demise was met with cheers.

The local police had Dmitri Makarova in custody. His mug shot was making international news. Homeland Security was taking over the case. The preliminary investigation found surveillance footage from The Legend, showing Dmitri going into Volkov's condo earlier Friday morning. The authorities suspect that someone altered the footage. Their report shows that the next ten hours were replaced by footage from a few days earlier. The cameras didn't record live again until after 8:15 p.m. There were experts working to recover the missing data.

"It won't be recovered," Rei said. "Catching Dmitri on tape was too good to pass up. Sebastián and I made sure that the other footage is gone. They only use in-house storage, no cloud. We were able to scramble their data in a way that would be impossible to recover."

While the Volkov bratva was listed by Homeland Security as a known terrorist organization, the investigators believe this double homicide was not the result of the recent turf wars between bratvas but instead the result of a jealous husband. The investigation is ongoing.

Other outlets were reporting from Kozlov's home in Hidden Hills and Volkov's home in La Jolla. Yachts and cars. It was the same ploy—to expose their extreme wealth bought with the sale of ill-gotten goods.

"The people," Jano said, "following the news want to sleep at night. They want to reason that organizations such as ours don't exist. The bratvas and famiglias are a thing of fiction. If a simple story like an affair can ease their concerns about safety in the streets, they will latch on to it like a baby to a tit. They don't give a fuck if it's real or not."

"What about their hideout?" I asked, "Volkov's."

"We're monitoring it," Silas said. "Not surprisingly, his men are lying low."

"I'll give them a choice," Adrian said. "They swear an oath to Ivanov, or they die."

Andros Ivanov was getting most of the power from

this operation. The good news was that he was now part of our growing alliance. *El Patrón*, the capo, and Ivanov would work out the arrangements. The most important factor was that each entity would operate within their boundaries, be those merchandise, crews, or territories. Together we were stronger.

I spoke, saying what I'd been told to say. "After the successful operation with Volkov, a select few of our chiefs and soldiers carried out a raid on an abandoned building in Barrio Logan."

My father's jaw clenched. This was part of his territory.

"The intel came in late yesterday," I said. "Adrian heard chatter. It was how we first learned of Volkov's location. He visited the building. We hoped we might find Herrera. To be honest, there was a chance it could have been a setup. It wasn't.

"As you know, Herrera wasn't there but on Volkov's yacht. We found a large shipment of weapons and ten women."

Adrian continued, "Your soldiers took the women to the warehouse south of here. I went down there to speak to them and gave them the choice to go back to where they came from or to travel to Detroit and work for Ivanov."

Uncle Nicolas shook his head. "Jano, we could make a fortune with Russian women at Wanderland. It sounds like Ivanov is getting away with more than we are."

Jano stood. "*El Patrón*."

Red seeped upward from Nicolas's neck. "*El Patrón*."

"I considered Wanderland. I decided to send them where they could communicate."

"You don't need to talk to spread your legs."

Jano quirked his brow. "My decision is made. It will not be discussed further." He sat back in his chair as silence prevailed and my uncle steamed. "This afternoon," Jano said, "we will meet at the big warehouse and tell our soldiers our version of what you've learned today." He looked at Adrian and back to us. "The alliance with Ivanov is too young to make common knowledge." He looked at Piero and Lorenzo. "Currently, this was an operation between our cartel and the Luciano famiglia."

They nodded.

"We're not done," *el Patrón* continued. "We're not done until Elizondro Herrera rots in hell."

Rei spoke. "This news doesn't leave this room. *Sí?*"

"*Sí*," came from around the office.

"We have intel that Herrera fled early this morning from a yacht registered to an LLC that can be traced to Volkov. He must have gotten word of Volkov's death. Soon that boat will be viral on social media. The boat was roughly twenty miles off the shore of Baja California."

He had our attention.

"Helicopter?" my father asked.

"No, speedboat." Rei shook his head. "The boat took him to Isla San Martin. It's fucking crowded with tourists, cruise ships, and rich assholes. We have two men on the ground. If he's there, they'll find him. If he left, they'll find where he went."

"When they find him, they bring him to me," *el*

Patrón said. "Or I'll fucking go to him. He's going to die by my hand."

"No word about Herrera," Rei said, "to the soldiers. We haven't been this close in a long time. We can't risk a leak."

I thought back to Cat and Dario's wedding. "We should have gutted him at Cat's wedding."

Jano grinned. "Hindsight." He turned to the room of men. "*Váyanse.* Do your jobs, spread the word. Everyone who isn't essential where they are will be at the warehouse at four." He looked at Nick and me. "*Ustedes se quedan.*"

We hung back as did Adrian and the others who took part in last night's mission.

Silas closed the office door and walked the others out to their cars.

Jano leaned back and looked at Nick. "*Su fucking padre.*" His jaw clenched.

Nick inhaled. "He sees the Roríguez cartel first and only."

Jano slammed his palm on the desk. "I see our cartel first *Only* is a mistake. Without Adrian and Kozlov's men, we wouldn't have found Volkov. Without Piero and Lorenzo, we might not have pulled off last night's operation. The bratva's and famiglia's assistance deserves to be rewarded."

Nick nodded. "I totally agree, *el Patrón.*"

Inhaling, Jano leaned back and looked at his brother. "Dmitri." He laughed. "Fucking perfect."

"Lockdown?" I asked.

Jano ran his hand through his hair. "We give this one more week. If it doesn't turn on us, it will be over."

"My wedding?"

He arched his eyebrows. "I thought you were married. No doubt why you were late."

"I am married. My mother is planning a ceremony tomorrow." I cocked my head. "Fuck, did you not approve that?"

Jano smiled. "Fucking with you, Em. Mia filled me in." He sat forward and rephrased. "She asked for approval. It will be good to see the capo in person. We have much to discuss."

I exhaled. "How big will you allow Mom to go?"

"Family." He shook his head. "No fucking mariachi band. The wedding and food. I don't want to create a target in case Volkov's men plan an attack."

"We'll have them contained by then," Adrian said.

THIRTY-SEVEN

Isabella

Although it felt wrong to shop for a wedding dress without my mother, I was a little excited. I'd told Mia the truth when I said I never dreamt of a big wedding. Valentina warned me that this wouldn't be as big as Mia and *el Patrón*'s. She also promised me that she and Mia would do their best to make it special.

As the different associates from the boutique brought us an array of dresses, that small part of me who had possibly dreamed of a white dress took over. When I saw the dress with cap sleeves with the floral embroidery and shimmering embellishments that flowed over the bodice and tulle skirt, I had to try it on.

When I came out of the dressing room, I was shocked

to see Mia and Liliana sitting with Valentina. Tears came to my eyes as they all rushed me, filling my ears with their ecstatic reviews.

The boutique assistant came closer, tugging here and there. "If we get you some high heels, I don't think we'd need to do any further alterations."

"Not too high. I'd probably fall."

"May I get any of you champagne while we work to accessorize Miss Luciano's excellent choice?"

Valentina accepted.

When the associate looked at me, I replied, "I'm not twenty-one."

"But you're the bride. We won't tell anyone."

"I'll have a glass too," Liliana volunteered.

"Mia?" Valentina asked.

She waved her off. "Still breastfeeding."

Over the next hour, we sipped champagne while choosing my blue garter, the perfect necklace and earrings, and lastly, the veil. I didn't want one of the extravagant options. This wedding wasn't going to be in a chapel or cathedral. And the dress was too beautiful to cover. I chose a simple one made out of tulle that would cover my face until Papà removed it.

A part of me feared he wouldn't oblige.

Before I could let that ruin my day, I decided Emiliano could be the one to lift it.

Beyond the private dressing room sat three of the most intimidating men anyone would want to encounter. I almost giggled. The boutique was by appointment only. If it wasn't, the sight of them would probably turn away prospective clients.

"Where's Horace?" I asked.

"He's watching the back entrance," José said.

I nodded as I recognized Diego, one of Mia's bodyguards and the man I met this morning.

As the owner packaged our purchases and secured the dress in a zippered long bag, Miguel came to Valentina's side. "Señora, would you like me to take these packages to the car?"

We waited until Miguel and Horace came to the front door, escorting Valentina and me to our car. Diego and José drove Mia and Liliana. Our next stop was back at Valentina's home—which I supposed was now my home for the time being.

Valentina, Mia, and Lola were joined by Viviana, Mia's housekeeper. As we ate lunch, the four of them discussed food and the number of guests, given the short notice. About halfway into the discussion, I gave up. They were all speaking both English and Spanish—even Mia. I turned to Liliana. "What are they talking about?"

Liliana laughed. "Mia is advocating for an Italian menu. Valentina is saying that the wedding is at her house."

I shook my head.

Liliana reached for my hand and lowered her voice. "I didn't want to ask in front of everyone." We both turned to the discussion. They obviously weren't paying attention to us. Liliana went on, "Are you...?" She took a breath. "I hoped you were all right."

"I'm good. A little tired and nervous about my parents coming here."

"No. I mean...was Em kind?"

My cheeks rose in a smile. "Thank you, Liliana. He was. I'm still tender, but yes. Like we predicted, he's a good man."

Her shoulders relaxed. "I'm happy to hear that." She rolled her eyes. "If I'd been given the option of a second chance to say my vows, I would have said, hell no."

"I'm sorry you weren't. But in a way you have been."

She opened her eyes wider.

"Don't marry again unless it's what you want to do."

My phone in my pocket vibrated. When I pulled it out, I read my father's name. My air escaped my lungs as I worried what he might say.

"What is it, Izzy?" Mia asked.

I lifted the phone. "It's my father."

Everyone around the table stared.

"You should answer," Mia said.

Inhaling, I pushed the green icon. "Papà."

"We're here, in San Diego." His voice was robotic, without emotion.

"You're here already?"

"We're staying at Hotel Del Coronado, where we stayed for Mia's wedding. Where are you?"

"I'm" —I looked at Mia— "I'm having lunch at the Ruizes' home, Em's parents."

"Rafaele will be there in half an hour to pick you up. You'll spend tonight with your family."

My heart twisted in my chest. I wanted so badly to see Noemi, Tony, and Mom. "Papà, you know Em and I married last night. Tomorrow is for family."

"We can discuss that. Have your things ready." The call disconnected.

I swallowed as I tried not to cry.

"What did he say?" Mia asked.

"He did know that we married, didn't he?"

Mia nodded. "Dario told him. I know because Aunt Aurora called me."

"He said he's sending Rafaele here to pick me up. He wants me to spend tonight with my family and we'll *discuss*" —I emphasized the word— "my marriage."

Mia's shoulders slouched and then straightened. "What do you want to do?"

"I don't know," I answered honestly. "I want to be with Em, but I've missed my sister, my brother, and my mother."

"Your father?" Valentina asked.

"Right now, he scares me."

She tossed her napkin on the table and walked toward me. When she reached my chair, she spread her arms. "Come here, child."

I stood. "I'm not a child."

"You always will be to me. Em is a child in my eyes as are Cat and Camila."

I nodded and took a step toward her. She wrapped me in her arms and pulled me close. "We are all children sometimes even when you're as old as I am." She rubbed my back. "And sometimes we need a parent's shoulder."

My tears started.

"Mine will always be here."

I gasped for air and stood straighter. "Thank you."

Valentina teased my hair away from my face. "What do you want to do? You're right. As an adult, where you go and what you do is your choice."

"I want to see them. I'm afraid he'll force me back to Missouri."

"Where are they staying?" Mia asked.

"Hotel Del Coronado."

Mia stood and walked away.

Liliana laid her hand on top of mine.

When Mia returned, she had Diego, José, and Horace with her. "Don't go anywhere until you talk to Em. I've come up with an option. When Rafaele arrives, Horace will offer to drive you. He'll offer to follow Rafaele."

"My father—"

"Isn't making your decisions. You and your husband are. Diego will go with Horace."

"What about you?"

Mia shook her head. "Viviana and I are safe here. We'll work on tomorrow's menu. If you're not back, I'll call Silas or Felipe. With this plan, you have both Horace and Diego to make sure you leave the Del when you're ready to leave. And above all, they won't allow you to be taken back to Missouri."

"Papà said I was spending the night."

"Is that what you want?"

I shook my head. "I want to be here with my husband."

Valentina nodded toward my phone. "Call Emiliano. Listen to his point of view, and the two of you decide what you will do."

Exhaling, I took the phone toward the back of the house. The room that had couches last night was undergoing a transformation. The regular furniture was gone, and a crew of people were setting up round and long tables on the right side.

What if Valentina is going through all this trouble, and my family tries to steal me away?

I went back into my call log and called *Your husband.* Em answered on the second ring. "Am I bothering you?"

THIRTY-EIGHT

Emiliano

I stopped walking on the sidewalk in the Barrio Logan neighborhood. I was near the location where the raid went down last night. My job was to scout around to find out who was aware of what happened and if anyone saw our crew.

There was something in my wife's voice. "Isabella, are you all right?"

"I don't know."

I stepped to the side of the walk and leaned against a brick building. "Did something happen? Where's Horace?"

"My father just called..." She spoke fast, telling me about their phone call and her concerns.

With each word, I gripped the phone tighter. If that son of a bitch thought he could come and take my wife away from me, to do something to dissolve our marriage... It would be over my dead body. No, make that *his* dead body.

"Take a breath, beautiful." I spoke as calmly as I could muster. "What's Mia's plan?" I nodded as she told me. "What do you want to do?"

"I want to see them. I've missed them."

I sucked in a breath. This was one of those occasions where I could tell her no. It wouldn't be without cause. Carmine Luciano could fucking be planning a kidnapping. "Do you want to stay the night?"

"No," she answered immediately. "I want to be with you."

That answer helped my rising blood pressure. I checked my GPS on my phone. I could be at the Del in under twenty minutes. "Izzy, I love you. If you want to see your family, go. Please follow Mia's instructions and ride with Horace and Diego. If you have the slightest bit of trepidation, notify them or call me."

"You? You need to work, settling dust."

"Nothing is more important than you."

I heard a ragged breath.

"If I was there, I'd wrap you in my arms."

"Papà couldn't take me away if you were here."

"He's not taking you away."

"I love you." Isabella disconnected the call.

I turned toward the building and slammed my hand against it.

Fuck.

My next text was a group text to both Horace and Diego.

. . .

"TEXT me when you leave my home. Stay with my wife until she enters their room at the Del. Stay outside the door and text me the room number."

THEY BOTH RESPONDED.

I had enough time for one more stop. It was a hole-in-the-wall bar down a side street. Barrio Logan or sometimes referred to as Logan Heights was one of the oldest neighborhoods in San Diego. As downtown grew bigger and taller, this neighborhood fell behind. Currently, it was going through gentrification. The plan would push all the longtime residents out, tear down places like the one I was about to enter, and rebuild with construction ten to a hundred times the current inhabitants' budget. Property this close to the ocean was valuable. Making it more livable was all in the name of progress.

It also stole homes that had been in the same family for generations. When you entered a place like Bud's, you weren't there to listen to loud music, dance, or talk stock market. You were with old and young men who knew this neighborhood backward and forward.

Opening the door, I could smell the stale smoke in the air. It took a minute for my eyes to adjust as I scanned the mostly empty room.

Taking a seat at the bar, I spoke in Spanish to the bartender. *"Dame una cerveza."*

He nodded and then wiped the bar in front of me

with a dirty wet rag. The glass looked clean as he held it under the tap. "*Cinco dolares*," he said as he set the pint down in front of me.

I pulled a wad of low-denomination bills from my pocket and peeled off a five and three ones.

"*Gracias.*"

I sipped the beer and lit a cigarette as the bartender refilled two beers down at the end of the bar. When he returned to check on me, I casually mentioned I heard something happened last night and asked if he knew anything.

It wouldn't be that easy.

We went back and forth a few times. He was feeling me out, seeing if I could be an undercover cop. It was when I said I'd heard it was near that abandoned old store at Newton and South Twenty-seventh Street that he started to open up.

He corrected me.

It was Boston Avenue and South Twenty-seventh Street. He proceeded to tell me that after news of Volkov's death, some people think the Detroit bratva was trying to make a move out here. He thinks it was Detroit's men who took away whatever Volkov had in there. He told me that half his customers were afraid to come out. Before I left, he warned me about asking questions.

"It's not safe."

I nodded as I laid another five on the bar. "Thanks for the advice."

When I slipped into my car two blocks away, I checked my phone. Horace sent the text message.

. . .

"Luciano's man wasn't happy with the change of plans. Senora Izzy stayed strong. She told him she would only go if she went with us. He finally gave up. From a car behind, it looks like he's been talking the whole time. I'd guess Carmine Luciano is chewing his ass."

It would take them longer than me to get to the Del. The timestamp on the text message said they had been en route for nearly ten minutes. We could arrive at the same time. I slowed intentionally. I didn't want Isabella to think I didn't trust her. On the contrary, I wanted her to know that I would move heaven and hell to keep her safe.

I sent a text message to Jano, telling him what I'd learned. The locals were blaming the Detroit bratva.

The Del was fucking huge. They could have stayed in a normal five-star hotel, but that wasn't good enough for Carmine Luciano. The Del had recently reopened the original structure, called the Victorian. There were five differently named sections to this beachfront resort. I parked by Seaforth Marina off Glorietta Bay and waited for Isabella's location.

THIRTY-NINE

Isabella

Diego pulled our car into a parking space next to Rafaele's. Horace turned, looking at me in the back seat. "Lieutenant Ruiz instructed us to stay with you. We'll wait outside your parents' room."

I nodded. "I'd like that."

Rafaele opened the door as Diego and Horace were getting out of the car. "Miss Izzy," he said offering me his hand as he'd done a million times in my life.

I laid my left hand in his.

His gaze immediately went to the ring on my fourth finger. Yet, as I stepped out, he didn't offer me congratulations. Once I was standing on the parking lot, all three men were surrounding me.

Rafaele spoke, "Thank you for driving Miss Luciano. I

can assure you she will be safe in my care as she has always been."

Horace shook his head. "We told you back at the house. Mrs. Ruiz is our responsibility, and we won't be leaving here without her."

"Very well." Rafaele gestured with his hand. "Enjoy the resort. You can even charge your drinks to Carmine Luciano. Miss Luciano may inform you when she's ready to be taken back."

I lifted my hands. "Honestly, you're giving me a headache." I had three sets of eyes on me. "Rafaele, take me to my family." He smiled with a nod. I turned to Diego and Horace. "You two follow. I'd hate to lose you to this extravagant beach resort."

"Gladly, Mrs. Ruiz," Horace replied.

"It isn't necessary—" Rafaele began.

"Which way?" I interrupted. "I'm anxious to see Noemi and Tony."

Rafaele and I walked the paths, trailed by my new bodyguards. We seemed to be following the signs to a structure called The View. Once inside, all four of us awkwardly entered an elevator. Rafaele flashed a key and pushed the button for the seventh floor. I rolled my eyes. Of course, my father would have to be on the top floor.

The doors opened to an eerie silence. We stepped from the elevator bay into the hallway. Only the hum of the air conditioner could be heard. "It seems empty."

"Your father rented the entire floor. Mr. Salvatore and his family haven't yet arrived," Rafaele said.

"They're coming too?" My mind filled with thoughts

of my cousins. Not only would I see my siblings, but also Marisa, Aria, and Cenzi.

We came to a stop in front of the door to suite 704. I turned to Diego and Horace. "Thank you. I'll be fine inside."

"If you need us, Mrs. Ruiz..."

I nodded with a smile "Thank you."

When I turned, the door was open, and my father was standing within the doorframe. His gaze wasn't on me but on Diego and Horace. "Leave or I'll have you thrown off the property."

"Papà, these are my bodyguards."

"Rafaele is perfectly capable of watching over you." He scanned the floor. "Where are your things—an overnight bag?"

"I'm not spending the night." I lifted my left hand. "I'm married. I'll spend the night with my husband."

I didn't see his hand, but Horace must have. I heard the swoosh of air as Horace pulled me backward against his hard chest, saving me from an open-handed slap. Before I could blink, Diego had a gun pointed at my father, and Rafaele had a gun pointed at Diego.

"Stop," I demanded, moving away from Horace. I looked at my father. "Where are Mom, Noemi, and Tony?"

The darkness in his eyes intensified. "We need to clear up matters." His scowl deepened as lines formed, spidering from the corners of his squinted eyes. His words came through clenched teeth. "I told you about Aldo Ricci with the Esposito famiglia in St. Louis."

I lifted my chin. "I'm already married." I tried to peer around him. "Mom," I called out. The reality hit me. "They're not here, are they?"

"Working with whores turned you into one." He scanned me up and down. "Did he ruin you?"

I gasped. "I'm married, by a priest."

"Isabella Luciano." He used his father voice, the one that came out when he was upset about something. "Come into this suite right now. You and I are going to talk. Aurora and the kids are on their way with Sal and Giulia."

I sucked in a breath, refusing to shed a tear. "I would like to see you tomorrow for the ceremony. I was hoping you'd walk me down the aisle." A red hue filled his face as capillaries glistened in his complexion. "It's all right if you don't. Maybe I'll ask *el Patrón*."

Papà cursed and reached for my arm. His grip tightened as he pulled me toward the suite. I was a wishing bone with Papà on one side and Horace on the other. The earlier silence was gone, replaced with shouting. Guns were raised. It was mayhem until I heard another voice I recognized.

"Get your fucking hands off my wife."

My heart skipped a beat as I turned to see Em walking toward us with a weapon in his outstretched steady hand.

Papà cursed and released my arm, pulling his own gun.

Em pushed me back toward Horace. My bodyguard

tried to make me walk away, but I couldn't. My father and lifelong bodyguard were in a showdown with my husband and a cartel guard.

"Mrs. Ruiz, I need to get you to safety."

"Papà, this isn't right," I called. "I love Emiliano Ruiz. We're married. I want you to accept it."

Finally, he lowered his gun and told Rafaele to do the same. Ignoring Em, he turned my way. "How? How could you embarrass the family like this?" He motioned to Em. "With him. I told you what the cartel does. You married a criminal—a murderer."

Before my husband could respond, I stepped up to Em, held tight to his arm, and lifted my chin. "I married a man who tells me the truth. When I first got here, Emiliano was honest with me about what he does and about the cartel." I looked my father in the eye. "In eighteen years, you were never honest about what you do, about what the Luciano famiglia does."

"You were always too young to understand."

"I'm not too young to marry. The ceremony is tomorrow at one o'clock. I still want you to be there." I turned my attention to the gun in his grasp at his side. "Just don't bring the gun." Em and Diego lowered their weapons. "Tell Mom and everyone that I'll see them tomorrow. I don't care what she wears, but I'd like Noemi to stand up with me." With that, Emiliano and I turned and walked toward the elevators.

Diego and Horace watched Papà and Rafaele until we turned the corner into the elevator bay. Em wrapped his arm around me, and I leaned against his chest.

"He couldn't take me," I said, "because you did what you promised to do."

He squeezed me tighter. "Wrap you in my arms." He lifted my chin. "I'm so sorry, Isabella."

I shook my head. "Don't be. I'm where I want to be and with the man I want to be with." Looking at the elevators, I asked, "How did you get up here without a key?"

My husband just grinned.

That evening, Viviana cooked a delicious rehearsal dinner even though we didn't need to rehearse. Em and I were already married. *El Patrón* and Mia's home was filled with people who a month earlier I would never have spoken to but who welcomed me and showed me the true meaning of family.

I stood back against the dining room wall and stared at the room. Em and Rei were talking. *El Patrón* seemed more relaxed than I'd ever seen him. He had Jorge in his arms as he talked with Andrés and Nick's father, Nicolas. Mia was helping Viviana prepare dessert in the kitchen. Valentina and Nicolas's wife, Maria, were sitting at the kitchen island with glasses of wine. Liliana was deep in conversation with Sofia and Sofia's cousin Mireya.

I hoped they'd work things out.

When I turned to the pool deck, I saw Jasmine sitting by herself in one of the outdoor chairs. I walked toward her. "Do you mind if I sit out here?"

Her blue eyes met mine. "I don't mind."

"Are you all right? I mean, you're by yourself."

"I'm good," she said. "I'm processing news about

someone and…" She inhaled. "I'm sorry if I'm not festive."

I tried a different subject. "Is it true? Em told me that you and Rei are expecting."

Her cheeks turned as red as her hair and her smile grew. "We are. I'm just out of the first trimester. Catalina tells me the nausea will get better."

I scrunched my nose. "That doesn't sound fun." I took a breath. "You know, coming out here—to San Diego—has opened my eyes to a lot of things."

She looked out over the ocean. "Yeah, it's beautiful out here."

"I'm sorry for the way I've treated you," I blurted out.

Jasmine turned to me. "Don't be."

"I am. I've learned that not everything I was told was true." I leaned back. "Honestly, I feel like my whole life has been a lie." I turned to her. "You don't have to forgive me. You probably shouldn't. I just wanted to tell you that we were mean." I inhaled. "I was mean. It was wrong."

She smiled as Rei came and stood beside her chair.

"Is everything all right out here?" he asked.

Jasmine nodded and looked up at him. The love I saw in both their gazes made me hope that was how Em and I appeared.

"Catching up is all," she said.

He leaned down and kissed her lips. "Mia is getting the dessert ready. It's flan."

"Flan," I said. "Liliana told me about that."

Jasmine stood. "It's the best. I don't even care if the sugar gives me heartburn."

"Does sugar give heartburn?"

She laughed. "Everything gives me heartburn."

Em reached for my hand as we entered the living room. Tugging me toward him, he leaned down and kissed my lips. "I can do that anytime I want," he whispered.

"*Sí, jefe*, anytime."

His eyes sparkled as he curled his lips into a menacing smile.

CHAPTER
FORTY

Isabella

My things from Mia's house were now in our bedroom. My new home was filled with more people than I could imagine. The capo, Catalina, Ariadna Gia, Dante, and Camila arrived late last night, all of them staying here. If I had known that Dario was down the hall, I would have been a lot more self-conscious about the sounds that came from my lips during the night.

It wasn't my fault.

According to Em, I was a good girl, and good girls get to come.

I did, over and over.

It's strange how I'd been trying to prove to everyone that I was an adult and the words *good girl* from my husband caused my insides to twist and my nipples to bead. Em stayed true to his word; everything was oral. I told him I wanted to try part two again after our ceremony.

He proclaimed he was going to exhaust me with orgasms so I would tell him about the wedding dress we bought. He did his part, but I stayed strong. Well, strong until I passed out in his protective arms. When I woke this morning, I found a note telling me that we were to not see one another until the ceremony. He told me that he was going over to *el Patrón's* until closer to the event.

Imagine my surprise when I entered the kitchen in the morning and was met by none other than my cousin, the capo.

I continued my boundary pushing and walked up to him and his cup of coffee. "Thank you, Dario, for approving our wedding."

He nodded in the way that said, yes, I am God of all those around me.

I turned to walk away when he spoke. "Isabella, I didn't send you out here to fail."

I spun toward him. "Did Mia tell you...?"

"She did. I never thought you would fail. Mia needed help. I was recently reminded that no matter how much we want to clip children's wings, they deserve to fly."

"Thank you. My parents?" I asked.

"Emiliano asked me not to influence their decision."

Nodding, I pressed my lips together. "Seems like everyone is talking to you about me."

He showed me a rare smile. "It's all been good. You're making the famiglia proud."

I could be upset that Em shared what I'd told him about the capo not forcing my parents, but I wasn't. If they attended, I'd know it was of their own volition. By eleven thirty, I was in my new bedroom with a hairstylist and makeup artist. Liliana, Mia, Catalina, Camila, and Valentina were all present to help me dress. The hairstylist pulled my hair up on the sides with diamond hair combs that belonged to Em's grandmother on his father's side.

While everyone went on and on about the dress, my hair, and my makeup, there was a void that ached in my chest. Looking at my hands, I saw the wedding ring from last night. I handed it to Valentina.

"You decided you don't want it?"

"No." I opened my eyes wide. "I want you to give it to Em so he can place it on my finger again today."

She smiled and took the ring. "I'll give it to him."

"Is he here?"

"*Sí*." Her smile grew. "Everyone is here. Father Gallo, Josefina—Jano's mother—the harpist…It will be beautiful."

No mention of my family.

"I thought *el Patrón* said no band."

"He did." She grinned. "There's no mariachi band. Only a harpist." She winked. "You'll learn to see the loopholes."

I reached for her hand. "Thank you for being so nice to me."

Valentina kissed my cheek. "Thank you for making my son happy."

"I'll do my best."

"I know you will." She looked around. "Is there anything you need?"

I shook my head.

Valentina cupped my cheek. "I see sadness." She shook her head. "Tell it to go away. Today is too special for sadness."

I nodded.

Liliana came up behind me. "You're beautiful. I'm so happy for you."

I met her gaze. "It's kind of last minute, but I was hoping my sister..." I exhaled and forced a smile. "Would you stand up with me?"

She looked down at her sundress. "I-I."

"You're beautiful, Liliana. And you helped to open my eyes. I'd be honored if you would be my matron of honor."

"Sure. I'd love to. But if your sister makes it, the job is hers."

I looked at the clock. The ceremony was set to begin in half an hour. "Yeah, I don't think she will, but that's all right. I have people here who love me."

Liliana hugged me. "You do." She winked. "Sofia and I made up last night."

"That's great."

"She also helped me sneak a few people in under the radar."

"Who?" I asked.

"Celeste and Reina."

My eyes opened wide. "Oh my God. What if Nicolas recognizes them?"

"He won't. I hardly recognize them. They won't stay

past the ceremony, but they wanted to see you and Em wed.”

I nibbled my lip. “Maybe it’s better my family isn’t here.”

“You won’t even spot them in the crowd. I just wanted you to know.”

“I’m glad you got them in.”

Everyone else had cleared out of the room, claiming it was time to be seated. Liliana squeezed my hand. “Do you want me to stay up here with you?”

As I debated, the bedroom door opened. I saw Horace open the door a millisecond before Mom, Noemi, Aunt Giulia, Marisa, Aria, and Cenzi came rushing in.

My mother cried, lifting her hands to her face. “You’re so beautiful, Izzy.”

I tried to blink away the tears as my sister and cousins attacked me with hugs. I held tight to Noemi and whispered, “Is Papà here?”

She nodded. “He wants to walk you down the aisle.”

My gaze went to my mother’s. “Tell him yes. I want him to walk me.”

Mom nodded and hurried from the room.

Liliana waved.

“Wait,” I called to her. “Everyone, this is my best friend out here. This is Liliana.”

Noemi, Marisa, Aria, and Vincenza all said, “Hi.”

One by one, I introduced each family member to Liliana.

“I’ve missed you,” Noemi said. “And now you’re not coming home.”

“I’ll come home if Papà and Mom will welcome Em.”

"We will."

We all turned to the deep voice.

"Girls, let me talk to Isabella."

I smiled as Horace peeked in. "I'm good."

He nodded.

Once we were alone, Papà came toward me. "You're beautiful, Isabella. I'm sorry." He shook his head. "For what I said." His nostrils flared. "For so many things. The capo told me years ago that I was wrong about them."

"The cartel?"

"Yes. Dante told me. I didn't believe them." He cupped my cheek. "I believe you. I can't promise miracles, but I'll try. You and whomever you love are welcome in our home."

"You're making me cry," I said as we hugged.

He framed my cheeks and rubbed his thumb under my eyes. "No more crying. After the ceremony, I hope Emiliano and I can try again."

"You can, Papà. Emiliano is a good man."

I scanned the room as we arrived at the beginning of the aisle in Valentina's large living room. The right side was filled with the tables I'd seen earlier. The left side was filled with chairs—chairs filled with people. Everyone stood as the harpist played the wedding march.

My gaze immediately went to Em. In a custom suit that tapered from his wide shoulders to his slim torso, he was the personification of everything I knew about him —a murderer, a criminal, a gentleman, a man capable of extremes, and the man I wanted to spend the rest of my life with. I didn't have to imagine what was under that suit. I knew. And there wasn't one inch of him I didn't love.

With his clenched jaw and dark eyes, I saw an inferno, one about to burn out of control. He was looking at my father. My smile grew, catching his attention and dousing his fury. As we got closer to the altar, I mouthed 'faith.'

Em smiled, his eyes showing a different kind of fire, the one of desire.

To my surprise, Noemi and Liliana were both standing on the right side of Father Gallo. Nick and Rei were beside Emiliano. Three of the top men in the Roríguez cartel. Three men who should intimidate me. Two men I now considered friends and the other, my husband.

Father Gallo spoke, but my mind was consumed with the tall dark-haired man staring at me, the most handsome of the lineup, the man who was already my husband.

"Who gives this woman to be wed?"

The room took a collective breath as Papà reached for my hand and passed it on to Emiliano. "With pride, her mother and I."

FORTY-ONE

Isabella

It was only a little after eight p.m. when Emiliano and I made our way up the stairs. While most of the guests were gone, there was an informal meeting occurring in Andrés's office. Something big had happened, but I knew I wouldn't get details until we were alone. Em closed the bedroom door and turned the lock in the knob. He was handsome with his suit coat gone, his tie loosened, and the sleeves of his white button-down rolled to near his elbows.

I spun toward him and smiled. "I couldn't be happier."

He stalked toward me and reached for my shoulders. "Do you have any idea how fucking stunning you are in that dress?"

"I'm glad you like it."

"I've wanted to get you out of it since you appeared with your father."

I took a deep breath. "Thank you."

"For not killing him? You're welcome."

"For giving him another chance. He apologized to me. And when he gave me away, he said it was with great pride." I wiped a tear from my cheek. "Yesterday, he told me I was an embarrassment."

A vein in Em's forehead throbbed. "I heard."

"No, don't be mad. Dario told me that you told him not to insist on my family's presence."

"Well, damn. He wasn't supposed to tell you."

I ran my palm over his cheek. "We tell the truth."

"We tell the truth. I was just going to leave that part out."

"I'm glad I knew because when Papà walked in here—"

"Your father was in our bedroom?" Em grinned. "Where I fucked his daughter?"

I slapped his chest. "Where you're not going to do it again if you don't let me tell you what he said."

He inhaled. "Then by all means, Mrs. Ruiz, tell me what your father said feet away from the bed where I took his daughter's virginity."

"You're awful."

"I'm not. What did he say?"

"He said that Dario and Dante have told him that he's been wrong about the cartel, but he refused to believe them. He said he believes me, and he'll try."

Em nodded.

"He also said that I'm always welcome in their home and so is anyone that I love."

"That's me, right?"

"Yes." My cheeks rose as my lips curled. "I thought about it. I think he means others too."

"What others?"

"Well, if we try part two again tonight and it's better, we might want to try it again and again."

"I like the way you're talking."

"If we do that, in a year or two when we visit Kansas City, there could be more than two of us."

His gaze turned sultry. "Are you sure you want children?"

I shrugged. "I've always imagined having them. I guess before you, I didn't realize how dangerous the world can be."

"It's less dangerous than it was yesterday."

"Why is that?"

Em took my hand and led me to the bed. We both sat on the edge. "This is one of those times I'm being truthful, but for now, it is only between the two of us. Don't tell your father."

"Why would I tell him?"

"I don't know. If he would ask, pretend you don't know."

"What don't I know?"

"Not long after we completed the ceremony, Jano received a message from our men in Mexico."

"You have men in Mexico?"

"He received an important message. Elizondro Herrera was captured."

I sucked in a breath. "He's the one *el Patrón* wanted."

Em nodded. "Jano believed that Herrera was responsible for many horrible things. He believed he called the hit on his father." Em took a breath. "When we found Volkov, Jano's only condition was that he be the one to take his life. He wanted the same thing with Herrera. He told our men to keep him detained, and that he'd be down to Saint Martin tomorrow."

"Is he going?"

"No."

"Why not?"

"Dario thought something was suspicious. He and Rei followed Jano to the other room. They heard enough of the conversation to figure out what was happening. Rei and Dario talked Jano out of traveling out of the country. While you and I were cutting cake, the three of them were strategizing. According to Rei, Dario laid it on the line. Leaving the country would be dangerous for Jano. He's right. Dario said that Jano could pick up the phone and tell his men to execute Herrera, just as Herrera had done to Jorge. Jano would be the reason Herrera was finally dead."

It was like listening to a movie plot. "Did *el Patrón* do it? Did he call for Herrera's death?"

"He did. He has photos to verify that Herrera is finally gone."

"And this is good, right?"

"Yes, my love, it is very good. The Roríguez cartel is stronger than ever."

Our lips collided. I lifted my arms to his shoulder and ran my fingers through his styled hair. Keeping our hips together, I leaned back and smiled. "I've wanted to do that all night. I think the messy look is sexy."

He arched an eyebrow. "Messy hair, the scent of tobacco. What other aphrodisiacs turn you on, Mrs. Ruiz?"

"Just being in your presence." I looked down at my left hand. Above Em's great-grandmother's band was a sparkling, gorgeous round diamond.

Em reached for my hand. "You like it?"

"I do. We need to get you a ring."

"Lockdown is over. We can go do whatever you want to do."

I spun around and peered at him over my shoulder. "I'd rather stay here tonight." I batted my eyelashes. "Could you maybe help me out of this dress?"

"Fuck yeah."

I expected him to reach for the line of pearl buttons. Instead, Em pulled a knife from a leg holster. I spun back around. "You are *not* cutting this dress."

"Isn't that what would happen if you married in the Mafia?"

My smile quirked. "I didn't marry into the Mafia. I married into the cartel."

"Yes, you did." Em encouraged me to turn until he had access to the line of buttons. With each button, he kissed my back, lower and lower. By the time I removed my arms from the cap sleeves, the dress pooled around my feet, leaving me in the new white high-heeled sandals and new lace lingerie. "You're too fucking good for me."

"I'm not. I was raised in a dangerous world without knowing it. I prefer knowing what's happening, no matter how dangerous." I took a step toward my husband. "My turn." I started with the top button that was secured on Em's shirt. One by one, I released them, adding my kisses to his chest until I reached the waist of his pants.

Kneeling, I reached for his belt.

Em laid his hand over mine. "Stand up, Izzy."

I looked up at him. "You don't want...?"

"A fucking blow job? Yes. But not tonight. You're a fucking princess, and tonight we're going to make part two pleasurable. Tonight, I want to come in that tight pink pussy of yours." He ran his thumb over my lip. "I can wait to feel those lips around me." He lifted his eyebrows. "Because I know it will be worth the wait."

I nodded.

Pleasurable.

I wanted that.

Together we continued to undress. He helped me. I helped him. It was a mating dance. By the time we were nude, our hands were a frenzy of movement. Me touching him and him touching me.

I did what I hadn't done the first night, looking closer at what would soon be inside me. While I didn't suck, I kissed and licked. Em's intense reaction twisted my core and was enough to make me want to do more.

Soon the roles reversed. It was Em's face buried between my legs. The sparks that had come to life as I kissed and licked were fanned by the fervor of his actions. My hips bucked as his tongue, lips, and teeth worked in an alliance to bring me pleasure. It was as he added his hands, circling my clit, that I came unwound.

Nerve endings sparked, sending a trail of explosions through my body. I reached for his head, pushing him away to no avail. The orgasms were overpowering. When I didn't think I could possibly take any more, Em moved over me.

My body was too worn out to notice the pressure at my entrance. By the time my mind and body came together, I felt full. No pain. I opened my eyes meeting Em's concerned gaze, nodded, and smiled.

"Are you good?"

I shook my head. "Not good. I'm better than good."

"Not sore?"

"No. I feel full, and it feels wonderful."

"I'll make it better."

I wasn't sure there was a better.

I was wrong. Better came as we moved together, the push and pull, the arching of my back, and the movement of his torso. Each position felt different in the best of ways. Then all of a sudden, without warning, my body seized, sending detonations throughout my nervous system. From the top of my head to the curling of my toes, I was alive like I'd never known.

Our room filled with noises from me and curses from Em as he pushed my knees back and pounded harder. Soon, his expression morphed as he filled me to overflowing. When Em collapsed at my side, he reached for my chin, turning it toward him.

"Better?"

"The best."

He kissed my nose. "What if I told you it will keep getting better?"

"I'd say you're setting a high bar."

He pulled me into his arms. I listened to the sound of his heartbeat as he stroked my hair. "I love you, Isabella. I want to have and hold you forever."

I rolled in his arms. "I like the sound of that." I lifted my left hand and wiggled my finger. You didn't need to get me a diamond."

"I did."

"Does it have a story?"

"I bought it yesterday. That means this is just the first chapter." He kissed me. "We have a lifetime to write the rest of the story."

Rolling toward him, I lifted my lips to his. "As long as it ends with 'They lived happily ever after.'"

And they did.

Thank you for reading TO HAVE AND TO HOLD. I hope you've enjoyed the Brutal Vows series. If you missed any of the individual stories, you could start with NOW AND FOREVER, Dario and Catalina's story. Then, TILL DEATH DO US PART, Alejandro and Mia's story. BOUND BY A PROMISE, Dante and Camila's story. Next, QUEENS AND MONSTERS, Reinaldo and Jasmine's story. The final book of the series is TO HAVE AND TO HOLD.

Roriguez - Ruiz / Luciano Family Tree

At the end of book five, TO HAVE AND TO HOLD

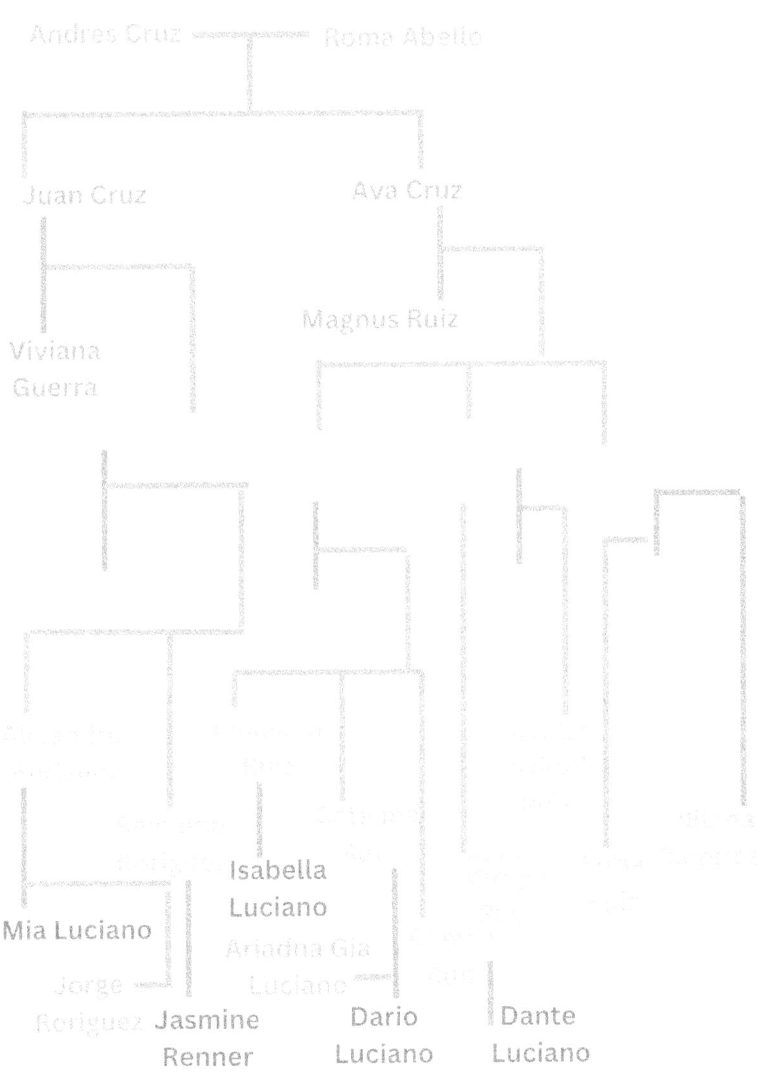

WHAT TO DO NOW

Visit Aleatha's store to purchase e-books, signed books, and store exclusive items.

LEND IT: Did you enjoy *TO HAVE AND TO HOLD*? Do you have a friend who'd enjoy *TO HAVE AND TO HOLD?* *TO HAVE AND TO HOLD* may be lent one time. Sharing is caring!

RECOMMEND IT: Do you have multiple friends who'd enjoy my dark romance with twists and turns and an all new sexy and infuriating anti-hero? Tell them about it! Call, text, post, tweet...your recommendation is the nicest gift you can give to an author!

REVIEW IT: Tell the world. Please go to the retailer where you purchased this book, as well as Goodreads, and write a review. Please share your thoughts about *TO HAVE AND TO HOLD* on:

*Amazon, *TO HAVE AND TO HOLD* Customer Reviews

*Barnes & Noble, *TO HAVE AND TO HOLD,* Customer Reviews

*Apple Books, *TO HAVE AND TO HOLD* Customer Reviews

* BookBub, *TO HAVE AND TO HOLD* Customer Reviews

*Goodreads.com/Aleatha Romig

All also available on Aleatha's store

BRUTAL VOWS:

NOW AND FOREVER

May 2024

TILL DEATH DO US PART

June 2024

BOUND BY A PROMISE

October 2024

QUEENS AND MONSTERS

January 2025

TO HAVE AND TO HOLD

March 2025

SINCLAIR DUET:

REMEMBERING PASSION

September 2023

REKINDLING DESIRE

October 2023

ROYAL REFLECTIONS SERIES:

RUTHLESS REIGN

November 2022

RESILIENT REIGN

January 2023

RAVISHING REIGN

April 2023

RELEVANT REIGN

June 2023

SIN SERIES:

RED SIN

October 2021

GREEN ENVY

January 2022

GOLD LUST

April 2022

BLACK KNIGHT

June 2022

~

STAND-ALONE ROMANTIC SUSPENSE:

LIGHT DARK

Republished 2024

Previously: INTO THE LIGHT and AWAY FROM THE DARK

SILVER LINING

October 2022

KINGDOM COME

November 2021

~

DEVIL'S SERIES (Duet):

DEVIL'S DEAL

May 2021

ANGEL'S PROMISE

June 2021

~

SPARROW WEBS

WEB OF SIN:

SECRETS

October 2018

LIES

December 2018

PROMISES

January 2019

TANGLED WEB:

TWISTED

May 2019

OBSESSED

July 2019

BOUND

August 2019

WEB OF DESIRE:

SPARK

Jan. 14, 2020

FLAME

February 25, 2020

ASHES

April 7, 2020

DANGEROUS WEB:

Prequel: "Danger's First Kiss"

DUSK

November 2020

DARK

January 2021

DAWN

February 2021

THE INFIDELITY SERIES:

BETRAYAL

Book #1

October 2015

CUNNING

Book #2

January 2016

DECEPTION

Book #3

May 2016

ENTRAPMENT

Book #4

September 2016

FIDELITY

Book #5

January 2017

THE CONSEQUENCES SERIES:

CONSEQUENCES

(Book #1)

August 2011

TRUTH

(Book #2)

October 2012

CONVICTED

(Book #3)

October 2013

REVEALED

(Book #4)

Previously titled: Behind His Eyes Convicted: The Missing Years

June 2014

BEYOND THE CONSEQUENCES

(Book #5)

January 2015

RIPPLES **(Consequences stand-alone)**

October 2017

CONSEQUENCES COMPANION READS:

BEHIND HIS EYES-CONSEQUENCES

January 2014

BEHIND HIS EYES-TRUTH

March 2014

~

STAND ALONE MAFIA THRILLER:

PRICE OF HONOR

Available Now

~

STAND-ALONE YA ROMANTIC THRILLER:

ON THE EDGE

May 2022

~

TALES FROM THE DARK SIDE SERIES:

INSIDIOUS

(All books in this series are stand-alone erotic thrillers)

Released October 2014

~

ALEATHA'S LIGHTER ONES:

PLUS ONE

Stand-alone fun, sexy romance

May 2017

ANOTHER ONE

Stand-alone fun, sexy romance

May 2018

ONE NIGHT

Stand-alone, sexy contemporary romance

September 2017

A SECRET ONE

Prequel to MY ALWAYS ONE

April 2018

MY ALWAYS ONE

Stand-Alone, sexy friends to lovers contemporary romance

July 2021

*QUINTESSENTIALLY THE ONE

Stand-alone, small-town, second-chance, secret baby
contemporary romance

July 2022

*ONE KISS

Stand-alone, small-town, best friend's sister, grump/sunshine
contemporary romance.

July 2023

*ONE STRING

Second-chance, enemies-to-lovers, fake-date, little-sister's-
best-friend, forbidden, stand-alone contemporary romance

July 2024

*All Riverbend interconnected stories

INDULGENCE SERIES:

UNEXPECTED

August 2018

UNCONVENTIONAL

January 2018

UNFORGETTABLE

October 2019

UNDENIABLE

August 2020

ABOUT THE AUTHOR

Visit Aleatha's store to purchase e-books, signed books, and store exclusive items.

Aleatha Romig is a New York Times, Wall Street Journal, and USA Today bestselling author who lives in Indiana, USA. She has raised three children with her high school sweetheart and husband of over thirty years. Before she became a full-time author, she worked days as a dental hygienist and spent her nights writing. Now, when she's not imagining mind-blowing twists and turns, she likes to spend her time with her family and friends. Her other pastimes include reading and creating heroes/anti-heroes who haunt your dreams!

Aleatha impresses with her versatility in writing. She released her first novel, CONSEQUENCES, in August of 2011. CONSEQUENCES, a dark romance, became a best-selling series with five novels and two companions released from 2011 through 2015. The compelling and epic story of Anthony and Claire Rawlings has graced more than half a million e-readers. Her first stand-alone smart, sexy thriller INSIDIOUS was next. Then Aleatha released the five-novel INFIDELITY series, a romantic suspense saga, that took the reading world by storm, the final book landing on three of the top bestseller lists. She ventured into traditional publishing with Thomas and

Mercer. Her books INTO THE LIGHT and AWAY FROM THE DARK were published through this mystery/thriller publisher in 2016.

In the spring of 2017, Aleatha again ventured into a different genre with her first fun and sexy stand-alone romantic comedy with the USA Today bestseller PLUS ONE. She continued the "Ones" series with additional standalones, ONE NIGHT, ANOTHER ONE, MY ALWAYS ONE, QUINTESSENTIALLY THE ONE, ONE KISS, and ONE STRING.

If you like fun, sexy, novellas that make your heart pound, try her "Indulgence series" with UNCONVEN-TIONAL. UNEXPECTED, UNFORGETTABLE, and UNDENIABLE.

In 2018 Aleatha returned to her dark romance roots with SPARROW WEBS. And continued with the mafia romance DEVIL'S DUET, and most recently her Brutal Vows series.

You may find all Aleatha's titles on her website.

Aleatha is a "Published Author's Network" member of the Romance Writers of America and PEN America. She is represented by SBR Media and Dani Sanchez with Wildfire Marketing.

facebook.com/aleatharomig

instagram.com/aleatharomig

* 9 7 8 1 9 6 5 9 8 4 1 6 1 *